ELLIE JORDAN, GHOST TRAPPER

by

J.L. Bryan

Published 2014
JLBryanbooks.com

Copyright 2014 J.L. Bryan

All rights reserved.

This book or any portion thereof may not be reproduced or used in any manner whatsoever without the express written permission of the publisher except for the use of brief quotations in a book review.

All characters appearing in this work are fictitious. Any resemblance to real persons, living or dead, is purely coincidental.

ISBN-10: 1500977004
ISBN-13: 978-1500977009

Foreword

Thanks so much for picking up this copy of *Ellie Jordan, Ghost Trapper*. It's the first in a new series for which I have high hopes, because it's been a lot of fun to write so far.

I thought ghosts would be an interesting area to explore because, unlike other paranormal types like vampires, werewolves, creatures from black lagoons, and so on, we can't be completely sure that ghosts don't exist in the real world. In fact, my wife and I once heard a voice that couldn't be explained except as some kind of ghost, so I half-believe in them myself.

For this series, I try to keep it as close to reality as possible. My characters, for the most part, use methods and equipment employed by the countless ghost-hunter and paranormal groups that exist in the real world. The setting is contemporary Savannah, Georgia, a city where most of the downtown buildings are said to be haunted.

I look forward to Ellie's future adventures, and I hope you will, too! Thanks for reading!

-J.L. Bryan

Acknowledgments

I appreciate everyone who has helped with this book. Several authors beta read it for me, including Daniel Arenson, Alexia Purdy, Robert Duperre, and Michelle Muto. The final proofing was done by Thelia Kelly. The cover is by PhatPuppy Art.

Most of all, I appreciate the book bloggers and readers who keep coming back for more! The book bloggers who've supported me over the years include Danny, Heather, and Heather from Bewitched Bookworks; Mandy from I Read Indie; Michelle from Much Loved Books; Shirley from Creative Deeds; Katie and Krisha from Inkk Reviews; Lori from Contagious Reads; Heather from Buried in Books; Kristina from Ladybug Storytime; Chandra from Unabridged Bookshelf; Kelly from Reading the Paranormal; AimeeKay from Reviews from My First Reads Shelf and Melissa from Books and Things; Kristin from Blood, Sweat, and Books; Lauren from Lose Time Reading; Kat from Aussie Zombie; Andra from Unabridged Andralyn; Jennifer from A Tale of Many Reviews; Giselle from Xpresso Reads; Ashley from Bookish Brunette; Loretta from Between the Pages; Ashley from Bibliophile's Corner; Lili from Lili Lost in a Book; Line from Moonstar's Fantasy World; Lindsay from The Violet Hour; Rebecca from Bending the Spine; Holly from Geek Glitter; Louise from Nerdette Reviews; Isalys from Book Soulmates; Jennifer from The Feminist Fairy; Heidi from Rainy Day Ramblings; Kristilyn from Reading in Winter; Kelsey from Kelsey's Cluttered Bookshelf; Lizzy from Lizzy's Dark Fiction; Shanon from Escaping with Fiction; Savannah from Books with Bite; Tara from Basically Books; Toni from My Book Addiction; and anyone else I missed!

For Christina

Also by J.L. Bryan:

The Ellie Jordan, Ghost Trapper series
Ellie Jordan, Ghost Trapper
Cold Shadows
The Crawling Darkness
Terminal
House of Whispers
Maze of Souls
Lullaby

The Jenny Pox series (supernatural/horror)
Jenny Pox
Tommy Nightmare
Alexander Death
Jenny Plague-Bringer

Urban Fantasy/Horror
Inferno Park
The Unseen

Science Fiction Novels
Nomad
Helix

Chapter One

"Why do ghosts wear clothes?" Stacey asked as we drove toward the possibly-haunted house.

Stacey was twenty-two, four years younger than me and much prettier, her blond hair cropped short and simple, carelessly styled, but her makeup was immaculate. She looked like what she was: a tomboy despite being raised by a former beauty-queen socialite in Montgomery, Alabama. She was a very recent graduate of the Savannah College of Art and Design film school, but she'd been eager to join Eckhart Investigations and hunt ghosts rather than pursue a more sane and profitable career.

I had to wonder how Alabama-socialite mom felt about that.

"Well?" Stacey asked, raising an eyebrow. She rode shotgun as I drove our unmarked blue cargo van through the streets of Savannah. It was June, and rich sunlight fell through the thick, gnarled branches of ancient live oaks dripping with Spanish moss and crepe myrtles heavy with red blossoms. The stately old trees shaded columned mansions and gardens filled with summer blooms.

"I don't know, Stacey," I said, trying not to sigh. "You tell me why ghosts wear clothes."

"I'm asking you!"

"I thought you were setting up a joke," I said.

"Nope, totally serious."

"I don't get the question," I told Stacey. "Why wouldn't they?"

"Well...think about it," Stacey said. "The living wear them to keep warm or whatever. If you're a ghost, you don't have a body."

"Does *that* keep you warm?" I smirked at her low-cut tank top, which wasn't quite appropriate for work. I've been scratched and bruised by enough angry spirits that I wear turtlenecks, leather, and denim even in hot weather. I've tried to warn Stacey about this, but she hasn't listened so far.

"Uh, no..." Stacey looked down at her shirt as if puzzled.

"So why do you wear it?"

"Because I don't want to be naked?"

"Question answered," I said. "Next?"

"Why do ghosts wrap themselves in bedsheets?" Stacey asked.

"They don't do that. Why would you even think--?"

"So they can rest in peace." Stacey beamed, then her smile faltered a little. "*That's* a joke."

"No, jokes make you laugh."

"That one killed at my second-grade Halloween party."

"Only because your audience was high on sugar," I said.

"Here's another one: why do ghosts come out at night?"

"Because their electromagnetic fields are sensitive to dense concentrations of photons."

"Joke-ruiner," Stacey said.

We drove north and west, away from the city center. The Treadwell house was in an odd area of town, upriver, near empty brick warehouses and a few old factory shells dating back more than a hundred years. The nearest residential neighborhood was a row of decrepit bungalows on narrow, weedy lots, some of them clearly abandoned or foreclosed. They'd probably been inhabited by factory and dock workers at some point.

One old factory did show some signs of remodeling and gentrification, with a clothing boutique and one of those restaurants where you can buy a cruelty-free mushroom sandwich on sprouted-grain bread for just fifteen bucks. Maybe the area was on its way back.

I dropped the sun visor and opened the mirror to double-check myself before meeting the new clients. I always kept it pretty simple—minimal make-up, long brown hair pulled back in a ponytail. I can't do much more than that with my crazy coarse hair, anyway.

Back in high school, I'd let it grow too shaggy and thick, and it combined with my old armor-thick glasses to create a real Mad Scientist Girl look.

Unlike Stacey, I hadn't been trained in a thousand subtle varieties of cosmetics and hair products. After my parents died when I was fifteen, I didn't really care about normal adolescent stuff like parties, dances, or dating, anyway. I'd stay up late at night studying everything from William James and Spiritualism to Tarot cards and Aleister Crowley.

Even then, I was training myself to be a ghost trapper.

"I don't see any houses down this way..." Stacey said. We passed a low brick warehouse choked with vines, its windows boarded over and spraypainted with graffiti.

"Maybe there." I pointed to an overgrown lot with a screen of massive old trees and a wilderness of overgrown shrubs. A narrow, cracked brick drive led from the street into the darkness behind the trees.

We had to slow down and squint to read the old letters rusting off the ivy-choked brick mailbox. It was the right address.

I turned and eased the van up the cracked driveway, nosing aside low-lying limbs.

"Doesn't look like anybody's lived here in a long time," Stacey whispered. "Do you think it'll be a real ghost this time? I'm tired of duds."

"Careful what you wish for," I told her. More than half our calls come from people who are just plain ghost-happy. They think their place is haunted, and they haven't bothered to eliminate other options. Sometimes that eerie, moaning cold spot is just a clunky air conditioner; sometimes those strange footsteps in the attic are just squirrels. Our first job is to check for any non-paranormal causes for the alleged haunting.

Stacey hadn't seen much in the way of real ghosts in the three weeks since she'd been hired full-time. If she had seen the kinds of things I've seen, she would have been less eager to find a true haunting.

The house lay beyond a jungle of green that had once been a lawn and gardens. Here in coastal Georgia, with the hot sun and constant rain, the wilderness is always ready to sprout back at the first sign of neglect.

I slowed to a halt as the front of the house came into view.

"Wow," Stacey whispered.

A three-story brick mansion loomed above us, much of it hidden by the shadows of the old trees overhead, and even more of it concealed by moss and wild vines. It was a Gothic Revival style house, made of dark brick and heavy wood, with treacherously steep roofs and sharp, high gables rising toward the dim tree canopy above. It had a medieval castle look to it, maybe the kind of neglected castle where Beauty would find the Beast hanging out, just waiting for the remodeling power of love to turn it all into a gorgeous palace.

A team of three men worked on the roof, repairing years of broken shingles and rotten wood. A pair of paint-spattered pick-up trucks sat in the drive below them. I idled beside the trucks for a moment.

"This place looks creepy," Stacey whispered. "Does it feel cold to you?"

"There's enough shade to lower the temperature a few degrees," I said. "Don't get worked up and spook yourself. Keep your mind empty."

"An empty mind is an open mind," Stacey intoned solemnly, imitating our boss, Calvin Eckhart. We both broke down into snickering. Stacey is a pretty convincing mimic, and Calvin's occasional bouts of Zen are always amusing, delivered in his earthy good-old-boy accent.

"It's true," I said, straightening up in my seat. "They said to pull around to the side."

"Ooh, we have to use the servants' entrance?" Stacey made a face as we followed the weedy brick drive back around to the two-story east wing of the house. The east wing had its own chimney and looked to be in much better repair than the main facade, with no mold or vines on the bricks, the trim freshly painted a dark brown. "They must not want the neighbors to know they called the ghost exterminators."

"What neighbors?" I asked, thinking of the empty warehouse we'd just passed.

I parked near a likely-looking side door. The door was heavy and red, built of solid wood and shielded by a screen door. It was sunken at the back of a small brick porch under the shadows of a sharply peak roof. The door itself looked new, and the brick looked worn but recently pressure-washed.

Two more cars were parked there, a silver Jaguar and a small black Mercedes. Good. Eckhart Investigations charges on a rough sliding scale, so people and businesses who can afford it pay more, while poor people pay less. We also do some free work for people who obviously can't afford anything.

I sort of hoped the Treadwells had a true haunting. The ghost business had been slow for a few weeks, and I could use a decent paycheck at the end of the month.

Stacey and I got out of the van. I grabbed my black toolbox, while she brought her camera bag.

"Are you the ghost catchers?" a small, whispery voice asked, and I jumped. Maybe I was a little more affected by the dark, creepy old mansion than I wanted to admit to Stacey.

A girl in a yellow dress emerged from the shadows under the roofed doorway, clutching a cloth doll in her hands. She twisted the doll nervously as she stared at us. She was nine or ten, and she had purple bags under her eyes as if she hadn't slept in a long time. It was unsettling to see that on a kid so young. She could have been the cover girl for Sad Orphan Monthly, if not for the brightly-printed Cavalli dress that probably cost as much as a month's rent on my apartment.

"We are the ghost catchers," I replied. "I'm Ellie, and this is Stacey Ray."

"Just call me Stacey!" Stacey said. She waved and gave the exaggerated smile people use when clumsily trying to ingratiate themselves to small children. "What's your name?"

"Can you make her go away?" the girl asked me, and for a moment I thought she was talking about Stacey. The little girl's face was pale and solemn.

"Make who go away?" I asked.

The girl glanced back at the door behind her, as if to check whether anyone was watching. Then she whispered, looking down at her doll: "The lady who comes at night."

"Is she scary?" Stacey asked. The girl looked at Stacey like she was incredibly stupid.

"Is your mom Anna Treadwell?" I asked.

"Yes."

"Would you get her for us?"

"Mom!" The little girl turned and screamed at the door, but she did not move closer to it. "The ghost people are here!" She turned back and stared at us. "I don't like to go inside."

A minute later, a woman stepped out of the red door. She looked to be in her late thirties or early forties, her dark hair in a stylish professional bob. She was attractive and fit—I pegged her as the Pilates type. She wore old sneakers, worn jeans, and a t-shirt that read *Southeastern Wireless: Team-Building Camp 2013!* Every bit of her, from her hair to her toes, was spattered with light blue paint.

"I'm so sorry, I'm a mess," the woman said, blushing hard and trying to adjust her hair. "Is it ten already? It's so easy to lose track of time in this house."

"That's fine, please don't worry about it. Doing some renovations?" I pointed to the guys working on the roof.

"You have no idea." She shook her head as if overwhelmed. She wiped a paint-crusted hand on her jeans. "I'm Anna. I'd shake your hand, but you probably don't want to stain your clothes Daydream Azure, so..."

"I'm Ellie Jordan, senior investigator for Eckhart," I told her. "We spoke on the phone yesterday."

"Oh, yes!" She smiled, but it looked forced, like she was trying to hide some serious apprehension. "Nice to meet you."

"This is Stacey Ray Tolbert, our tech manager." I delivered our job titles with a straight face, as if our company consisted of more than three people. It was just me, Stacey, and our boss Calvin Eckhart, a retired homicide detective who had fallen into paranormal investigations and ghost-trapping years ago. Calvin had hired Stacey because he wanted to withdraw from fieldwork, claiming that he was tired of trying to chase ghosts in rickety attics and basements while confined to a wheelchair.

"You can call me Stacey," Stacey told her. I don't know why I even bother introducing Stacey by her full name. It's just kind of fun to say: *Stacey Ray Tolbert.*

"I guess you've already met Lexa," Anna Treadwell said, giving her daughter a half-hug with one arm. Lexa ducked away, looking annoyed. "Come on inside, everyone. Please ignore the mess, we're still unpacking and organizing...everything's been crazy lately." I took it she didn't mean *crazy* in a fun way.

"Did you recently move here?" I asked as we followed Anna and Lexa inside. Anna had a gentle Midwestern sort of accent, so I knew she wasn't from Georgia originally.

"Oh, yes. About six weeks ago." The hallway was tall but fairly narrow, with a dark hardwood floor that made our footsteps echo. A hammer banged overhead. Light bulbs burned in a chandelier, but the heavy shadows of the corridor seemed to absorb the glow, leaving the upper corners dark. Heavy wooden doors lined both sides of the hall. One opened onto a dining room with a long, polished cherry table and matching chairs, plus cardboard boxes heaped in the corner. The opposing door opened onto a living room with a long leather couch, a big flatscreen on the wall, and more boxes waiting to be unpacked.

The hall seemed to end abruptly. On the right side, a flight of polished wooden stairs led up and out of sight. Just past the steps, at the very end of the hall, was another heavy door like the one through which we'd entered. Three industrial-sized deadbolts were built into it, and one was locked into place. The wall around the door seemed a slightly different color than those around it, as though the wall and door were not original to the house and had been added later.

"Dale!" Anna shouted up the stairs. The hammering paused for a moment, then resumed. "Dale, the ghost detectives are here!"

The hammering continued.

"My husband will be down in a second," Anna said with an apologetic smile. Though she was putting up a calm front, her hands were trembling.

"No rush," I said. I wanted to put her at ease but wasn't sure how. "Where did you move from?"

"Oh, Marietta. Outside Atlanta?" She pointed back over her shoulder.

"I'm familiar."

"Chicago before that. Dale grew up there." Anna took a deep breath and screamed: "Dale, get down here *right now!*"

The hammering stopped, and there was another loud bang, as if someone had thrown a hammer on the floor. Footsteps clomped on the stairs. A thin man about Anna's age, his dark hair speckled with gray, stomped down from the landing.

"Anna, I can't leave a bookshelf half-hung!" he snapped at his wife. He definitely had a Chicago accent. There was a lot of nose in that voice. "I had to finish that second nail. Maybe if you helped out more, you would understand—"

"Dale, the detectives are here," Anna interrupted, pointing at us.

"What's that?" Dale saw us, then straightened up. A look of confusion crossed his face as he looked at me and Stacey.

I knew that look. I saw it most often among older males—they get thrown off-balance by the idea of a female detective.

We introduced ourselves quickly. Dale's voice became less whiny now that he wasn't alone with his family.

"You have a beautiful home, Mr. and Mrs. Treadwell," I added, eager to defuse any tension.

"It's a wreck," Dale said, shaking his head. "Real money pit, just like I said before we bought it. And that was before all the..." He shrugged, as if deciding he didn't want to finish his sentence.

"Is there somewhere we can sit and talk?" I asked, glancing at the dining room, where eight chairs were spaced around the table.

"Maybe the dining room." Anna and her family stepped around the piles of boxes to sit on one side of the table. Stacey and I took the opposite side, our backs to the two narrow windows that barely let in enough sunlight to pierce the gloom.

"I'm sorry about the clutter," Anna added, gesturing helplessly at the pile of unpacked boxes beside her.

"If you don't mind me asking, how did you end up moving to Savannah?" I asked.

"Oh, well, in our past life, Dale was vice-president of product development at AlgoSystems Data Management. Have you heard of them?"

I shook my head.

"Well, they're a...software company, basically," Anna continued. "And I was a corporate accounts executive at Southeastern Wireless. With our commutes and our careers, we barely saw each other, and Lexa practically lived at the daycare center. Together, Dale and I decided it was too much. We wanted to escape the rat race." She touched her husband's hand. He looked at the floor and slouched, as though maybe he wasn't so happy about escaping that particular race. "We'd visited Savannah a couple of times, and it was just such a beautiful city...We decided to buy one of these big old houses and turn it into a bed and breakfast. We bought this place for a steal, even when you consider how dilapidated it is."

"Yeah, we've stayed at some bed-and-breakfast spots around the country, and they're usually run by idiots," Dale said, perking up a little. "Just complete idiots. So we figured we could do it smarter. Imagine this: wife comes to husband, says she wants to spend a weekend at some fruity-fruit bed and breakfast in Savannah, so she can shop for antiques, visit museums, junk like that. Husband says no way. But wait, wife says. *This* one's got a sports lounge right on the ground floor—we're talking big-screen TV, beer on tap. Now husband's like, heck yeah, I can catch the Bears game, let's go!"

"Something to appeal to the whole family," Anna explained.

"Can we make this quick?" Dale asked. "We have a lot to do around here. The girls say they've seen ghosts, but I don't think so. I don't believe in ghosts."

"We'll move as fast as we can, Mr. Treadwell." I said, mentally noting how he referred to both his wife and daughter as *the girls*.

I gently set my black steel toolbox on the floor, since I didn't want to risk scratching their dining table. I popped the lid and brought out a long yellow legal pad, two pens, and a digital voice recorder.

I asked if it was okay to record the interview. Dale rolled his eyes, but nobody objected. I placed the device in the center of the table and tapped the record button.

"Okay, Mrs. Treadwell," I said, since it was clear that Dale was the family skeptic. "Can you tell us why you believe your house is haunted?"

Chapter Two

"It started about two or three weeks after we moved in," Anna Treadwell said.

"Sooner than that," her daughter Lexa interrupted, shaking her head. "Like the first week."

"Lexa was the first to experience it," Anna said. "She heard a couple of noises at night, but we thought it was just an old house with a lot of unfamiliar sounds. Settling, creaking..."

"I still say that's all it is," Dale interrupted. "The girls are just hearing things and scaring themselves."

"It is not!" Lexa snapped. "*She* wants us to leave. She wants us to move back home."

"This is our home now, sweetie," Anna told her daughter.

"It's not *my* home. Or Maggie's." Lexa clutched the doll close to her chest. "Maggie doesn't like it here."

"We've heard enough of that, Lexa!" Dale snapped at his daughter. "We told you, we moved here, we're staying here, and it's all final. Damned kid's regressing, carrying that doll around," Dale said to me, as if Lexa weren't even in the room.

"Dale, calm down," the wife said, looking shaken. "We're trying to figure this out."

"Nothing to figure out," Dale said. "You want to spend more money we don't have on stuff we don't need. Ghost hunters, Anna? Really?" He turned to look across the table at Stacey and me. "How much is this gonna set me back?"

"We haven't even determined whether there's an actual ghost," I replied. "Our fees depend on a variety of factors—"

"Already sounds expensive," Dale grunted.

"Dale, *please*," Anna snapped at her husband. "This is important."

Dale sighed and rolled his eyes again. "Couple of doors bang in the night, you girls get hysterical."

"I am not crazy!" Anna shouted. "Lexa is not crazy. If you would just listen--"

"All I do is listen! I listen to you two complaining and griping all day long. Always some stupid thing or some other thing that's even stupider than the last thing--"

"Why do you always think you know better than everyone else?" Anna hissed at him.

"Because I always do!" He slammed his fist on the table. "It's not my fault I'm surrounded by idiots!"

Lexa had curled up in her chair, tucking her knees up to her chest and clutching the doll tight. She looked a little flushed. I couldn't tell if the poor girl was scared or embarrassed. Maybe both.

Stacey and I were doing our best to keep our eyes on the table and pretend we weren't in the room while our clients had their family argument. It was awkward.

"That's enough of this crap." Dale stood up. His voice was getting whiny again. "You can all sit here wasting time and scaring each other if you want. Somebody has to get some real work done." He left the room and stomped away up the stairs.

"I'm sorry," Anna told us, her voice quiet. "It's been very stressful around here. I think he knows something's wrong, but he doesn't want to admit it..."

"Should we come back another time?" I asked, hoping she would say no.

"No!" Lexa shouted, sitting up in her chair. "You have to help us! You have to make her go away!"

"It's okay, sweetie." Anna tried to comfort the girl by patting her on the head again, but again Lexa pulled away from her. Anna looked at me. "We may as well go ahead."

"Why don't we start over?" I suggested.

"Okay." Anna took a deep breath. "After we moved in, Lexa started having bad dreams. We thought it was because, you know, a new house in a new city..."

"It was the lady," Lexa whispered. "Her eyes are like holes in the ground."

"One night, Lexa came to our bedroom and woke us up," Anna said. "She said there was somebody in the house."

"I heard her footsteps," Lexa added. "They came up the stairs. They stopped at my room. It was just footsteps that time."

A loud banging sounded overhead. Dale was hammering again, louder and harder than before, as though trying to make some kind of point.

"We got out of bed and searched around," Anna said. "We were a little worried about vandals and vagrants, since the house had been empty for a few years before we bought it. We didn't find anybody, but then we checked downstairs, and the door to the main house was open."

"Which door?" I asked.

"Down at the end of the hall."

"The one with all the deadbolts?" Stacey asked. "I was wondering about that..."

"At some point, the east wing was walled off from the rest of the house," Anna said. "It was a caretaker's apartment. Only one door connects it to the main house, and that's the door I'm talking about. It already had the deadbolts when we moved in, but two of the three are rusted and stuck open."

"Was it locked when you went to bed that night?" I asked.

"We assumed we must have left it unlocked, so we threw the bolt and went back to bed," Anna said. "I didn't think too much about it then. We thought the footsteps were just another of Lexa's bad dreams, and we expected those to stop once she got used to the house."

"It wasn't a *dream*," Lexa insisted. "I heard the door open. It went cree-eeeeak. Then her footsteps."

"It happened again the next night," Anna said. "Lexa came into our room talking about footsteps. We found the door to the main house wide open, with a cold draft blowing in. I know the door was deadbolted that second night, because I double-checked before bed. My husband insisted I must have been wrong." Anna rolled her eyes a little. "He said it must be the draft blowing open the door. So, the next night, I made *him* bolt the door and double-check it before bed."

"And how did that go?" I asked.

"We actually didn't have a problem that night," Anna said. "But the next night--"

"She came back," Lexa whispered. "I heard it from my bed. The door opened, the footsteps....Then I saw her." Lexa crumpled up in her chair, not looking directly at anyone.

"You don't have to talk about it if you don't want to," her mother said.

"First I heard the door, and I knew she was coming." Lexa was barely speaking above a whisper, and Stacey and I had to lean in to hear her. "Then her footsteps. It was usually just a couple of steps, but this time they came all the way up the stairs." Lexa was shivering, and she looked close to crying. "Then she came to my door and looked at me."

"What did you see?" Stacey asked, clearly enthralled as if hearing a campfire story. I cut her a warning look. *Don't look so happy*, I thought.

"You don't have to tell us if it's too scary," I told Lexa. "But it would help if you did."

Lexa whispered something, swallowing her words.

"It's okay, sweetie." Anna rubbed the girl's back. "Can you say it a little louder?"

"I said she looked dead," Lexa said, her eyes lifting to stare into mine. "She looked rotten. Her whole face. She had a raggy dress and her hair was really dirty. I couldn't see too much because all the lights were out, but I could feel her looking at me."

"What did you do?" I asked.

"I couldn't move!" Lexa's face screwed up and turned red. "I tried. I couldn't even yell. I was too scared. So I just stayed there and wished she would go away. She was gone after a minute."

"Back down the stairs?" I asked.

"Noooo..." Lexa shook her head furiously to emphasize how wrong I was. "She was just gone. I waited and waited and waited and then I tiptoed and looked out the door. She wasn't in the hall. She wasn't on the stairs. I ran to Mom and Dad's room."

"Lexa was really upset that time," Anna said. "We searched all over the east wing again, but nobody was there."

"And the security door downstairs?" I asked.

"Wide open again." Anna shook her head and rubbed the fresh goosebumps on her arms. "Dale and I had both checked to make sure it was locked before sleep."

I nodded. It was possible, I thought, that the girl was behind it all—first running downstairs and opening the door, then waking her parents and claiming to see and hear scary things. Lexa didn't seem like she was lying to me, but you have to consider these possibilities.

"The lady started coming every night," Lexa said. "Sometimes just footsteps. Sometimes I see her. She's mean."

"So we barricaded the door the next night," Anna said. "Furniture and heavy boxes full of hardback books. Dale thought there must be some kind of problem with the deadbolt. I thought so, too. It was the only thing that made sense, you understand?"

"Of course," I said.

"A loud crash woke me up later that night," Anna said.

"It woke up *everybody*," Lexa added.

"We told Lexa to stay in her room, then Dale and I ran downstairs." Anna folded her hands on the dining table. She was trying to act calm, but her hands were trembling and her face had lost all its color.

"Downstairs, the boxes and chairs had fallen over, and some of the boxes had spilled open. It looked like someone had given the door a hard shove and knocked it all down, but only a really strong person could have pulled that off. And the deadbolt was wide open again. A draft came from the main house, and it smelled like...just rot and decay. Death."

"She didn't like that," Lexa said. "When we tried to lock her out like that."

"Dale called the police," Anna said. "He was convinced it was a break-in. 'Probably teenagers,' he kept saying. 'Probably just some idiot teenagers.' The police looked around, but they didn't find anybody. All the doors were locked and the windows latched, so nobody had broken in—not in the main house, or here in the east wing. There was no explanation. Lexa told them about the disappearing woman she'd seen."

"Dad didn't want me to tell the police about her," Lexa said. "He got mad at me."

"I tried to laugh it off, but I guess I wasn't very convincing." Anna forced a laugh. "Just before they left, one of the officers—an older man—pulled me aside and told me that if it kept happening, I might call your detective agency. He said Eckhart Investigations had cleared up a few hauntings around town. I just looked at him like he was crazy. Now I feel pretty bad about that."

I'd been taking notes the whole time. Footsteps: possible auditory manifestation. The door opening, even when bolted and barricaded: possible psychokinetic activity. The vanishing dead woman: a full apparition. If the haunting was real, it was a major one, but nothing we couldn't handle.

The only other explanation was an elaborate prank, which is more likely than it sounds. More than a few cases have turned out to be kids faking a ghost. I doubted Lexa was lying—she looked pretty scared and sleep-deprived—but logically I had to consider it.

"Let's back up a second," I said. "What exactly did you and your husband do after the crash woke you up? I mean from the first moment you were awake."

"Well..." Anna tapped her fingernails as she thought about it. "First, we looked at each other. Kind of a 'did you hear that?' moment, but we didn't have to say anything. We both ran to the hall, and we checked on Lexa first, of course--"

"How much time passed between the crash and when you reached her room?" I asked.

"Not long. Five seconds, maybe. Less than ten, I'm sure. Why?"

"Just being thorough..." I jotted down her time estimate. "How did you find Lexa when you reached her room?"

"She was upset."

"I was scared," Lexa said, nodding.

"I mean, where in the room was she? Near the door?"

"Lexa was still in bed," Anna said.

"You think I'm lying about the ghost," Lexa said, scowling at me. "Just like Dad."

"I didn't say that, Lexa," I told her. "I'm just trying to understand what happened that night."

"Yeah, right." She crossed her arms. "Are you going to help us or not?"

"I will if I can, Lexa. Have you seen anything else since that night?"

"She keeps coming to my room," Lexa said. "Even if I lock the door, it opens. Sometimes I can see her. Sometimes it's just footsteps."

"Has anyone else had strange experiences?" I asked Anna.

"Dale says he's never seen or heard anything, but I..." Anna hesitated and glanced at her daughter. "Lexa, do you want to go and play now?"

"No," Lexa said.

"I need to speak with the detectives alone, sweetie."

"You saw her." Lexa turned her scowl on her mom. "You saw her and you don't want me or Dad to know about it."

"I just...have had strange feelings, especially at night." Anna's fingers twisted together on the table while she spoke. "Like there's someone here who isn't supposed to be here. Someone watching me." She shuddered. "That's all. But...well what do you think?" Anna looked at me. "Do you think we have a ghost?"

She and Lexa both watched me closely. So did Stacey, who'd stayed quiet during the interview because she was still learning the process. Anna and Lexa looked worried; Stacey was barely able to hide her excitement.

"It sounds very possible to me," I said. The family didn't strike me as particularly crazy or ghost-happy. It's a little awkward when you meet new clients and part of your job is assessing whether or not they're completely in touch with reality. I got my degree in psychology to help me work with ghosts, but it's handy when studying potential clients, too. "Can you show us the places where you've had activity? The door, the stairs, maybe Lexa's room?"

"This way!" Lexa said, shoving herself out of her chair as if eager to get things moving.

"Do you mind if Stacey takes some video, Mrs. Treadwell?" I asked. I nodded at Stacey, who was already opening her camera bag to grab her video recorder. "It's part of the process."

"Of course." She gave me a tight, fake smile. "And you can call me Anna."

As we left the room, Stacey was on the balls of her feet. She probably felt what I felt—there was something wrong in this house, a sense that the shadows were too dark and the air too cold and heavy. Stacey was probably thrilled about that.

Chapter Three

Anna began our tour with the downstairs kitchen and living room, explaining how they'd started with the bathrooms and kitchen to make the caretaker's apartment livable.

"Everything was a wreck at first," she told me. "We brought in new appliances, of course, and we had to scrub and re-stain all the woodwork...the floor's new, obviously...we have contractors in and out all the time."

I nodded politely while she demonstrated the drawers and cabinets, and how they opened and closed and had shelves inside them. She brightened up as she talked about her struggles with picking new cabinet pulls. It seemed to calm her down, so I didn't interrupt.

Finally, we walked down the short hallway and faced the door. Anna's chatty smile faded into a quiet frown. Lexa stayed behind her, crossing her arms and glaring at the door.

"It looks like a serious security door," I said, stepping close to study the three bolts. "Is it thick?"

"A few inches, I think," Anna said. "It's a bear to haul it open."

"It would take a pretty strong draft to do that," Stacey said.

"I wonder why somebody would put this here," I said.

"We think somebody used to rent out rooms here," Anna said. "In the main house, each bedroom has a lock with a key. The master suite on the third floor was cut up into rooms that can be locked against each other."

"But you don't know for sure?" I asked.

"The realtor didn't know much about the house's past, but it looks that way to me," Anna said. "Somebody lived in the east-wing apartment and rented out the bedrooms. Maybe he didn't trust his tenants."

"That's something we'll have to find out." I knocked on the door, then reached for the closed deadbolt. "Do you mind if I open it?"

Anna and Lexa looked even more pale. Anna attempted to speak twice before she managed to say, in a very reluctant voice, "Go ahead."

I grasped the cold, rust-speckled iron knob. I pulled, and it scraped heavily against its housing, reluctant to move. I had to grit my teeth and wrench it hard, and it finally slid open with a shriek.

"Creepy," Stacey said, smiling behind her camera.

"Shh," I told her. "I just want to test the door."

The door's curved handle was also heavy, cold iron. I wrapped my fingers around it and pulled hard.

The heavy door opened onto a dark hallway, much of which had been stripped down to studs for remodeling.

"I don't think a breeze would nudge that door open," Stacey mentioned again.

"No," I said. "The lock and handle are both iron, though. Highly conductive."

"What does that mean?" Anna asked.

"Ghosts are dense electromagnetic energy," I said. "It may be easier for them to manipulate conductive materials."

"So we should change the lock?" Anna asked.

"It could help a little, but I want to learn more before I start giving advice." I peered ahead into the dark main-house hallway. "Do you ever see or hear anything strange in there? Besides this door opening?"

"Sure, some creaking and settling at night," Anna said. "We don't go over to the main house after dark. We work over there during the day, but of course we're making a lot of noise then, hammering and sawing....Plus, I like to blast music when I work."

I nodded, eased the door closed, and slid the deadbolt back into place.

"These are the stairs where you hear footsteps?" I pointed to the staircase. Lexa nodded, with a deep frown on her face.

"Those are the only steps in the east wing," Anna told me.

"Let's check them out." I ascended the stairs slowly. They were made of beautiful dark wood, surrounded by matching paneling on the walls. The Treadwells had already hung family pictures here, showing their little family at younger ages, as well as posing with others I assumed to be family friends and relatives. I wondered if the household ghost felt annoyed at this territorial marking by the new owners.

A huge antique chandelier dripping with crystal hung at the landing. I had to turn around to climb the next flight of steps up to the second floor. The wood squeaked and groaned beneath my shoes.

"Lexa's room is the first door you see," Anna told me as I reached the upstairs hall. Like the downstairs hall just below it, it was oddly short for its width. There was no door at the end of this one, just a blank wall where the east wing had been severed from the main house.

I stopped in front of Lexa's bedroom. "Lexa, can you show me where you saw the lady?"

"She stops right here." Lexa slowly opened the door. "She stands right here and watches me in bed."

Her room was particularly nice, spacious with a high ceiling, a queen-sized bed, a brick fireplace with a hand-carved mantel, and a row of narrow medieval-style windows. It was painted a shade of yellow that seemed like it was trying too hard to be cheerful and sunny.

I asked Lexa to describe the ghost woman again, and she mostly repeated what she'd said earlier—ragged dress, dead face with some decay, hair like dry straw. I nodded, quietly checking her story for consistency. One old cop trick I'd learned from Calvin: people who are telling the truth tend to keep their story consistent, while those who aren't tend to change and embellish the story each time they tell it. I always like to ask witnesses to recount their experiences a few times over, just to check.

"What do you do when you see her?" I asked Lexa.

"I just stay there and keep quiet," Lexa said, nodding at her canopy bed, which was occupied by a large stuffed bear in a tuxedo. "I'm too scared to close my eyes and I'm too scared to yell for help."

"Does she say or do anything while she's here?"

"No. But she doesn't like us. She wants us to leave."

"How do you know that?" I asked.

"I can tell by how she looks at me." Lexa shrugged. "By everything she does. Slamming the door open and trying to scare us."

"Has she ever hurt anybody?" I looked from Lexa to Anna, but they both shook their heads.

"Listen, Lexa," Anna said. "Why don't you show Stacey your room for a minute?"

Lexa gave her mother a suspicious look.

"Oh, good idea!" Stacey agreed. "And you can tell me more about the ghost..." Stacey's warm, smiling attention seemed to relax Lexa a little bit, and Lexa led Stacey into her room.

I looked at Anna, wondering why she'd wanted to send them away. Anna took my arm and led me into the master bedroom. The windows were open, and I could hear Anna's husband outside, barking orders at the roofers in his Chicago accent.

"He thinks he knows everything," Anna whispered. She led me past the king-size bed. The polished antique furniture was mostly heavy, dark wood. A few bookshelves had been nailed to the wall, but that project looked half-completed, with nails and sawdust on the carpet below. It looked like they'd put in new carpet before renovating the walls—not the smartest choice.

Anna took me into the spacious master bath. The tub was Jacuzzi sized, and there was a separate shower stall tucked into the corner. A big picture window overlooked the dense, tangled greenery of the back yard. A little sunlight seeped in through the wide glass pane, but the canopy of leafy, twisted limbs outside seemed to absorb most of the light before it ever touched the house.

I shivered. Despite the seeping sunlight, the master bath was much colder than the master bedroom. I waved my hand in front of the air-conditioner vent, but no air was blowing out.

"It's cold, isn't it?" Anna whispered. "It's not just me?"

"No, it's not." I crossed my arms, feeling a little ill. "This room doesn't feel right."

"I didn't want to scare Lexa, and I know Dale would just call me crazy, but..." Anna took a breath. She gestured toward the shower stall, which was walled with clear panes of glass. Not much privacy there, especially when you considered the giant picture window just across from the shower.

"Did something happen to you?" I asked her, speaking as gently as I could.

"Two nights ago," Anna said. Her voice was so soft I had to lean in to listen. "We'd been doing cabinets and painting all day—I like to do the painting—so I thought I'd have a long, hot shower before stumbling to bed. I was exhausted.

"In the middle of the shower, everything turned cold," Anna said. "First the water, like the water heater had conked out, which is totally possible since Dale installed it himself. Then the *air* got cold. I could feel the temperature plunge. I opened my mouth to yell at Dale, and that's when the lights turned out. So I'm standing there in the dark, freezing, with my hair full of shampoo.

"I called out to Dale to see if he'd turned off the light by accident, or maybe as a prank, but Dale doesn't really do pranks. I called for him a few times, but nobody answered.

"I washed out my hair as fast as I could in that freezing water, then I turned it off. I opened the shower door and sort of felt along in the dark until I found the towel rod.

"After I wiped my face and opened my eyes...that's when I realized I wasn't alone. Someone else was in the room, but it wasn't Dale. It wasn't Lexa, either. It was an adult woman. She stood right there, like a solid black shadow in front of the window. She was facing me, and she wasn't moving at all." Anna wrapped her arms around herself, and I could see goosebumps all over her.

"Can you describe her a little more?" I asked.

Anna shook her head. "She blocked out most of the moonlight. I could sort of see her hair—stringy, messy hair like dry straw...sort of like a crazed drug addict's hair, you know? She was staring right at me."

"What did you do?"

"You'd think I would scream, right? But I didn't. I could barely catch my breath. I couldn't even move, except for my knees. They wouldn't stop wobbling. I just stood there and clutched my towel and stared back at her."

"How long did that go on?" I asked.

"I don't know—a few seconds, a minute? It felt like a long time. And she still didn't move *at all*. Then she spoke to me. Just a whisper, and I heard it right in my ear. She said..." Anna swallowed, then spoke in a harsh whisper: "She said, '*Leave this house.*' That was it, just three words."

"When I heard her voice, I screamed. I could move again, so I ran to the door and pulled it open." Anna demonstrated by opening the bathroom door and gesturing into her bedroom. "The light was on in there, and it didn't feel cold at all. Dale was just lying in bed with his reading glasses and his new issue of *Motor Trend.*

"He jumped up, and I told him there was someone in the bathroom...The lights flickered back on just as he came in here to check. He acted like I was crazy. She was gone."

"That sounds pretty upsetting," I said, looking over the picture window. "I don't see any way someone could sneak in or out of here...the windows don't open..."

"Exactly. So, do you think I'm crazy?"

"I think something is obviously happening in this house."

"Me, too." Anna seemed relieved. "Do you think it was the same woman Lexa keeps talking about?"

"There's no way to tell yet, but maybe you should discuss that with her."

"I don't want to scare her."

"She's already scared," I said. "I think she'll feel better if she knows she's not alone, that you've seen things, too. Especially since your husband doesn't seem to believe any of it."

"Maybe I'll talk it over with her." Anna hurried out of the cold bathroom. The bedroom beyond it had to be ten or fifteen degrees warmer. "Should I tell Dale about it first?"

"Tell Dale about what?" Dale leaned in through one of the big, open bedroom windows, apparently taking a break from harassing the roofers. "This better not cost a heap of money, Anna."

"There's no charge for the initial consultation, Mr. Treadwell," I said.

"Yeah, right." He stepped in through the window.

"Is there anything else you wanted to show me?" I asked Anna.

"That's the worst of it," Anna said.

"Are you still talking about that light going out in the bathroom?" Dale asked. "I told you, Anna, we're still repairing the electricity. It's all a big rat's nest down at the fuse box. Stuff's gonna happen."

"And I told you I saw somebody in there," Anna said. "A

woman."

"Oh, right. The 'move out now' lady. We aren't moving out, so she better give up." Dale smirked and shouted into the bathroom, his hands cupped around his mouth. "Hear that, ghost lady? We aren't moving!"

"Don't make her mad," Anna whispered, and Dale just snorted and shook his head. He walked past us and clambered on down the stairs, and turned on the television to watch a golf game. He must have been exhausted from all the minutes he'd spent watching the roofers work.

"Do you think you can help us?" Anna asked me as we walked into the hall.

"She says they can!" Lexa said, dashing out from her room. Stacey followed behind her with the little video camera, and she gave me an apologetic smile.

"There must be something we can do, right?" Stacey asked. She was blushing—she'd overstepped her bounds a little bit, and she knew it. I was supposed to be the one who determined whether the alleged haunting needed further investigation.

Fortunately for Stacey, she was right this time. I did think something nasty had moved into the Treadwell house.

"Here's what I would like to do," I said. "Let's schedule a night when Stacey and I can stay over. We'll do a full observation of all the hotspots—video, audio, thermal, electromagnetic frequencies. We'll have cameras in the hallway, the stairs, and of course the door that keeps opening..." I led them downstairs as I spoke, then I gestured at the heavy security door with the deadbolts. "I'll probably camp out in your hall to keep an eye on that door."

"Maybe we could rig a camera on the other side, too," Stacey said. "You know, in the main house over there? We might catch the ghost coming or going."

I nodded. "And I'll look into the history of the house and see if we might find a cause for a haunting. Maybe some clues to the ghost's identity, if we're lucky. It's so much easier to trap ghosts when you know who they are. What do you think, Anna?"

Anna and Lexa looked at each other.

"Can we start tonight?" Anna asked me.

"Let me check my schedule..." I opened the calender app on my phone and pretended to look through it, even though the only appointments were meeting with the Treadwells this morning and my kickboxing class at four in the afternoon. "We could come back around seven or eight."

"Yes!" Stacey said, grinning and nodding like a goofball. She was eager to catch a ghost. "I can start the set-up right now, if you want..." She looked between Anna and me.

"We'll have plenty of time when we come back," I said.

"And then you'll get rid of the ghost?" Lexa asked.

"First we have to know what kind of ghost we're dealing with," I said. "But, yes, Lexa. We'll get rid of this ghost even if we have to drag her out by her hair. You're going to be perfectly safe."

For the first time since I'd met her, Lexa smiled.

Chapter Four

"Full apparition with multiple witnesses, psychokinetic disturbances...sounds promising," Calvin Eckhart said. He sat at the scuffed wooden worktable in our office, which was actually more of an industrial space out on Telfair Road. Not exactly a central or historic spot—our next-door neighbor is a car-crushing place—but building and maintaining ghost traps has elements of heavy industry, so Calvin rents his space away from the more populated areas.

Our clients rarely come to the office, anyway. We mostly do house calls. It's not like they can bring their ghosts to us.

There's a semi-professional-looking area out front, with some actual carpet, a few old chairs for visitors, and few dog-eared magazines that are even older than the chairs. The largest area is the workshop in back, where we were eating lunch. Here, the floor is bare concrete and power tools hang on the walls. There are coils of copper wire and a big blue Paragon kiln for glassmaking.

I'd brought Calvin some pork fried rice from Happy King China. I'd ordered myself some of their vegetables, but more importantly, I had a large Styrofoam cup of sweet tea. Happy King China has the best sweet tea in town. Not many people know that secret.

Calvin's dog, a droopy-faced bloodhound named Hunter, sat

under the table sniffing fried-rice aroma with his super-sensitive nose.

"So what's your plan of attack?" Calvin asked. He dug his chopsticks into his rice again.

"Pretty standard so far. I'll hit the library and see what I can dig up about that house. I already called the Savannah Historical Association, but nobody can meet with me until tomorrow. The family's ready for us to set up a full-spectrum observation tonight...well, the wife's ready. The husband thinks it's all nonsense."

"He's probably just in denial to hide his fear," Calvin said. "He knows something is opening that door at night, and he knows he can't stop it."

I nodded. "So that's the plan. I'm going to sit by that door all night."

"I've been concerned about you going to these jobs by yourself," Calvin said.

"I know, so you hired Stacey, and now I'm stuck training a ghost-happy paranormal fangirl."

"Stacey has plenty of good qualities for this job."

"Name one," I said.

"She'll work for cheap," he replied.

"Name two."

"She's good at collecting audio-video evidence."

"Name three."

"Stop moving the goalposts," Calvin said. "My point is, I don't want you to get hurt investigating these hauntings. Stacey sits out in the van with the monitors while you're alone inside."

"I can handle whatever any ghost wants to throw at me."

"I used to think that, too." Calvin glanced at his thin legs, sitting useless in his wheelchair. Calvin had grown out his gray hair a bit since leaving the force, but he still had the square shoulders and rigid bearing of a cop. Even wearing his granny glasses and sitting in his wheelchair, he still projected authority.

"I get it, Calvin," I said. "I really do. You think you're sending a couple of girls into danger, but I promise you, we can handle it. If we can't, we'll get out of there. This doesn't even sound like a very dangerous haunting—maybe a territorial ghost trying to drive out the living, but she hasn't hurt anyone..."

"I am responsible for your safety," he said. "But I also think the team could use an extra perspective. An extra set of hands, too."

"I don't know if you've checked the ledger lately, but we aren't exactly rolling in spare cash right now. So even if we did need somebody else, which we don't, we can't afford it. We're lucky Stacey is a trust-fund baby willing to work for peanuts."

"Then we're doubly lucky that the young man I have in mind is willing to work for free—for now, at least—as part of his therapy."

"Therapy? What is he, a phasmophobic?"

"He doesn't have an irrational fear of ghosts," Calvin said. "If he's afraid of them, it's because he finds himself surrounded by them. Purely rational, really."

"I don't think I like where this is going." I put down my fork and sat up on my old wooden workbench stool.

"He was in an airline crash," Calvin said. "One of only a few survivors. Since then, he's been in almost constant contact with the dead--"

"No, no, come on. You know what I think about using psychics."

"I've had some great help from them in the past," Calvin said.

"And we've been burned by them, too. Subtract out the frauds, the crazies, and the ones who maybe *are* psychic but are still obviously crazy--"

"An old friend recommended him to me," Calvin said. "She thinks working with us would help him gain control over his abilities."

"That's why he'll work for free, then," I said. "Because he doesn't know what he's doing."

"Exactly. You said yourself this is a minor case with limited danger. It sounds like a good test for him. We can just see what he finds."

"I like to keep it scientific, Calvin. Things you can observe and measure."

"This city's full of colleges. Why don't you call around and see how many professional scientists agree that applied parapsychology is related in any way to actual hard science?"

"I just don't like the idea of some guy wandering around pretending to download information into his brain. It can distract you from the real evidence."

"Or break the case," Calvin said. "I had one or two psychics help with that even when I was still on the job. Missing persons and homicide—police use psychics more than the public knows."

"You told me I'd be in charge of the field work now," I said.

"That was our agreement. You can't stick me with some crystal ball reader who'll just trip up my investigation." I stood up and tossed my greasy to-go box into the trash. "I have to run. The library closes at six today. You going to your poker game tonight?"

"Changing the subject and running away?" He raised an eyebrow at me.

"Exactly. I'll check in later." I opened the steel fire door at the back and hurried out before he could try to sell me on the psychic again. He really should have known better.

I left the big van at the office so Stacey could set it up when she returned from lunch. I drove my own car, a black 2002 Camaro that continues to run mainly by magic, I think. It has T-tops that pop out so I can soak up the roughly nine months of summer this city enjoys every year. And, when I get the chance, I can drive very, very fast. It's probably not the kind of car I would have bought for myself, but I inherited it from my dad, so I wouldn't trade it for anything.

I zipped a couple of exits down the interstate, then hit thick traffic downtown. I didn't have far to go, though.

The Bull Street Library is a thing of beauty, nearly a hundred years old, with a Grecian marble facade and Ionic columns. It's a gorgeous sunlit place to spend a few hours slogging through microfilm in search of murder and death.

Chapter Five

"I want to check whether you recognize any of these women," I said to Anna. We sat at her dining room table again, facing each other. I'd asked Lexa and Stacey to leave the room. It was eight-thirty, and the windows behind me showed solid darkness outside.

I opened the manila envelope and slid out ten black-and-white photos printed on regular computer paper, all of them drawn from the library's newspaper archives. They showed women with clothing and hairstyles from across the past century. I'd been at the library until closing time, mucking around in microfiche, which meant I'd missed my kickboxing class. I didn't totally regret it—kickboxing is a great workout but also kind of a pain.

Of the ten images on the table, only two really interested me. The other eight were filler. Since Anna had described a woman with straw-like hair, half the women were blond.

Anna watched with her brow furrowed as I spread out the pictures. She took a few minutes looking them over.

I sipped some of the coffee she'd thoughtfully brewed for Stacey and me. It was strong and rich, which was good. It was going to be a long night.

Finally, Anna touched one page and slid it over to me.

"That could be her," Anna said, tapping a pretty woman in a dark dress with long, unkempt yellow hair. The woman wore a flat, blank look. It was an arrest photo.

"Who?" I asked.

"The one I saw. If it's any of them, it's her."

"Okay. I'd like to ask Lexa the same thing, if that's all right." I slid the woman's picture back into place.

Anna nodded. She opened the door and brought Lexa inside. The house echoed with the sound of banging—Dale had picked the moment of our arrival to go hang drywall in the main house.

Stacey leaned in the door with a questioning look, and she obviously wanted to get in on the action. I gestured for her to stay where she was. She nodded, gave a conspiratorial wink and a thumbs-up, then raised the digital camera to continue recording us.

Lexa sat across from me. Her eyes were wide and solemn as she looked down at the pictures.

"Lexa," I said, "I just want to know if you happen to recognize any of these people."

"That's her." Lexa picked up the same printout and waved it at me. "Who is she?"

"Her name is Mercy Cutledge," I said. I hesitated to continue. What I was about to say was not exactly great conversation for a ten-year-old, but Lexa was already being haunted by the woman. Knowing the identity of a specter can give you a real sense of power over it—it's no longer some unknown evil tormenting you, but a specific person with a name and a past. If I were Lexa, I would have wanted to know. I had to see kids frightened or endangered by ghosts, and always feel a special need to protect them.

"Did she used to live here?" Lexa asked, still gazing at the grainy picture.

"I think so. The newspaper said she was a household employee of a past owner of this house, a sea captain named...Augustus Oliver Marsh." I drew out a picture of Captain Marsh, a bald, white-bearded man in a white suit, posing in a highbacked chair next to a telescope and a globe. His mouth was a hard, humorless line almost lost in his enormous beard, which curled down to his shoulders and chest. His eyes were bright and sharp, almost stabbing outward from the paper. "Have you heard of him?"

Anna shook her head.

"Do you recognize this woman?" I pointed to a scratchy image of a woman in a high-necked dress and a large hat decorated with feathers. It was the oldest picture of the group.

"No," Lexa said, and Anna shook her head again.

"This was Eugenia Marsh, his wife," I said. "She died in 1901. Sudden sickness and fever."

"Oh, no!" Anna said.

"Captain Marsh himself died in 1954...also in this house. He was murdered by this woman, Mercy Cutledge." I pointed to the picture that Anna and Lexa had both picked up.

"I just felt chills up and down my back," Anna whispered.

"Was it like someone was touching you?" Stacey asked, dashing toward her with the camera. "Like fingers, or a hand, or—"

"Calm down, Stacey Ray," I said.

"She's a murderer," Lexa whispered, staring at the blond woman.

"I don't understand something," Anna said. "If his wife died in 1901...how old was he in 1954?"

"According to his obituary, he was born in 1848." I brought out a copy of the old newspaper notice to show them. "He fought in the Confederate Navy as a teenager, and later he became a steamship captain. So he was a hundred and six when he died."

"Wow." Anna gaped at the picture.

"Why did she kill him?" Lexa asked. "What did he do?"

"I couldn't find that in the papers," I said. "She was committed to a state psychiatric hospital..." I leafed through more of the printouts. "Released in 1982. After which....Well, it's a little disturbing." I was already feeling bad for talking about the murders in front of the girl.

"Lexa, do you want to leave the room?" Anna asked.

"No!" Lexa scowled. "Tell me everything about her."

I glanced at Anna, who sighed and nodded.

"She paid a return visit to this house after she was released the mental hospital," I said. "By then, it was owned by Marsh's grandniece, Louisa Marsh. And...well, Mercy came back here and took her own life."

Anna gasped and looked at Lexa, who was just nodding and processing. She looked much calmer than her mother.

For Lexa's benefit, and maybe for Anna's, too, I spared the true gory details. I hadn't mentioned how Mercy Cutledge had stabbed the extremely elderly man thirty-three times with a butcher knife, or how she'd hanged herself from the second-floor landing in the foyer twenty-eight years later, leaving Marsh's grand niece to find the body.

I figured I would get into those specifics only if I needed to, and preferably when the little girl wasn't around.

"So that's our ghost," Anna whispered.

"It seems likely to me," I said. "Especially after you both picked her out of the line-up."

"Then how do we..." Lexa glanced around, then lowered her voice until it was barely audible, as if afraid the ghost would overhear her. "How do we make her go away?"

"First, we have to see what kind of ghost she is," I told them. "Some ghosts are more like recordings, just doing the same thing again and again. Some are more aware of what's going on around them. She's obviously territorial and trying to scare your family away. Maybe she thinks she's still living in this house. Stacey and I will do our observation tonight, and that should give us plenty of information about what we're dealing with."

"Are you going to stay all night?" Lexa asked.

"That's the plan," I said.

"Good." Lexa nodded.

"We'll both be watching out for you, Lexa," Stacey said. "You don't have to worry about anything tonight!"

That claim was a little exaggerated. It was entirely possible that our presence would anger the ghost, goading her into being more aggressive. Still, I nodded slightly, wanting to comfort the girl. Lexa gave me a suspicious look, but she did seem to relax a little in her chair.

"Should we get started?" I asked.

Since Dale was working over in the main house, with the security door ajar, we started upstairs. We set up twin cameras in the master bathroom, one regular digital video, one thermal to detect cold spots. Stacey hummed the *Ghostbusters* theme while she worked, until I gave her a look that told her to cut it out.

"I guess I'll be using the hallway bathroom tonight," Anna said, in a resigned, half-joking sort of tone.

"Remind Dale, too, please," Stacey said, and I had to swallow back a laugh. Stacey would be out in the van monitoring all the cameras and microphones together. She was probably worried about seeing Dale using the bathroom in the middle of the night. That would be less scary than a ghost, but not by much.

When Stacey was done there, we moved out into the upstairs

hallway. We set up a night vision camera outside Lexa's door. Stacey raised it high on its tripod and tilted it forward, so we could see anyone on the second flight of stairs or in the hallway by Lexa's room.

Lexa smiled and nodded a little, as if the camera made her feel a little safer.

We set up another pair of cameras in the downstairs hall, a night vision and a thermal, pointed right at the security door. I placed my little inflatable air mattress behind them. This way, I could watch the door with my own eyes, plus see the display screens of both cameras, all at a glance.

Through the security door, we could still hear Dale hammering away at the drywall in the main house, though it was almost ten o' clock now. Anna and I stepped through the door.

We stood in a dim hallway in the main house, lit by a couple of electric lanterns. The floor was ancient, heavily scuffed hardwood. If there had been any furniture here, it had been cleared out while the contractors stripped and replaced the walls. The hall had a few old wooden doors, all of them closed, and it led into darkness in both directions.

"Don't you think that's enough for tonight, Dale?" Anna asked. "The ghost hunters need to set up over here."

"Oh, almost forgot about them," Dale said, giving me a little sneer. "I hope you don't slow things down too much."

Here's what I wanted to say: *You're only being sarcastic and smarmy to hide your fear, Dale. You know something creepy is happening, and you're just making a pathetic attempt to cling to the denial stage.*

Here's what I actually said: "We don't mean to cause you any trouble at all, Mr. Treadwell. We just need to monitor this hallway tonight."

Dale made a show of sighing and putting down his tools.

"Whatever calms the girls down, I guess," he said. "I need to go take a shower, anyway."

Stacey looked worried as Dale walked through the open security door, back into the east wing. He tossed her a smile as he passed by.

"Use the hall bathroom!" Anna told him. "They put cameras in ours."

"Oh, come on!" Looking annoyed, Dale strode up the stairs. "Can't get any privacy around here..."

I kept my face calm and professional while he left, biting back the urge to make a snarky remark when he was out of range. Anna and Lexa were still his wife and daughter and might not appreciate such comments from an outsider, no matter how he was acting. All three family members were my clients and had to be treated with respect.

I caught Stacey's eye just as she opened her mouth to say something, and she seemed to think better of it and stayed quiet.

"It's dark in here," I said. Dale's two electric lanterns were feeble in the heavy gloom, like sputtering candles. I clicked on my flashlight, piercing the darkness with three thousand lumens of shimmering light.

A flashlight is a ghost trapper's sidearm. Seriously. You can chase a lot of nasties away with a solid blast of bright white. It doesn't hurt them, but it can bother them enough to make them slip off in search of darker pastures. A strong bright light interferes with the ghosts' electrical fields, making it harder for them to focus when they want to claw at you or throw dishes at your head. This is probably why ghosts prefer to do their haunting and harassing at night.

Lately, I've been carrying an MF Tactical PowerStar, a SWAT team flashlight with a hard aluminum casing and protruding steel ridges around the lens, which can help if you need to break in or out of a place quickly. It puts out up to thirty-three hundred lumens at a blast, like a beam of sunlight on a hot desert day.

Of course, my job is to find and remove the ghosts, not to send them scurrying away into hiding, so I only use the flashlight as a last resort, when the need to finish the job is momentarily overshadowed by danger. Or by fear—I get into a lot of very dark, scary situations in this line of work, and I'm not too ashamed to say I still get terrified when I encounter malevolent specters and spirits. I'm only human.

"I want to get the door from each direction," Stacey said. She raised a night vision camera on a tripod and pointed toward the back of the main house. "I'll do this one back there. Do you mind setting up the last thermal?"

"Sure. I want to check out the foyer, anyway." That was where Mercy, Captain Marsh's murderer, had hanged herself in 1982. It was bound to be a center of any activity.

Anna and Lexa stayed on their side of the house, but Lexa stood right in the doorway watching Stacey with large, fascinated eyes.

I carried the thermal camera up the hall toward the front of the house, swinging my flashlight from side to side. The house contractors still had a lot of work to do, but generally the hallway looked nice, with its high crown molding and plaster ceiling fully intact and recently restored.

From the public real estate records, I knew the house had gone through several owners since it left the Marsh family. The sale prices had ballooned during the real estate bubble, until the last owner suffered foreclosure during the downturn. The house had been empty and bank-owned since then, until the Treadwells had purchased it at a very reduced price a few months earlier.

I reached the end of the hall and put down the thermal camera, but I didn't set it up yet. Curiosity was driving me onward.

I nudged open the last door and stepped out into the foyer.

It was a large space, two stories with a row of narrow Gothic windows above the door. A wide, blocky staircase ran up the western wall and connected with a second-story walkway. Heavy oak double doors stood at the front of the room, with a fairly new steel chain looped and locked around the door handles, making entry from the outside impossible.

Unlike the rest of the house I'd seen, this spacious room appeared to have been hit hard by the corrosive effects of rain, wind, vagrants, and juvenile delinquents. Several of the second-story windows were boarded up, and many of them were surrounded by water damage and dark patches of mold. The room reeked of decay, probably because of the mold.

The walls were discolored and warped, and they looked like diseased skin. Graffiti was everywhere, all over the walls, floor, and stairs, some of it occult, most of it just puerile and pornographic.

I shined my light up the stairs. An ornate wooden handrail adorned the staircase. At the top, the handrail curved around and became the balustrade for the upstairs walkway, where a few doors and a central hallway led deeper into the house. The balusters were densely packed all along the way, two to a stair, and carved in ornate Victorian style.

The second-floor walkway ended at the eastern wall of the room. I could see a rectangular area where the hallway had been walled up and painted over to divide the east wing from the rest of the house. It looked oddly sunken, like a closed lid over a missing eye.

I swung the light back along the balustrade. Near the center, one of the thick wooden balusters had broken, and its lower half was missing. I wondered if that was the spot where Mercy Cutledge had hanged herself.

I was starting to feel ill. The rotten mold smell was aggressively forcing its way up my nostrils and down my throat. A sudden wave of sickness can indicate a ghost—typically a ghost who does not want you around.

"Mercy," I said, in case she could hear me. "Mercy Cutledge. We know you died in this room. We're here to help. We don't mean you any harm—we want to help you move on and leave this family in peace."

I didn't receive an answer, unless it was the second wave of nausea rolling through me, making me want to vomit between my boots. I covered my nose and mouth with my hand, my stomach heaved, and I ran back to the door through which I'd entered as fast as I could.

"Hey, you okay?" Stacey called out at the sound of my running into the hall. She blasted her flashlight at me. "Ellie?"

I waved my hand, afraid that if I spoke, it would be the final straw in making me throw up in a very embarrassing and entirely unprofessional fashion. I leaned against the wall and caught my breath. Compared to the foyer, the air in the side hall was like a crisp, clean mountain breeze.

"Earth calling Ellie," Stacey said. "Can you just say something? Say 'shut up, I'm fine.'"

"Shut up, I'm fine," I managed to breathe out. As the dizziness and nausea passed, I stood up and busied myself with the thermal camera. "That front room is a very bad place. Or at least a very rotten one. That could be the ghost's main lair."

"Should we stick a camera in there?" she asked.

"I'll just place this one at the very end of the hall. Maybe we'll catch something coming out of that room." I activated the camera and checked the little monitor to make sure it captured the length of the hall. Then I walked back to the open security door to join the others.

Stacey gave me a giddy, excited grin as we stepped back into the east wing hallway. "All set?"

"We're ready." I followed her through and pushed the security door shut, then slid the deadbolt and twisted the knob up to lock it into place. I double-checked to make sure the door was sealed tight.

Then I turned to face Anna and Lexa. Anna stood behind her daughter, her hands on the girl's shoulders. Lexa twisted the soft doll nervously in her hands.

"Okay, ladies," I told them. "You said it usually shows up between midnight and two, right? So we have about an hour. I'd recommend you follow your usual routine from here on."

"That means we should have gone to bed at nine," Anna said with a thin smile.

"I want to stay up with the ghost hunters," Lexa told her mom. "I want to see what they do."

"You won't miss much, Lexa," I said. "It's mostly a lot of sitting around. Like a police stakeout, but without the doughnuts, because Stacey and I are watching our carbs. If anything happens, Stacey will record it to show you in the morning."

"Yeah, you get to skip to the best parts, without the long boring parts in between," Stacey told her. "I'll cut together a special video of anything that's *not* boring, okay?" She flashed Lexa a cheerful smile, and the girl returned it, a little.

"Come on, sweetie," Anna told her daughter. "I'm ready for bed, too. We should let them work."

I watched the two of them depart up the stairs.

"Are we ready?" Stacey whispered. "Do you think we'll get one this time?"

"I hope so," I whispered back. "I've got bills to pay."

"Good luck to both of us, then." Stacey winked and clapped me on the shoulder. She left through the side door. I made sure it was closed behind her, but not locked. Stacey would be outside in the van, watching every camera at once. I wanted her to be able to come running if I needed help.

The house lay quiet. I turned out the lights, leaving only a single small lamp burning in the living room. It left the hall in a deep gloom, but not pitch dark. When my eyes adjusted, I could see the outline of the bolted security door.

I sat down on my inflated mattress on the hallway floor, facing the security door. I checked the display screens on the thermal and night vision cameras again. My cameras were recording the door at the end of the hall and a portion of the first flight of stairs. If anything came through the door and up the stairs to harass Lexa, there was a fair chance I'd capture a hint of it on camera.

I slipped on my headphones. While I waited for midnight, I read a thick paper copy of *Decline and Fall of the Roman Empire*. So sue me, I'm a nerd.

I kept my eyes on the locked security door, and I waited.

Chapter Six

It's a tricky business, ghost trapping. Ghosts have a funny way of not showing up when you want them, but instead creeping up on you when you don't. When you're alone in the house late at night, minding your own business, that's when you're likely to hear the unexplained footsteps, walk into a cold spot, or feel invisible fingers touch the back of your neck. When you're actually trying to find them, they can hide silently for days, even weeks.

The ghost at the Treadwell house, fortunately, did not keep us waiting long.

For a time, all I could hear was occasional creaks, and a slow drip of water somewhere as if a faucet had been left slightly open.

"Ellie," Stacey whispered over my headset. We stayed in touch through headphones with little microphones to keep our hands free. "Ellie, there's something happening in the main house."

"What is it?"

"It's a...oh, wow...uh...uh...holy cow..."

"You could be a littler clearer," I whispered.

"Sorry. The hall, over in the main house, by the foyer. I'm getting a rapid drop in temperature...it's been eighty-seven degrees but now it's seventy...sixty-eight..."

"What do you see?"

"Nothing on night vision. The thermal, though...it's like a deep blue cloud. It looks like it came from the foyer...now it's drifting down the hall...it's moving toward you, Ellie."

"Okay," I managed to say, while staring at the bolted door. My heart was already thumping faster in anticipation. I listened carefully, but I heard nothing on the other side. If an entity was moving toward me, it was doing so in complete silence.

"Getter closer now," Stacey whispered in my ear. "It's almost to the door."

"Can you see anything on night vision?"

"Nothing, sorry." Stacey took a breath. "It's at the door. It's stopping. Still just a blue mist on the thermal...the whole hallway is getting cold, like fifty degrees now, so it's hard to make out the shape..."

"Shh." I thought I'd heard something very small. A tiny metallic *plink*. The door was just a dark rectangle in the gloom, so I looked to the little screen of my night vision camera.

The room was quiet for a second...and then there was no mistaking the rusty, rasping sound as the bolt slid open. I could see it plainly on my night vision, the heavy bolt moved by an invisible hand.

I don't care how many ghosts you've encountered—the fear never goes away. I watched the bolt slide and felt myself shiver. A feeling of panic rose in my gut and had to be fought down. It was surreal, like a bad dream, watching that bolt scrape itself open.

I grabbed my flashlight from my open toolbox, just in case Mercy the ghost was in an angry, attacking sort of mood tonight, but I kept it turned off.

The door opened slowly and gently, as if nudged by a silent breeze, the hinges creaking. Behind the door lay a rectangle of solid darkness—even on my night vision camera, I couldn't see any details of the little hallway on the other side. There was just no light over there at all. It was unnerving to see that on my night vision, like staring into a black hole.

"Holy cow, the door's open!" Stacey gasped over my headset. "Right in front of you, Ellie!"

"Yeah, I noticed," I whispered back.

"We're picking up something on your thermal," Stacey added. "This could be it!"

I looked at the screen, and there it was—the blue mist shape

Stacey had mentioned, visible only by its cold temperature.

I didn't need the camera to tell me something was in the room with me. Already, the temperature was dropping hard. It's disturbing to be surrounded by hot summer air that abruptly begins to freeze. The air grows heavy and closes in around you like a big invisible hand.

I checked my Mel Meter, which detects electromagnetic fields as well as temperature. It's a critical tool. Parapsychology has never been an exact science—in fact, it's often called a pseudo-science or just plain delusion—but generally, a ghostly presence is strongly indicated when you have an unexplained surge in electromagnetic energy combined with a sudden drop in temperature.

I'd already checked the usual electrical hotspots, like outlets and appliances, so I had a general idea of what was normal for the room around me.

The EM portion of the meter spiked to six milligaus, indicating a high-energy presence. Readings of two to seven milligaus are often associated with ghosts. At the same time, the Mel Meter's temperature readings plummeted from ninety to sixty-seven degrees, confirming that the cold front prickling my skin and making me shiver wasn't just in my head.

"You okay in there?" Stacey asked. "Should I join you? I can totally come in if you want! I'm ready!"

"Stay in the van," I whispered. "I need your eyes all over the house."

On the thermal display, the mist rolled slowly toward the stairs, then drifted up along the first flight. I still couldn't see anything with my eyes or the night vision.

Then I heard the creak. It was just one stair, something like a light footstep made by a small woman. It may not sound like much, but at that moment, the single creak all but made my hair stand up.

Onscreen, the blue mist continued upward and out of sight. I quietly rose to my feet, flashlight in one hand and Mel Meter in the other. I grabbed my thermal goggles and perched the lenses on my forehead in case I needed them.

"She's out of sight," I whispered.

"Coming up the stairs," Stacey whispered back, and at that moment, I heard another creak, this one from the second flight that I couldn't see. I nearly jumped out of my skin. I forced myself to stay calm.

"She's a very active one," I whispered. "I'm following her."

"Are you sure? Should I come in now? Let me just grab my flashlight and my handheld camera, okay?" Stacey asked. She was trying to sound concerned, but she wasn't able to hide the excitement that wanted to bubble out. Stacey hadn't seen enough scary stuff to be cautious, but I knew she would eventually, if she stuck with me long enough.

"Hold your position," I said. That kind of talk comes by way of being trained by Calvin Eckhart. It's become automatic for me in these situations. "Just keep your eyes and ears open for me."

Gripping my flashlight in one hand and the Mel Meter in the other, I began to ascend the stairs. It grew colder with each step...sixty-one degrees on the first flight, fifty-three by the time I reached the midway landing. I started up the second flight.

"You're right behind her," Stacey whispered. "This is so freaky."

Forty-eight degrees. My own footsteps sounded as loud as gunshots in my ears as I climbed the stairs. Forty-five degrees. By the time I reached the top step, it was at forty degrees, and I could see a frosty plume each time I exhaled.

I stood in front of Lexa's door. The upstairs hallway was cold and silent around me, the moonlight thin from the windows, barely penetrating the darkness. The gloom felt oppressive, the air unnaturally heavy.

I was just about to drop the thermal goggles down over my eyes when I heard the tiny *click* from Lexa's door. Lexa's name was painted on a wooden square mounted in the middle of the door, surrounded by little flowers and butterflies in bright pigments.

The round doorknob gave the smallest squeak as it turned. The door to Lexa's room crept inward, again moving slowly, as if nudged by the lightest possible draft of air.

Lexa sat up in her bed, outlined by a feeble pink-flower nightlight plugged into the far wall near the fireplace. The room grew even darker around her, as if the nightlight were burning out.

"She's here," Lexa whispered to me. She raised a shaking arm and pointed at me. "She's right beside you."

The temperature was down to thirty-six degrees—my fingers would begin to freeze if it grew much worse.

I turned toward the freezing center of the cold spot and reached for my goggles again.

I didn't need them.

She took shape gradually, like a scrim of frost collecting in midair. At first, she was just a shape—female, petite, a little shorter than me, pale as ice. Then more details appeared. She wore a clingy, low-cut black dress, and some kind of teardrop-shaped pendant hung against her transparent white flesh. Her hair was colorless and stringy, hanging in thick clumps.

Then I could see rope burns on her neck, and I recognized her face from the picture. Mercy.

She stared at me with hollow eye sockets. Even at her most detailed, she was transparent, barely even there. I could plainly see the hallway behind her. I felt like, if I blinked, she might vanish again.

"Ellie, what's up?" Stacey asked. "Are you seeing something? These temp readings are down low, like deep-winter low...that whole upstairs hallways is like creepy-crawly with cold—"

"Sh," I whispered. Her chatting wasn't helping me. Every nerve in my body was tense, screaming at me to run away, to run straight out of the house and slam the door behind me. It was hard to ignore my instincts, but I had a job to do.

Resisting the desire to flee, I forced myself to speak instead.

"Mercy," I said. "Mercy Cutledge."

The ghost's hollow eyes widened a little, giving me a better view of the empty hallway behind her. Her mouth opened, and I thought I heard a cold buzzing in the air. For some reason, it made me think of the ice machines at cheap motels.

"Mercy," I said. "Leave this family alone. Your time here is done. You need to move on."

Her lips drew into a sneer. She had no visible teeth or tongue—as with her eyes, it was just empty hallway behind her when her mouth opened.

She blasted one word at me. I felt it strike me in the forehead like a gust of arctic air, and I heard the word inside my brain more than with my ears: *Leave.*

"You don't understand, Mercy," I said. "You're dead, you died--"

A howling shriek hit me right in the brain. The ghost charged at me, her misty face distorted and distending as she put on speed, her empty eye sockets and mouth hole stretching to inhuman shapes.

I raised my flashlight, but she slammed into me before I could click it. A rush of cold, rank air that smelled like a meat locker full of rotten carcasses blew back my hair, and I gagged, growing instantly sick and off-balance. Stacey shouted my name over the headset.

Then it was gone, an evil wind blowing away down the stairs. I didn't have the luxury of a moment to recover. I had to keep moving.

"What happened?" Lexa asked.

"Be right back," I told her, racing down the stairs. I heard footsteps from the lower flight below, but I couldn't see anyone there. The apparition was no longer visible.

I hate it when they turn invisible.

"Mercy, wait!" I shouted. "Show yourself again."

That got no response. I took the second flight of stairs two at a time. When I reached the bottom, I dropped my thermal goggles over my eyes in time to see flimsy blue tendrils of cold mist curling away into the open security door.

"Ellie!" Stacey shouted again over my headset.

"I'm following her. What do you see in the main house?"

"There's a shrinking cold...nothing," Stacey said. "I see nothing on either camera. It's like it melted away."

"Mercy?" I stepped through the open security door and looked up and down the hall. No blue mist, no cold spot racing away from me. The hallway felt warm, the way it should have on a June night in Savannah.

"Sorry, I lost her," Stacey said.

"She did what she came to do," I said. "She's retreated into the gray zone for now. Maybe for the night."

"Shoot," Stacey said, disappointed. "Well, what happened? I saw your hair blow back. You looked like you wanted to scream."

"I'm surprised I didn't," I told her. "She went right past me."

"Are you hurt?"

"I'm fine. A little shaken. I'd better go check on Lexa." I stepped back through the security door, then closed and bolted it.

"So what do you think?" Stacey asked.

"Yeah," I replied. "I'd say this house is definitely haunted."

Chapter Seven

Stacey and I stayed up the rest of the night, but there was no more activity at the house.

We joined the family for breakfast, which was bowls of cold cereal and some Pop-Tarts. The kitchen had a shiny new oven, but it looked like it had never been used.

Stacey had extracted and combined the important video clips from the various cameras, and she played them for the family while I ate my first bowl of Captain Crunch in who knows how many years. Hello, sugar-packed carbohydrates!

The family watched quietly as the cold blue mist drifted up the hallway in the main house and stopped at the security door. The footage flipped to the night vision camera on the other side, where I'd been sitting. An invisible hand drew open the bolt, and the heavy door creaked open by itself.

I watched Dale as he stared at the footage, wondering how he would take it. Not well, as it turned out. He turned pale, his spoonful of Oat Flakes forgotten halfway to his mouth. A little milk dribbled out of the spoon as his hand shook.

"That's...that's..." he said.

"Just what you and your family reported, Mr. Treadwell," I said.

"The entity opens the door a little after midnight."

"You can see it again on thermal." Stacey showed him the cold blue mist flowing out of the door and up the stairs, followed soon by my warmer, redder shape.

"That's what the ghost looks like?" Anna asked.

"That's where it's sucking heat out of the air," I told her. "Ghosts need energy to manifest, or to pull PK tricks—that's 'psychokinetic,' sorry—like opening a door. They pull the energy from the room, so you feel it growing cold. Sometimes they'll put out candles or small fires in their hunger for energy."

Anna shook her head. "I just can't believe I'm seeing this," she whispered.

The footage switched to another camera—the thermal one upstairs, showing the mist moving toward Lexa's room. It grew darker blue, bordering on purple, while my shape came up the steps after it.

"That's when she opened my door," Lexa whispered.

"Here it is on night vision." Stacey played another clip with the same time stamp. In the greenish world of night vision, I approached the door, taking the temperature and energy levels around me. Something small flickered across Lexa's doorknob—just a tiny orb, a pale circle no bigger than a shirt button. It vanished as Lexa's door opened.

I hadn't seen the orb in person, but that's why we use night vision. It's extremely sensitive.

We could hear Lexa's voice, then mine. The cold blue mist pulled itself together into a dense, dark shape vaguely suggesting a woman.

Her voice, seething with anger, played over the speakers on Stacey's laptop: "*Leave.*"

Anna gasped, and Dale finally lost control of his spoon. It dropped back into his cereal bowl, splashing him with oat flakes and driblets of milk. He jumped in surprise at the clanging and splashing.

"That was her," Lexa said.

"Lexa and I both saw an apparition here," I told them. "But the night vision camera didn't seem to catch it."

"Really annoying," Stacey commented, nodding. "I should have come in, brought my handheld—"

A ghostly shriek sounded from the speakers. On the screen, the cold mass flung itself at me. It rushed past, blew back my hair, and swirled away downstairs, trailing long threads of ice-blue cold behind it.

The family watched in rapt silence as I chased the ghost into the main house, where we lost all sign of it.

"And that's pretty much all that happened," Stacey said, sounding a little sad about it. She ejected a CD from her laptop and snapped it into a plastic jewel case. It was labeled ECKHART INVESTIGATIONS, with our contact info and the current date. She slid it it across the table toward Anna. "That's your copy."

Anna looked at the CD as if it were a maggoty fish lying on her breakfast table.

Dale was uncharacteristically silent.

"So...any questions?" I asked.

"Can we get rid of her now?" Lexa asked. Smart girl, right to the point.

"That's our next step," I said. "From what I've seen, it looks like we have a territorial ghost here—she's obviously trying to make you leave. That's what she said to me, too. We know that Mercy Cutledge was some kind of servant or employee to Captain Marsh in his later years. We don't know for sure whether she actually lived in this house...but if she did, she probably feels that you're intruders in her home."

Dale and Anna gave each other a worried look.

"What often happens is that ghosts don't realize they're dead," I continued. "If she understood that, she could move on from the house rather than clinging to it. In these situations, it's good to try and communicate with the spirit and make it understand that it has died. That's what I tried to do last night, but direct dialogue rarely works—the ghost is already in serious denial, obviously, and not ready to give up its delusion of being alive."

I took a breath, hoping I'd prepared them enough for my proposed solution. Some clients tend to freak out at the idea.

"Ritual and symbolism connect better with the dead than analysis and hard facts," I said. "In these situations, we can create what we call a 'mock funeral' for the restless spirit. This can help them realize they're dead and move on."

"Wait," Dale said. "You're telling me you want to have a funeral for this thing? With a minister and all that noise?" I could see the dollar signs weighing him down.

"No, Stacey and I can take care of it," I said. "You don't have to bring in anyone else. I'd recommend doing it in the front room of the main house. That's where she died."

"Can I wear my black dress?" Lexa asked, raising her eyebrows.

"I don't know if we should get in the way..." Anna looked at me.

"To be honest, it would help if the homeowners are there," I said. "Or at least one of you. Being the current owners gives your presence some authority."

"I'll go," Anna said. "I'll do whatever you want."

"Stacey and I can come back this evening and set things up," I said. "We'll do the funeral as soon as the sun goes down, make it an early night."

"And then all this will be over?" Dale asked. "That'll solve it?"

"I hope so," I said. "If we can't convince the ghost to leave, then we have to catch her and forcibly remove her. And that can get...messy. I recommend trying this first."

"It just sounds freaky," Dale said.

"You don't have to decide right now." I stood up, and Stacey stood with me. "But honestly, it would be better if you did. We need time to prepare."

"Dale?" Anna said. "If there's a chance it could work..."

Dale sighed. "I don't pretend to understand what's going on. I don't even know if I believe any of this...but yeah, if it'll fix the problem, we might as well fix the problem, huh? That's what we're paying you for."

"That's true." I nodded. "Then we'll be back tonight." That's me, closing the sale.

"Okay." Dale shook his head. "Just get it done."

I double-checked my toolbox on the way out—thermal goggles, night vision goggles, Mel Meter, flashlight...everything was there. We'd loaded all the cameras back into the van before breakfast.

I drove us back to the office. Hunter barked upstairs, where Calvin keeps his personal apartment on the second floor. The dog would probably wake Calvin, who might come down in his elevator.

I hurried to close the garage door and lock the van inside. I didn't want Calvin showing up and revisiting our conversation about the psychic guy.

Driving home in my own car through the sun-dappled streets, under archways of live oak dripping with moss, I could finally breathe freely again. After a dark night in a haunted house, there's nothing as sweet and soothing as golden Georgia sunlight.

I went home. I live in a second-story apartment on Liberty Street, in an old brick building that was a glass factory in the nineteenth century. That's what I've heard, anyway. Reaching my apartment required unlocking a gated side door, then climbing a flight of interior stairs to my door.

My cat dashed over to greet me when I walked inside, which meant he'd probably run out of dry food during the night. He purred and rubbed against my ankles.

"Morning, Bandit," I said, picking him up. He purred and batted at a long brown lock of my hair. Bandit is a black and white little creature with black patches around his eyes, giving him a raccoon-mask look. I've always thought he looked untrustworthy, hence the name.

I set him down, and he followed me to his two bowls at the corner of the kitchen nook. Plenty of water, no food. I poured him some kibble, and he immediately lost interest in me.

My apartment was a studio, shaped like a ship's galley and equally spacious. Two walls were raw nineteenth-century brick, while the other had been plastered over. At some point, I'm sure, some real estate developer had visions of selling the building off as high-priced condo lofts, like developers all over the city had tried to do at one point, but then the real estate bubble broke and the swarms of rich hipsters failed to materialize.

I could probably afford something bigger if I were willing to live with roommates, but I need my little pocket of privacy.

The walls are decorated with an assortment of dreamcatchers and Pennsylvania Dutch hex signs, like stars and trees. They're meant to be hung on the outside of barns to ward off bad luck and evil spirits. I painted the wall a color locally known as "haint blue," meant to resemble running water, which is also supposed to stop unwanted ghosts. I can't say whether any of this works, but I need all the help I can get. I also replaced my original cheapo window panes with heavy leaded glass, which I *know* is a barrier to ghosts.

I stripped out of my jeans and turtleneck, flopped down on my bed, and closed my eyes. Nap time. Sweet relief.

Naturally, my phone rang.

I grunted, annoyed, and clambered over to fish my phone out of my jeans. Even exhausted, though, I couldn't help but smile at the name on the caller ID. Grant Patterson.

"Good morning, Grant," I said, trying not to sound as grouchy as I felt.

"Good morning, dear," he said. Grant has all the grace and charm of a Southern lady from an old-line Savannah family. He's a research fellow at the Savannah Historical Association, which is a hobby for him. In his day job, he's a semi-practicing lawyer. His true calling, however, is gossip—whether it's two minutes old or two centuries, it's all juicy to him, as long as it's about our city.

Grant had helped us with our cases for years. Not only could he navigate the byzantine rooms of the Historical Association's old Federalist mansion, digging up long-lost details about old houses and properties, but he knew all the old, prominent families in town, since his family was one of them. He can dig out dirt with a few phone calls that nobody would ever share with lowborns like Calvin and me. Grant was always good for extra insight into the history of the haunted properties, and I think he gets a kick out of working with ghost hunters.

"Are we still meeting today? Tell me you're not calling to cancel," I said.

"Not to cancel, but merely to delay," Grant said. "Ellie, I am ashamed to say that I had no idea what a pit of sin and scandal we had in that Marsh house. I didn't even realize there still *was* a house under all that moss—I assumed it had rotted away years ago. You must tell me about the new owners."

"As long as you can tell me about the old ones," I said.

"And I will, but I want to collect just a bit more hearsay and rumor before I do," Grant said. "You've got me interested now. If you give me until lunch tomorrow, I will have unearthed the whole story for you."

"What are you learning?"

"It is wonderfully sordid, dear. I'll see you tomorrow."

I hung up, only mildly annoyed at his delay. It meant an extra hour of sleep today, after all.

I slept.

The events at the Marsh/Treadwell house replayed in my dreams—this kind of work brings lots of nightmares. In mine, the ghost didn't simply blow past me and vanish. Instead, I was trapped inside the old house, running through smoke-filled rooms while a fire swept through behind me. Somewhere, a dark voice was laughing.

Chapter Eight

So, you know what can get awkward? Putting together a mock funeral for a creepy ghost of a person who died decades earlier. It's especially awkward when you have to be the funeral director and also give the eulogy. My goal is usually to get it over with ASAP.

Stacey and I arrived at the Treadwell home about seven in the evening, with a vanload of weird stuff. Anna and Lexa watched from the kitchen as we carried it into the house and set it up in the foyer—Lexa looked curious, while Anna appeared disturbed. Natural reaction.

First, there were the flowers. A couple of wreaths, a pink and purple "memory bouquet" of lavender and pink carnation blossoms, a few baskets of assorted blooms, slightly withered. We set the wreaths on the flimsy wire stands from the florist, put a basket on an old wooden side table, and arrayed the rest of the flowers on the stairs.

The flowers cost us zilch because we'd dumpster-dived them from behind the Pierce Funeral Home. Well, Stacey did it while I stood guard—part of her initiation as the new kid.

Swiping used flowers from a funeral home or cemetery might sound both ghoulish and cheap, but we did it for a reason. They'd already been part of a funeral ritual, imbuing them with that particular tone and energy. Secondhand funeral flowers are better than fresh ones for our purposes.

We brought in a couple of little easels, where we set up large, blurry posters of Mercy Cutledge's face drawn from the newspaper account of her arrest, since it was the only image we had.

I found Dale on the couch in the living room, wearing a sweat-stained Cubs shirt while watching the Cubs on television. He also wore a Cubs cap and held his beer bottle in a Cubs cozy. Big Cubs fan, old Dale.

"Hi, are you busy, Mr. Treadwell?" I asked.

"Are you kidding?" he asked. "Cubbies are down by two, you got this Puerto Rican snake at bat for the Brewers—"

"I was hoping you could help us carry this coffin into your house." I tried not to crack a smile as his jaw dropped at my question.

"You guys have a real coffin?"

"A real one," I said with a solemn nod. It's not real, though it's carved and painted to look that way. It's made of plywood, just a stage-set coffin, but it's still hefty enough that I'd prefer to get a guy to lug it for me. It wouldn't kill Dale to help us out in between bouts of implying that we were all crazy.

"This is getting weirder all the time." Dale grunted and shook his head, but he paused the TV and stood up to join me.

I led Dale out to the blue cargo van, where I gestured through the open back door at the five-foot-long mock coffin waiting inside. I'd used this same one a few times, though usually with Calvin officiating instead of me.

"That thing looks heavy as an elephant," Dale complained. "I've got a bad back. Why don't you and the other girl carry it? What am I paying you for, anyway?"

"I'll get the other end for you," I said.

"It's just too big..." Dale slipped his fingers under the foot of the coffin, gritted his teeth, and tugged it upward, testing its weight. The light plywood coffin rose easily in his hands, clearly surprising him.

He helped me carried it inside.

"Is there a real dead person in there?" Lexa asked as we carried the coffin past the kitchen. She and her mother were at the round table by the old river-stone fireplace, ostensibly playing Uno but stopping to watch Stacey and me each time we passed.

"You bet it's a real dead person," Dale said, with a wink at me.

Ugh. "A scary dead person, and it's gonna get you!"

"Dale!" Anna snapped. "Not funny. Not right now." She took Lexa's hand—the girl looked thoroughly frightened.

"Nothing funny about missing the Cubbies, either," Dale grumbled as he carried the coffin down the hallway and through the security door.

As usual, the portion of the hallway past the door was noticeably dimmer and cooler than the portion before it.

In the foyer, Stacey had already set up the two sawhorse-like wooden supports for the coffin. Dale dropped the coffin into place and shook his head.

"Sick stuff," Dale muttered, looking around at the withering flowers and the row of folding director's chairs we'd brought. We could have used the Treadwells' own folding chairs, but it's better to remove every element of the mock funeral afterwards, to totally strike the set. Otherwise, the ghost might attach itself to some funerary object, and you don't want to leave your clients with a set of haunted lawn chairs. They really ruin the family barbecues.

"Thanks for carrying that," I said. "Can you open the windows and the front doors for us?"

"I have to get the key." Dale thumped the padlock and chain sealing the heavy double doors from the inside. He made no move to actually fetch the key, instead letting his comment hang in the air as if he'd identified some difficult or impossible obstacle.

"Please?" Stacey asked, giving one of her annoyingly cute grins. She was dressed in light summer clothes, a t-shirt and shorts, for the heavy-lifting portion of the evening.

Dale shrugged, looking indifferent to her perky hot blondness. "I'll send the girls to help out. I'm already behind on the game." He trudged out of the room.

"Thanks!" Stacey called after him, with an aggressive cheerfulness that made me want to laugh. "He's a chivalrous type," she whispered to me.

"Okay," I said, hurrying to change the subject from the lunky schlub Dale before we started really making fun of him. "Is the music ready?"

"I'm loaded up with old-school Gospel. All the old rugged crosses and trips across the River Jordan you could ever want." Stacey gestured at her iPad on a side table. We didn't really know anything about Mercy's religious beliefs, if any, so we were betting on statistical probability and going for a general Southern Protestant vibe, with elements she would likely have seen or heard at local funerals.

Anna and Lexa arrived, both of them looking a little stunned at how we'd turned their dank, dark foyer into a makeshift funeral parlor. It actually fit the motif pretty well, with all the old woodwork and narrow Gothic windows, if you ignored the graffiti on the walls.

"Dale said you needed this key?" Anna asked.

"We're going to open the doors and the windows," I told her.

She cast at doubtful look up at the second row of windows, some broken and leaking, high above us.

"Just the ones on the first floor," I added. "Open doors and windows will help encourage the ghost to leave."

"But can't they walk through walls?" Lexa asked. She was slowly approaching the mock coffin with a mixture of fear and fascination on her face. "Why do they need doors and windows?"

"They don't always need them," I explained. "It's a psychological thing for them. Especially with ghosts who may not fully realize they've died."

Lexa reached the coffin and stared.

"Can I open it?" she whispered.

"Lexa, don't get in the way," Anna said.

"There's nothing in there," I told Lexa. "But you can open it if it makes you feel better."

Lexa carefully placed her fingertips under the edge of the coffin lid. Shivering, she raised it up to peer inside. The lid's hinges squeaked, startling her.

"It's all fake inside." Lexa frowned. The interior was plain, unpainted plywood. "Can I get in?"

"Lexa!" her mother shouted, looking understandably disturbed by the question.

"That's not a good idea," I said. "It's flimsy. It could break or fall."

"Help me raise the windows, Lexa." Anna pushed open the double doors. Warm air and the rich, green smell of their overgrown jungle of a front yard wafted into the room. The place already felt a little better. Certainly less smelly, anyway. The music of thousands of crickets and cicadas filled the darkness outside.

"I guess we're ready," I said, after Stacey and I helped them open all the first-floor windows.

"Except for wardrobe." Stacey nodded at my jeans and black

turtleneck. "Unless we're doing a beatnik funeral."

"It's not a beach funeral, either," I said, pointing to Stacey's revealing work outfit.

"I'm wearing my black dress!" Lexa announced, dashing out of the room.

"We'll go get ready," Anna said. "I'll try to get Dale off the couch, too."

"Good luck," I told her.

Stacey and I changed in the van. She kept throwing nervous glances at the windshield, worried that Dale would creep out and try to spy on us. Something told me he probably wouldn't leave his Cubs game just for that, especially after his complete lack of reaction to her charming smile.

Stacey put on a black cocktail-style dress trimmed in black silk lace. It looked pricey. She also had matching stiletto heels and an actual hat with a little veil. I, on the other hand, wore a frumpy brown dress with a high collar and chunky old walking shoes. Don't laugh—I was going as a traveling tent evangelist type. That would have been the most common sort of Southern female preacher when Mercy Cutledge was growing up in the 1930s and 1940s. I mean, I couldn't exactly pretend to be a Catholic priest.

When it was time, we stood with the Treadwell family in their hall by the open security door. Anna and Lexa wore black dresses, too. Lexa kept mentioning hers until everyone had complimented it.

Dale wore a business suit, and weirdly, had applied a fresh splash of some oaky cologne, like he was really going out in public. I expected him to grouse and complain, but he now seemed deeply worried, like a man waiting for results from a cancer lab.

"Let's get it over with," he mumbled.

"We'll go in silently, as a procession," I said. "When we're done, we leave the same way. Once we step through that door, we need to act like this is real."

I led them through the door and up the hall toward the foyer. The electric lanterns spaced along the hallway cast tall, weird shadows on the walls.

Dale was behind me, then Anna and Lexa, the girl grasping her mother's hand tightly, with a look of determination on her face. Stacey followed at the end, keeping the family bookended in case of any sudden attack from the Other Side.

The foyer was silent despite the open doors and windows, as if all the night insects had gone on strike. Despite the electric lanterns, the cavernous room seemed much darker than the hallway. The air, as rank as ever, felt stiff and thick with a cold tension, like something tragic was waiting to happen.

Nobody said a word as we entered. The iPad played a rather sweet version of "In the Garden" sung by Dolly Parton. I paused it after Stacey and the Treadwell family members took their seats, Lexa perched in between her parents.

We'd arranged the coffin area at the dead center of the room. I stood behind it, facing the little congregation. The open doors behind them looked out onto blackness. Old, vine-choked trees blocked any view of us from the road, so the Treadwells didn't have to worry about passing motorists witnessing our bizarre funeral ritual through the open windows and doors.

Stacey had set up three cameras behind the chairs to capture the funeral—as you'd expect, there was one regular video, one thermal, and one night vision, just in case the ghost decided to attend her own funeral. We certainly hoped she would.

Next to me was one of the big, blown-up pictures of Mercy. Behind me were a couple of closed doors leading deeper into the house. Above them ran the second-floor walkway where Mercy had hanged herself.

I looked out over my congregation of four, and I raised the big old 1859 leather-bound Bible we use for this stuff. I opened it to a bookmarked page and set it on another easel beside me.

I adjusted my reading glasses and took a breath. *Get into character, holy roller.*

"Brothers and sisters," I began, "We are gathered today to celebrate the life of Mercy Cutledge, and more importantly, her return to her Creator. Mercy has passed away. Mercy has died." I was being repetitive for emphasis. Hey, I had a specific message to get across here. "Mercy is now free of this mortal world of suffering, and can now ascend into the Light of God. Mercy can leave behind this home, though she may have loved it well, because another, greater home awaits her. Peace and happiness await her the moment she departs."

Lexa smiled at me and seemed to relax in her chair, as if taking comfort from my words. That warmed my heart.

"We know a few things about Mercy," I continued. "We know she lived fifty-three years, and twenty-eight of them were spent in a state asylum. Her life could not have been an easy or pleasant one. We know she..." I paused, trying to think of a delicate way to say *murdered somebody*. "Had conflict and violence in her life. She must have felt great fear, and confusion, and pain, maybe sadness, regret, and guilt. We know she chose to end her life. We also know that she is now free to move on..." I made a sweeping gesture toward the open doors and windows. "Mercy can now leave us in peace, and go to find a greater peace of her own. Amen."

"Amen," Stacey and the Treadwells repeated, as I'd instructed.

"Now, let's pray..." The Twenty-Third Psalm is always a good one in situations like this, so I hefted the old Bible and read, "The Lord is my shepherd; I shall not want..."

When that was over, I started the music again, and Stacey and the Treadwells filed out. I left after them. The coffin remained in place—we would leave it all in place for the ghost to contemplate.

I was disappointed. The first time I'd done this, operating the cameras while Calvin performed the little ceremony, we'd all felt the spirit flee the room halfway through, parting the window curtains on its way out.

Nothing so obvious had happened this time. The room still felt cold, the air still oppressively heavy. It felt like a failure.

I blew out the candles as I left.

Chapter Nine

While we waited for that funeral to sink in—and for the ghost of Mercy to depart for happier trails, hopefully—Lexa invited us to play Uno with her and her mom. It didn't sound like a half-bad way to pass the time. Stacey and I sat down with them while the Cubs game blared in the other room, punctuated by Dale's frequent unnerving shouts, moans, and howling profanity.

"How many ghosts have you caught?" Lexa asked me while we played.

"I'd actually have to check the files at work," I said. "Maybe a hundred?"

"Whoa." She leaned back, widening her eyes, apparently impressed.

"Sometimes there's more than one ghost in a house, so that helps up your numbers," I told her with a smile. "I've been doing it for a few years, too."

"Don't you ever get scared?" she asked.

"Not her," Stacey said.

"I get scared all the time," I said. "It's scary work, but it's something people need, and there aren't many people who can do it for them."

"What's the scariest ghost you've ever seen?" Lexa asked.

I had a ready answer for that, but I wasn't going to talk about it, for a whole batch of reasons, only one of which was to avoid giving nightmares to my client's ten-year-old daughter.

"It's hard to pick," I said. "Most ghosts aren't really dangerous, though. They're like old memories that won't leave a house. A lot of them are just repeating parts of their lives again and again. They all seem kind of scary, but it's rare to find one who can really hurt you. Mostly they're just wrapped up in their own problems and not thinking about you at all."

"Like regular people," Lexa said. Combined with her serious, thoughtful nod, her comment made me laugh out loud. "What?" she asked, looking confused.

"You're smart, Lexa," I said.

She beamed at me.

Then the crashing and banging began.

First, it sounded like dishes spilling out of kitchen cabinets—a sound I've specifically heard before, it's a favorite trick of your more drama queen-ish ghosts—but we were sitting in the kitchen, and the cabinet doors hadn't stirred.

Then the true hammering started, like a series of cannonballs striking the front of the house, shaking the timbers, the walls, the old hardwood floorboards. It was like a stampede of angry bulls crossing through the house in the middle of an earthquake. Plaster crumbled and rained from the ceiling. Lexa screamed.

"Under the table!" I shouted, taking Lexa by the hand. All four of us crowded under the sturdy maple table while the house shook as if under attack. Dale clambered into the room, looking pale and screaming for his wife and kid. He finally saw us and crammed his way under.

Then everything stopped. I could hear scattered rattling and banging around the house as the last of the shuddering energy worked its way through and fell quiet.

"Is it over?" Lexa whispered.

"What the dog-crap was that?" Dale asked, his voice thin and reedy, his face as white as cream cheese. He grabbed my sleeve with a look of desperation. "Tell me!"

"I hope we got that on video!" Stacey gasped. The girl had her priorities. She scrambled out from under the table, grabbed a handheld camera and her flashlight, and dashed to the hallway.

"Wait!" I took off after her, grabbing my flashlight and Mel Meter from my toolbox.

"Dale, go with them," Anna said. I glanced at Dale, but he continued huddling under the table. His head moved slightly from one side to another, like he wanted to refuse but didn't want to admit it.

"You can all stay here," I said, mentally adding a few hundred bucks to Dale's bill. I ran to catch up with Stacey.

She was sliding open the bolt on the security door. We'd left it sealed, and regardless of whatever had just happened in the main house, the ghost hadn't come back through the security door this time. Stacey heaved it open.

"Come on!" she shouted, and then raced into the dim hallway, waving her digital video camera excitedly.

We ran together through the main house hall. The electric lanterns spaced along the wall had gone dim, as if all their batteries were dying. It was possible. While ghosts have always fed on ambient heat, fire, and even the physical energy of the living, some ghosts in modern times have also learned to suck energy from batteries and electrical devices. This can obviously cause huge problems, not just for the victims of the haunting but for ghost hunter equipment. That's why I prefer pneumatic ghost traps.

We flicked on our tactical flashlights, lancing the darkness with a pair of high-powered beams. By the time we reached the foyer, our flashlights were the only illumination. The electric lanterns we'd left had turned completely dark.

"Whoa, this place is trashed," Stacey whispered, slowly shining her light around the room. She was right. The folding chairs had been knocked over, as well as the antique table and most of the easels. The old flowers had been shredded as if by a mulcher-mower, then scattered like bright bits of confetti all over the room, their flimsy wire stands toppled and twisted. The three video cameras had been knocked down, too, their tripods jutting out like the stiff legs of dead insects. The coffin lay on the floor with its lid open, as though some zombie had escaped from it.

Only two things remained standing: an easel with a blown-up image of Mercy Cutledge, and the easel with the old Bible on it.

Turning toward the front of the house, I found the source of the barrage that had shaken the house. The front doors had slammed closed, and so had each one of the windows we'd opened.

Some of them had dropped hard enough to crack their panes.

"Well, that didn't work," Stacey said. She grabbed the iPad from the floor and shook off a few crumpled flower petals. We'd left it playing hymns, but now the tablet was dark and silent. "Looks like the battery's dead," she told me.

"Great," I said, taking in the mess. "We have a confirmed squatter. We'll have to evict."

"Ghost trap?" Stacey asked, raising her eyebrows.

"Unfortunately."

"I'll get one from the van!" She started for the door.

"Hold up, Stacey. Let's wait until we meet with Grant Patterson tomorrow. He might know something that helps us customize a trap for our ghost."

"Oh, fine." Stacey stopped where she was, shoulders slumped. "So what now?"

"We break the bad news to the family—this isn't over, and we have to come back for a third night. And then we clean up this mess."

"Thanks a lot, Mercy!" Stacey shouted up at the second-floor walkway.

We told the disappointed Treadwells we'd be happy to stay until sunrise and monitor the situation, and they accepted the offer.

After Stacey and I cleaned up the wreckage and reloaded all our funerary junk into the cargo van, we set up cameras inside the east wing hallway to watch the locked security door again. Stacey, bless her heart, offered to stay in the house with me for the night, instead of staying out in the van with all her monitors again.

I agreed. I didn't feel like sleeping alone with an angry tornado of a ghost lingering around.

We reviewed the footage from the three cameras in the foyer, which Stacey had fixed up again so she could watch them from her laptop all night. We didn't see much—the cameras had been knocked to the ground early, so all they really caught was bits of flowers raining onto the floor.

"Maybe we'll get some more tonight," Stacey said, disappointed.

She was wrong. For the rest of the night, nothing stirred. I didn't even hear much in the way of the usual creaks and cracks you might expect in an old house at night, no tree limbs scraping at windows, nothing. The house was silent as a tomb.

I imagined the ghost of Mercy Cutledge, exhausted from her

outburst, retreating into some dark and quiet corner of the house to plan her next move.

Chapter Ten

Stacey and I decamped at sunrise, leaving the quiet, exhausted Treadwell family to their breakfast. None of them looked like they'd slept well. Stacey and I hadn't slept at all, though, and we were ready for our own homes and beds.

"We'll be back before sunset," I assured the family as we stood by the door, ready to leave. "We're going to capture that ghost, I promise."

"Are we safe now?" Lexa asked.

"Your ghost doesn't come out during the day," I reminded her. "Most don't. By tonight, we'll be back, and we'll get rid of her for you."

"You'd better, or I'm not paying a dime," Dale said.

"I understand, Mr. Treadwell."

Stacey sighed as we pulled away in the van.

"That pretty much sucked. We look like amateurs," said Stacey, who'd been on the job for a whole three weeks.

"We'll take care of everything tonight," I told her.

We each had time to shower and nap before our lunch appointment with Grant. He wanted to meet at the Olde Pink House by Reynolds Square, which wasn't exactly the cheapest spot in town, but his information was free so we couldn't complain too much. He often insisted on picking up the check, anyway, with a large tip and a patrician indifference to the size of the bill. It's handy to come from old money, or so I assume. Grant was nominally an attorney, but I'm not sure how much time he spent doing any actual lawyering.

If you're not familiar with Savannah, the Historic District is laid out in twenty-two squares, following the planned grid initially laid down by the colony's founders in 1733. The squares are essentially little parks with gardens, brick paths, some very tall trees, and sometimes fountains, statues, features like that. They're usually surrounded by beautiful old mansions and churches, built in every imaginable architectural style. Reynolds Square's main adornment is a statue of John Wesley, the founder of Methodism, who lived right on that spot.

The Olde Pink House sits across from the square, an eighteenth-century Georgian mansion fronted with a Greek portico. The house is clad in a layer of stucco—I'll let you guess what color. The building might be more formally called the James Habersham house, after its first owner, who is supposed to haunt the house to this day. Nearly every building in the sprawling Historic District is said to have a ghost or ten. That keeps me busy.

Grant Patterson was already there, seated at one of the cheerful little outdoor tables, wearing dark glasses against the bright sunlight. As always, he looked perfectly put together: graying brown hair crisply coifed, his white summer suit and peachy silk shirt spotless, golden cufflinks polished, nails manicured.

I wished I ever looked that good when I left the house. I'm usually dashing around in old jeans with my hair in loose brown tangles around my face. Today, though, I'd put on some half-decent linen slacks for our lunch.

"There you are," Grant said as Stacey and I arrived together. Stacey had a light, breezy blue cotton dress that looked great on her. I don't do light and breezy. Or dresses, unless I have to.

"Thanks for meeting with us, Grant," I said. "It sounds like you put a lot of work into this."

"Digging up dirty, long-forgotten gossip and rumors hardly feels like work, dear," he said, rising to greet me. He looked at Stacey while he gently shook my hand. "Who is this pretty little thing?"

"Stacey Ray Tolbert. Eckhart just hired her."

"Oh, a new little ghost hunter," Grant said, smiling as he shook her hand. "Goodness knows our city could use a few more. How is Calvin? Too busy for lunch, I see."

"Still trying to make his retirement happen," I said.

"And that explains the new girl."

We took our seats as the waitress arrived. Grant was starting lunch with a Bloody Mary. I ordered coffee.

"I suppose we should get right to it," Grant said. "The Marsh house. Do you want the long version, or should I skip to the dirty parts?"

"Let's start with the dirty parts," I replied. Stacey snickered a little.

"I hoped you'd say that." Grant's eyes seemed to shine as he took a goodly sip of Bloody Mary. I wondered if it was his first drink of the day. "So. Augustus Marsh, born to a very minor family in 1848, joins the nautical life early, serves in the Confederate Navy. After that, a steamship captain—most of his routes would have been nothing too glamorous, hauling produce from the South up to Boston and New York so those folks could eat something besides fish. He may have traveled a bit farther—into the Caribbean, perhaps across the Atlantic. Records are spotty.

"He may have been involved in some sort of smuggling, because he amassed quite a lot of money. Bought that estate west of town, when the land was mostly woods and marsh, and built that house for his new bride. In 1890, he marries Eugenia Bremmer, daughter of a small-time shopkeeper. At nineteen, she's literally less than half his age. A bit of a beauty, from what anyone remembers, and she's devoutly religious and starts giving his money to the orphanage and other charities.

"Here's where the story turns dark," Grant said, relishing the moment. "In 1901, she develops an illness and dies almost overnight. Some people suspected Captain Marsh had poisoned her."

"Do you think it was murder?"

"I wouldn't know, but the examining doctor was a friend of the Captain's, and often attended the debauched parties at the mansion after the wife died. Captain Marsh *did* have a couple of possible motives to murder his wife."

"Like what?" I asked, and then the waitress arrived to take our lunch order. I'd barely looked at the menu. I asked for she-crab soup, Stacey ordered a wedge salad, and Grant asked for their BLT salad with fried green tomatoes. The waitress frowned a little as she left—

soups and salads for lunch don't lead to a large bill.

"You should come here for supper sometime," Grant advised us. "The seared sea scallops—amazing."

"Why would Marsh kill his wife?" I asked.

"Oh, well, nobody can say for sure that she *was* murdered, first of all. If she was, though, it could be because she was aggressively giving away his money, or because she failed to provide him any children. The soil at the Marsh estate was rich, dark, and fertile, and the crops grew tall, but nothing grew inside poor Eugenia except religious feeling and charity. So she's giving away all his money and not giving him any heirs. After eleven years of that, maybe he decides to poison her and have his doctor friend cover it up. Maybe not. It's interesting to speculate." Grant raised his eyebrows, watching for my reply.

"Is this the dark, sordid history you were hinting about?" I asked him. "It doesn't sound like much. One possible murder?"

"Oh, no, dear." Grant leaned back, smiling like I'd stepped into some little conversational trap he'd set. "Not at all. The scandals begin after Eugenia died. Apparently all the godliness left the house with her."

Stacey inclined her head a little closer to Grant, listening intently.

"The marriage must have reined in Captain Marsh's lower instincts, you see," Grant continued. "After she was gone, he did not seem interested in remarrying. Within a year or two, his house had become a den of excess for young men of wealthy families. There was drinking, gambling, possibly opium, and certainly girls. His home evolved into something of a high-class brothel." Grant delivered this with a satisfied smile.

"Did anyone else die there?" I asked.

"My, aren't we all business?" Grant shook his head. "Over time, as Marsh's reputation grew worse and worse, the parties at the Marsh mansion lost that 'high-class' tone. He gambled away much of his money and land, and his former gardens and fields became warehouses and factories. The crowd at his mansion grew, let's say, less civilized year by year. Yet the dirty festivities never stopped, though Marsh grew older and older. It's shocking he lived past a hundred. In fact, it's amazing he lived past fifty, given his reputation for drinking, feasting, smoking, and keeping company with the professional ladies.

"Even when he died—you must know this by now—it had

nothing to do with his health and lifestyle. He was stabbed to death by one of his working girls in 1954."

"Mercy Cutledge," I said. "A household servant, right?"

"Well, she did live there, but she was no maid," Grant said. "She performed other services for Marsh and his, well, gentleman visitors."

"Oh, wow." Stacey looked at me with wide eyes. "We didn't know that."

"So why would Mercy kill him?" I asked.

"One can imagine any number of conflicts arising in that situation," Grant said. "However, what she told the police, after they arrested her, was that the elderly Captain Marsh was an 'occult wizard in league with demons.'" Grant looked amused as he said it. "Her exact words."

"Was her claim investigated?" I asked, just in case, and Grant laughed.

"Well, no," he said. "When you stab an old man to death, then tell the police about black magic and demons, they tend to call in the psychiatrists, not the demonologists. To answer your question, though, nobody can remember any evidence or corroborating witnesses, and I've spoken to a few very old folks who were alive then. The judge decided she'd flipped her lid, and people generally seemed to agree with the verdict. They shipped her off to Lassiter State Asylum near Milledgeville.

"Marsh's grand-niece, Louisa, inherited the big old house and ran it as a boarding house. Apparently the house continued to attract the lowest sort of people during her era. Drifters, drug addicts, prostitutes. It's a wonder the city didn't shut it down earlier than they did. There were more deaths there, you'll be interested to know. Murders, overdoses, suicides. The house seems to have been a magnet for misery.

"Now, Lassiter State Asylum abruptly closed in 1982. Budget cuts. A whole flock of loonies was released that year. And I suppose you know she returned to the scene of her crime and hanged herself. The city told Louisa Marsh she would have to bring the rotten old house up to code if she wanted to continue renting it out—really, I think, they just wanted to finally close the place down. Louisa stopped renting rooms and eventually sold the house and moved away. Since then, the house has changed owners several times, with nobody settling in for very long."

"Did Louisa experience anything unusual in all those years?" I asked.

"It's possible, but I couldn't find anyone still living who knows much about her," Grant said. "Maybe you could ask her yourself. She's still alive, in a nursing home in Waycross. I have the information in your file folder, don't let me forget." He tapped his briefcase, down on the bricks beside his chair.

"Thanks," I said. "I wonder if she's the one who divided the house." I described how the east wing was walled off from the main house except for one thick security with multiple locks.

"Maybe she was trying to lock out ghosts," Grant said, looking amused.

"Or, from what you've told us, maybe she wanted security against her own tenants," I said.

"Or both!" Stacey offered.

"Mercy didn't die until 1982," I said, "So I'm betting Louisa divided the house to protect herself against her living tenants, not Mercy's ghost. We're pretty certain Mercy is the one haunting the house. She's rejected our invitation to scoot out of there peacefully and quietly. What we could really use now is some kind of object that belonged to her in life. Anything of significance that might draw her interest. Bait for a ghost trap."

Grant blew between his lips and shook his head.

"That's a tall order," Grant said. "Maybe Calvin has a friend who can dig through old police evidence storage, but we're talking about an open-and-shut murder from sixty years ago..."

"Calvin's doing that," I said. "Any other ideas? Where did Mercy live before the Marsh house? Where did she grow up?"

"I wish I could help." Grant tapped his fingers on the table, thinking. "Nobody I spoke to knows where she came from—there's an idea she came from a farm in central or west Georgia, probably looking for some city adventures, but that's all I've heard. If you can't find out from her police records, you might track down her doctor from the asylum, if he's still alive. Or check the records at the asylum yourself."

"But you said it closed in 1982."

"Exactly. Closed, but neither demolished nor refurbished. Left to rot instead. You may find it's a little bit of a time capsule inside, if vandals or arsonists haven't destroyed it."

"Wait," Stacey said. "You're suggesting we break into an abandoned mental hospital—"

"I suggest no such thing, dear girl!" Grant shook out his cloth napkin and laid it on his lap as our food arrived. "I'm simply sharing what I know. The two of you can do whatever you think best. Don't these tomatoes look delicious? A crispy golden crust on the outside, sweet and juicy on the inside. My mother used to make them with these big red homegrown beauties from her garden. Try one, Ellie." Before I could reply, he transferred one of the fried green tomato slices from his plate to the edge of my soup saucer.

"You said there were more deaths in the house," I said. "What do we know about them?"

"As I said, drifters, drug addicts, and good-time girls," Grant said. "Not the sort of individuals closely tracked by the newspapers. We do know it was considered a dangerous place, renting rooms to the rougher sorts."

"Sounds like it could be a very haunted house," Stacey said.

"We've only seen one ghost so far," I told her. "No need to panic our clients with too many extra details right now. All we have to do is remove the ghost of Mercy Cutledge, and their house should fall quiet." I looked at Grant. "Is there anything else you can tell me about her?"

"I have heard that Captain Marsh was stabbed to death while lying asleep in his bed," Grant said. "Do be careful with this ghost, Ellie. She sounds like a nasty one to me."

Chapter Eleven

Tips for breaking into an abandoned mental hospital: first, get permission from the current owner, probably a bank or government agency. Second: go during the daytime. Third: go with a large group.

Stacey and I followed one of these three suggestions. We wanted to get over there and back before sunset, and Milledgeville is two hours from Savannah if you stomp on it. I drove my Camaro to make better time. The company cargo van is a reliable old horse, but a slow one.

Naturally, zipping out to a dark, long-abandoned loony bin on a likely wild goose chase was not how I would have preferred to spend my afternoon. Calvin had tugged at his contacts in the police department, but if there was anything belonging to Mercy in deep storage somewhere, it was going to take days to even find out if it still existed.

It would have been handy to find the butcher knife she'd used to stab Captain Marsh, or some related piece of evidence. Her ghost wouldn't be able to ignore a highly personal object like that, but we didn't want to make our clients wait.

We had other options. According to police records, Mercy was originally from Camilla, a little peanut-and-cotton town in deep southeastern Georgia, two hundred and fifty miles away. Not exactly an afternoon trip. Plus, it would take some poking after we arrived there, since nobody named Cutledge currently resided in the town, as far as we could find. I'd put in some calls to local police and newspapers trying to find out about her family. If anyone was going to call me back with useful information, they hadn't done it yet.

We could poke around the Treadwells' house for any remnant of Mercy's life, but it would be better to find an artifact she hadn't encountered in many years, rather than something that was located in the same house she'd been haunting for the past three decades. It would be more likely to grab her attention.

For now, the old hospital seemed like the best bet. We could get out there and back in half a day. Even if we didn't find any of Mercy's personal belongings, we could probably find all kinds of artifacts that would be familiar to her. She'd spent more of her life there than anywhere else.

Calvin had also pushed for me to meet with the supposed psychic guy again, but I was still resisting. I just think a self-proclaimed psychic walking around my client's home had too much potential to muddy the waters, and it seemed like we would soon be closing the case, anyway.

The dark, massive shape of Lassiter State Asylum squatted on a lot badly overgrown with waist-high weeds, brambles, and tall pine saplings that were well on their way to becoming trees. A chain-link fence surrounded the complex of old brick buildings. We were heading for the central administration building, which was four stories at the center with two-story wings sprawling out on either side. The windows were all barred, and the building resembled an old fortress covered with graffiti.

"Looks inviting," Stacey said, taking a picture as we drove past. "You think they have greeters at the front like Wal-Mart?"

"I hope not." I pulled off the single-lane country highway and onto a service road that took us around back. There was no good reason to park out front and advertise our presence to local police. It would have been handy to get permission first, but who has time for red tape?

The service road was badly overgrown and potholed, so we drove slowly, mowing down high weeds as we went. Not exactly inconspicuous, leaving a wide, broken trail behind like that. I hoped no police or security-conscious citizen happened to notice.

We parked at the back of the chain-link, where sections had been ripped open by years of weather and trespassers. Stacey frowned as we stepped out of the car. The empty buildings loomed ahead of us, casting deep shadows like the towers of a crumbling fortress.

"You think it's safe in there?" she whispered, even though we were a long walk from the building. "What about, like, dangerous vagrants and drug addicts?"

"You should go to kickboxing class with me." I opened my black toolbox in the trunk and began to load things onto my belt—my SWAT flashlight, Mel Meter, night vision goggles. I have a utility belt that would make Batman jealous, but I rarely use it because it's uncomfortably heavy.

"That's your plan? Seriously?" Stacey gaped at me while grabbing out her own tactical flashlight and a backpack.

"I also brought this." I showed her my stun gun and thumbed the button. An arc of electricity crackled between the two sharp little metal prongs.

"Does that work against ghosts, too?" Stacey asked.

"I haven't tried it." I holstered it on my belt. "Interesting idea, though. It could disrupt their electromagnetic fields. Let's get moving, the daylight's slipping." It was already mid-afternoon and our shadows were long and dark.

We didn't have much trouble finding our way through a collapsed section of the damaged fence. We had to wade through dense weeds across the long-broken parking lot. A thorny green vine tangled around Stacey's leg, and she had to whack it away with her flashlight.

"Should've brought a machete," she grumbled.

The day had grown intensely hot, without a cloud in the sky, so I welcomed the shade as we reached the back wall of the building. Broken beer bottles were scattered all through the weeds here—good thing Stacey and I had worn boots. Some of the labels were fairly new, too. Somebody had been drinking and smashing here within the past few days. Great.

The windows back here were barred, too, but that hadn't stopped people from smashing the glass over the years. I was conscious of how isolated we were as we poked through the tall weeds, pushing and stomping through knots of thorny jungle as we explored the back of the extremely long brick building. Our efforts to hide ourselves from the road also meant that no one would know if some former asylum inmate decided to murder us and leave us in the bushes.

We found a steel door that stood slightly ajar, its handle and lock broken away so long ago that the remnants of the lock had turned to rust. I grabbed the edge of the door and pulled. It gave a loud, rusty shriek as I opened it wide enough for us to fit through.

"Great," Stacey whispered. "Now all the crazies know we're here." I didn't know whether she meant possible vagrants or the ghosts of old patients, and at the moment, it wasn't an area of conversation I wanted to explore.

I flipped on my flashlight and stabbed the high-powered beam deep into the darkness. It looked like what you'd expect—more graffiti on the old brick walls, a layer of nameless filth coating the floor. The light fixtures hung on chains high above us, their bulbs shattered into jagged pieces.

There was a smell of must in the damp air, and a distant sound of dripping water, though it hadn't rained in a day or two.

Stacey and I walked shoulder to shoulder up a wide brick corridor scattered with debris—broken sticks of old office furniture, a rolling hospital bed jammed against one wall, its sheets black with grime.

"Ugh," Stacey whispered. "Look up there."

Her flashlight had found something we did not want to see. Several steps ahead of us, a thin old mattress, maybe the one from the old hospital bed, lay on the ground. A heap of wadded, filthy clothing sat beside it, as well as an open coffee can filled with dark gunk. Cigarette butts were scattered all around.

Stacey gave me a questioning look—stay or go?

I raised my stun gun, and she frowned and nodded.

We continued onward, into the thick darkness of the old asylum, stepping over ripped hospital gowns, a dirty slipper, an overturned cafeteria tray. Noises scuffled and scratched in the dark rooms we passed. They were probably possums or rats, but I stayed on guard, ready to zap an attacker or stab him with the protruding steel edges around my flashlight lens.

We checked each doorway, peering into more decay, more crumbling plaster ceilings stained dark with water damage. The sound of dripping grew louder.

I was looking for some kind of filing room, which I reasoned would exist somewhere near the center of the admin building. I hoped there would be something about Mercy I could use.

If it sounds like we were grasping at straws, I'd call that a pretty accurate assessment. However, finding just one little object with emotional value to Mercy would make it all worthwhile.

We pushed open door after door, ready to stun anyone who attacked us. We found the remnants of old cubicles and an occasional office chair overgrown with mold.

Finally, we reached a big room crowded with old filing cabinets, some of them knocked over with their contents spilled into mildewed heaps on the floor.

"Hooray," Stacey whispered in a flat tone.

We dug through the mess, looking for patient records. Stacey found some likely suspects in a row of old cabinets against the back wall.

"Careful," she said when I started to look through a drawer. "Some of them are all moldy and stuck together."

"Great." I found a cabinet full of patients with "C" surnames and checked each drawer in turn. Shuffling through the file folders was like peeling apart the layers of a rotten sandwich, complete with the stench of decay. "Hey, what should we grab for dinner tonight? Subway?" I asked Stacey.

"Ugh," Stacey said from the file cabinet next to me, holding her nose. "Don't even joke."

"I can't believe it," I whispered. I gently lifted out the manila folder, which had the slimy consistency of old lettuce excavated from the very back of a produce drawer. With my scorching-bright flashlight beam, we could make out a portion of the text on the blurry and faded label on the tab: *Cutledge, Me....* The rest of the name was illegible.

"That has to be her," Stacey whispered. "Right?"

I laid the folder on top of the dirty filing cabinet and gently pried the pages open.

It looked like our girl. There was a black and white photograph of her in a patient's gown, her blond hair chopped short, her eyes dark and vacant-looking. I could easily imagine her as the transparent specter who had accosted me in the hallway outside Lexa's room.

I skimmed her file. She'd been treated as a schizophrenic, including heavy 1950's-style doses of first-generation antipsychotic drugs, later followed by years of brain-zapping electroconvulsive therapy. That's a serious neurological beating. If she wasn't insane when they put her into the hospital, she definitely was by the time they let her go.

"What are we looking for?" Stacey whispered over my shoulder.

"We want to find her old room, for one thing."

"Do we really want to do that?" Stacey asked. "That could get dangerous. This is a huge building, we could get lost..."

"All true," I said, still reading. "Here we go. Her room was over in building C, apparently the secure ward for dangerous patients. Her personal effects were put into storage when she checked in. There's a code number for finding it in the storage area."

"Where's that?"

"Don't hospitals usually post maps on the walls? For fires and stuff? Help me look." I shined my light along the corroded plaster walls, stepping gingerly through the rotten muck on the floor.

We found a pair of big, laminated maps, though I had to wipe grime away with a slightly less grimy scrap of carpet to make them at all legible.

"Here are our options, Stacey. We can go outside and across the hospital complex, break into the secure ward, and find her room up on the second floor. Or we can go down to the basement of this building and check the storage rooms."

"Those aren't great options," Stacey said. "Why would any of her stuff still be stored in the basement? Wouldn't they have returned it to her when she left?"

"Possibly, but she was released when the whole hospital closed," I said. "Maybe some things were left behind in the confusion. The employees might have been more concerned about getting out of here and finding new jobs for themselves than with reuniting all the released patients with their long-forgotten possessions. Let's check the basement first. It's closer."

"Whatever gets us out of here fast. I'd rather not get torture-killed by vagrants if we can avoid it."

"Good attitude," I told her. I slid the moldy file folder into Stacey's backpack, and she wrinkled her nose.

We walked out of the file room and back into the main hall, avoiding rotten debris while we walked to the hallway intersection ahead. The map had told us we'd find the stairs there.

"How about we take the elevators?" Stacey snickered as her flashlight landed on the closed steel double doors. She even jabbed the round button with her thumb.

"I think you'll be waiting a long time. If it does show up, it's probably haunted." I pushed open the heavy stairwell door under the dead EXIT sign.

Stacey and I hesitated, shining our lights down the filthy, damp concrete stairs into the darkness below. It was a cinderblock stairwell, with years of accumulated graffiti on the walls. A streak of dark liquid oozed down one side to accumulate in a puddle on the concrete landing below.

"What is that gunk?" Stacey whispered.

"I'm guessing rainwater," I said. "It's slowly worked its way down from the roof, getting nastier all along the way."

"Sweet," Stacey said. "Well, let's go check out the dark basement of the abandoned insane asylum. Nothing could possibly go wrong down there."

"Stay close." I started down the steps, and Stacey followed right behind me.

Our footsteps echoed through the stairwell. I glanced upward with my flashlight, but could only see the underside of more concrete stairs zagging back and forth into solid darkness above. If any dangerous guys were up there, listening to us, there were plenty of places for them to hide.

We crept down the stairs, avoiding the dank puddle that had collected on the landing. Unfortunately, the puddle had overflowed, sending a thin but nasty trickle of foul water down the second flight and into the basement. We stayed to one side of it.

The basement had solid brick walls, with heavy brick columns supporting the building above us. There were lots and lots and *lots* of spiderwebs down here, plus more of the dank puddles made of water dripping from the ceiling.

"It feels cold," Stacey whispered.

"Temperature is ten degrees lower than upstairs," I said, checking my Mel Meter. "Not shocking since we're underground, though. Nothing special on the electromagnetic side."

The basement's layout was less rational than the hallway grid upstairs. It was more like a catacombs, or something carved underground by blind moles, clusters of brick rooms opening onto each other. We could not walk in a straight line, but instead had to pass from chamber to chamber, picking and choosing doorways. I used glow-in-the-dark chalk to mark an arrow by each doorway through which we passed so we'd have less chance of getting hopelessly lost.

The rooms farther in were more cluttered, and we had to navigate around old beds and antiquated equipment draped in dusty sheets. Great hiding places for psycho killers. We lifted the edges of the sheets, looking for storage boxes or bins, but the first room held only rusting hospital beds, plus dusty cardboard boxes of surgical gloves, gowns, scrubs, cotton balls, and sutures.

In the next room, Stacey lifted an old sheet and grimaced.

"Uh, what's that, Ellie?" Her flashlight revealed a roughly hewn chair. Its arms and legs were abnormally wide, with thick leather restraints built into them.

Stacey wasn't looking at the leather straps, though, but at a wooden box that protruded from the chair's high back. If you'd sat down in the old chair, the box would completely cover your head. There was a kind of knob or crank built into either side of the box, about where your temples would be.

"Is that an electric chair?" Stacey whispered.

"I doubt it." I raised the box on its hinges to look at its underside.

The knobs on the outside of the box were attached to metal rods on the inside, each of which ended in a small, flat block of wood. The patient could be placed inside, and the wooden blocks used to lock the patient's head into place.

"You wouldn't be able to see anything in there," Stacey whispered. "You'd just sit there, seeing nothing, not able to move your head or anything else..."

"That must have been awful."

"I wonder how long they kept people locked up like that." Stacey shuddered as she dropped the sheet back into place.

We continued in our generally southward direction. The next doorway was so low I almost bumped my head going through it, and I'm not particularly tall. The arched wooden door had long since rotten from its hinges and fallen flat on the floor.

The room beyond it was narrow, the brick ceiling uncomfortably low and sloping all the way to the dirt-covered floor. Rickety, uneven shelves and tables lined the room, making it almost impassable.

Stacey and I silently passed our lights over the shelves. My skin crawled at what we found there—studded leather flails, rusty chains with cuffs and weights, rusty iron collars, leather masks for muzzling humans.

The room was particularly cold—nine degrees colder than the last one. My Mel Meter also picked up a quick spike of electromagnetic energy. I felt dizzy and off balance.

"I'm going to be sick," Stacey whispered. "We have to get out of here."

She didn't say aloud what we were both thinking: that a strong negative entity, an evil or dangerous ghost, can make you feel ill with its presence.

I shined my flashlight deeper into the room. It was narrow and long, almost like a hallway.

"Come on! Please, Ellie!" Stacey was pulling hard on my sleeve. "Let's go!"

"It looks like this room's a dead end, anyway," I said. "We need to double back."

"Or maybe get upstairs and outside," Stacey said, towing me along as she hurried out of the room. "I need to get out into the sunlight."

"Calm down. Stacey, stop." I planted my feet. She gave me a couple of frustrated tugs.

"Are you kidding? There is something in there!" Stacey hissed, pointing her flashlight back into the extra-cold room we'd just left. The shelves of old straightjackets and human muzzles cast creepy, human-shaped shadows high on the walls as her light whipped among them.

"I agree," I whispered, making my voice sound as calm as possible. I wanted to run and scream, too, the natural human reaction to walking into a dark supernatural presence. It's not the professional reaction, though, and I had to make that clear to Stacey.

"So let's go!" she said.

"We walked into its nest, but it didn't bother us," I told her. "You don't want to show fear. You don't want to draw its interest. We have work to do down here."

"Are you crazy?"

"This is the job," I said. "You can go back to being a cheerleader if this is too rough for you."

"I was *never* a cheerleader!" Stacey looked offended. Well, good. Anger was a little better than fear.

"Then stop trying to run away, and be aggressive. B-E-aggressive," I said.

"Okay, enough."

Since we'd reached a dead end, we doubled back. I kept marked the doors, now using a glowing "X" to indicate where we'd already been.

We passed through the chamber with the restraint chair again, but this time we took a different doorway out of that room. Another, larger room seemed to be what we wanted. It had rows of metal shelves that reached almost to the ceiling above. It was resembled a library, but with the shelves packed full of cardboard boxes instead of books. Over the years, boxes had fallen or been ripped apart by vandals, leaving each aisle full of debris.

"We're looking for lot number S146," I reminded Stacey.

"Doubt we'll find anything in this mess," she said.

Searching from one aisle to the next, we finally found a few boxes marked with an "S" and a number in faded black marker. The first one I saw was S12, which lay ruptured open on the floor. Through a rip in the side, I could see part of a rotten leather loafer and a plaid coil of necktie.

We had to push aside boxes and little rat-nests of clothing as we crept down the long aisle. I saw boxes labeled S47, S78, and S91 among the mess, but many of the numbers in between were missing.

Stacey stopped walking and went stiff, holding up a hand. I froze.

A footstep echoed from somewhere, as if someone had been walking along with us and stopped abruptly when we did.

"Did you hear that?" Stacey whispered. "It sounded like the next aisle over."

We stood in place, listening. I didn't hear anything. I tried to peer into the next aisle, but more boxes blocked my view.

I shrugged and kept walking.

Once we started moving again, I thought I heard another footstep from the next aisle. Stacey looked at me, and I brought the zapper out of its holster on my hip. If the thing stalking us was alive and weighed less than four hundred pounds, I could deal with it.

We moved along until we hit a big pile of fallen boxes, including one marked S132 and another marked S155.

"You should dig through here," I said. "I'll keep watch."

"Ugh." Stacey crouched and began pulling the heap apart, looking for the elusive S146, if it was still here at all.

I heard something further up the aisle, like cardboard shifting and scrubbing against metal. My flashlight revealed nothing but cardboard, metal shelves, and empty space.

"What was that?" Stacey asked.

"I'm not sure."

"I can't find anything down here!"

I holstered my stun gun and knelt to help her paw through the debris. The room was growing chillier. I wondered if the dark presence in the room of flails and masks had decided to leave its lair and come bother us.

Something made a sound near my ear. It was almost like a grunt, like a man lifting a heavy weight. I turned with my light, but again I didn't see anything.

Then there was a feeling of something crawling across my hair, like a spider. I slapped at it, but didn't find anything.

"You okay?" Stacey asked.

"Yeah." I tried to shake it off as I pushed more rotten cardboard. "Look, Stacey! This is it."

The box was almost flattened from being trapped under the weight of the pile, but I could read the black marker scrawled on its side. S146, Mercy's lot number. It was where they'd stored whatever possessions she'd brought from the outside world.

"Is it empty?" Stacey whispered.

"Hope not." I lifted the box free and folded it open.

Clearly, the hospital had not cared very much about preserving its patients' property, simply tossing their belongings into cardboard boxes in the basement while patients spent years and decades locked away in the cells upstairs.

Mercy's clothes were moth-eaten, the remnants of a dress, maybe some pants, some leather-strap sandals coated in mold.

I did find one thing that wasn't rotten to dust, though, and I couldn't help taking a sharp breath when I saw it.

"What's wrong?" Stacey asked.

I held up a tarnished necklace with a silver pendant shaped like a raindrop.

"I've seen this before," I told her. "An image of it, I mean. I think Mercy's ghost was wearing--"

A loud crash sounded as a heavy box fell somewhere up the aisle. While I turned toward it, Stacey screamed and toppled forward, landing on her hands and knees in the heap of rotten clothing and cardboard.

"What happened?" I turned my light toward her, in time to catch something shadowy pass behind her and vanish into the shelves.

"Something grabbed my pants!" Stacey pushed to her feet, swinging her light. "Seriously, there's some kind of pervy ghost in here!"

More crashes sounded, like boxes falling in the aisles on either side of us. The deep male voice groaned again, as if in agony, from the direction where I'd seen the shadow vanish. The high metal shelves where I'd last seen it began to shake hard, like a prisoner rattling his cage bars.

The voice groaned louder, and the room grew even colder. Whispers echoed in the darkness all around us. One voice was high-pitched and sharp, like an evil clown, while the one was like a rapid hiss. Their words were too distorted to understand, if there were any words at all and not just meaningless guttural sounds. They were not the voices of the living, but of the insane dead.

"Now can we panic and run away?" Stacey asked, her face completely pale and her jaw trembling. She was barely holding it together...but she *was* holding it together, which impressed me.

"Yeah, let's panic and run." I shoved the silver necklace into my pocket and jumped to my feet.

We ran together up the aisle, our flashlight beams barely piercing the inky blackness ahead. That meant the air was getting thicker and darker. A manifestation might be imminent. I wanted to be out of there before that happened.

As we reached the end of the aisle, cold, sharp fingers sank into my arm, just above the elbow. I turned to face it, raising my flashlight alongside my head at eye level, like a cop approaching a drunk in a dark parking lot.

My light caught broken pieces of a face floating in the air beside me—a fragment of a jaw, a single colorless eye, a sharp-boned cheek, all loosely held together by pale spectral mist. The thing recoiled from the three-thousand-lumen direct blast, and it vanished.

That didn't mean it was gone, though. It just meant I had no idea where it might appear next.

Old Groany's voice sounded again, but louder, deeper, and apparently in even greater agony this time. Stacey, a few steps ahead of me, suddenly twisted and fell sideways as if something had rammed hard into her right hip. She crashed into the shelves as I ran to catch up with her.

"Are you okay?" I asked.

"It's heavy," she gasped as I helped her up. She looked around, her eyes huge with fright, jabbing her flashlight at the darkness like a spear. "It's *strong*. Did you see it?"

"I didn't see anything."

We ran, our flashlights now about as useful as a pair of tiny wax birthday candles against the darkness. The air had grown so thick that it was hard to breathe, and hard to move, like in one of those nightmares where something is chasing you while your feet are somehow trapped or mysteriously heavy.

The host of creeps closed in around us. I'd heard at least three distinct voices, but there could have been more specters than that. It felt like a dark cloud of them, a cluster of ghosts that had more or less lost their individual identities, their yearnings merging into a combined pool of hunger, anger, pain, or whatever emotions motivated them to stick around instead of moving on. A "cluster haunting" is Calvin's term for this.

We pushed through the thick, dark air and passed through another doorway. We should have seen at least one of the glowing green arrows I had drawn, but we didn't. The darkness was like heavy, cold smoke, crushing in to choke us while we walked blindly through it.

Then the groan sounded again, followed by the other voices. They grabbed at us from every side, with hands that were invisible and insubstantial until they clawed into you. I felt icy fingers on my legs, another hand grabbing at my stomach, and another seized the back of my neck. That one made me scream.

Stacey screamed beside me, but I could barely even seen her. Pale, distended, half-formed faces rose in the darkness, their eye sockets hollow, the dark misshapen holes of their mouths wide open as if they expected to feed.

"They're all over me!" Stacey shouted.

Since our flashlights weren't helping much, I had to switch tactics. I holstered my flashlight and traded it for a wireless palm-sized Bose speaker. Then I touched the iPod on my belt to activate my emergency playlist.

I held out the little speaker like a weapon toward the nearest creepy, pale half-face.

A slice of Handel's "Messiah" blasted out at ear-crashing volume. It was the Hallelujah Chorus, one of the loudest and most potent sections of the song—I didn't have two hours for build-up.

The hallelujahs, as sung by hundreds of voices in the Mormon Tabernacle Choir backed by a full orchestra, rang out into the lightless basement room, echoing back from the walls around us.

Ghosts in long-abandoned properties like the old asylum are accustomed to years of darkness and quiet. This is why a powerful tactical flashlight beam can jar them. So can the right kind of music. My little speaker created a wall of sound—strings, brass, and voices organized and brimming with power, the song itself glowing with religious intent. It wouldn't harm the ghosts, but like a sudden burst of light, it might chase them away for a moment or two.

The faces spun around us, losing shape, their voices crying out in shock and surprise.

The dark cloud filling the room thinned a bit. It didn't disperse or vanish, but suddenly we could see a bright green arrow drawn in glowing chalk.

"That way!" I said.

Stacey and I hurried. Our flashlights were blasting at full power again rather than getting absorbed by the darkness. I didn't know how long it would take the ghosts to adapt to the powerful music filling their lair—maybe a few minutes, maybe just a couple of seconds. Then, I had no doubt, they would close in around us again, much angrier than before.

We had to get out of there before that happened.

The faintly glowing arrows guided us back to the steel fire door for the stairwell. I pulled on the handle. At this point, I half-expected the door to be stuck or locked by the specters, trapping us in the basement.

Fortunately, I was wrong about that. The door swung open, and we dashed up the concrete stairs, stomping carelessly through the stream of dark, nasty water that dripped from step to step. Though it was still pitch black in the stairwell, the air was much warmer and thinner, and nothing seemed to interfere with the glow of our flashlights.

We ran up to the main level and down the dim corridor. The weak, dusty light seeping in through the barred windows seemed glorious to my eyes.

We turned a corner, kicked open the same door through which we'd entered the asylum, and spilled out into orange, late-afternoon sunlight. We kept running through the high weeds until we reached the chain-link fence, and then we finally stopped to catch our breath.

"Holy...mother of...cows," Stacey panted, holstering her flashlight as she looked back at the sprawling old hospital. "Let's never go in there again."

"Agreed," I said.

"Have you ever seen anything like that before?"

"It can happen in long-abandoned places like this, especially institutions like prisons and hospitals," I said. "Some of the ghosts were people who were already intensely disturbed, maybe violent, when they were alive. Decades of isolation, trapped with just each other and their own memories...well, it's not therapeutic for them, let's put it that way."

"That was the scariest thing I've ever seen. I feel like I have a bad bruise here." She delicately touched her hip where Old Groany had slammed into her.

"Want me to look at it?"

"I'd rather get the hell out of here first," Stacey said. "I don't want to be here at sunset."

She had a point. We loaded our stuff into my car, and I pulled away down the massively deteriorated and overgrown service road. I had to resist the urge to shove the accelerator to the floor and leave the place behind as quickly as possible—we didn't want to hit a bad pothole and blow a tire or break an axle. The car bobbed up and down like a canoe on a choppy sea.

"Was it worth it?" Stacey asked after a minute. She was still shuddering, still traumatized from our experience. So was I.

"We'll find out." I fished out the tarnished silver necklace and held it up in the dying afternoon sunlight. "If not, we're going to have some real problems on our hands."

Chapter Twelve

The sun was low in the sky, and I called the Treadwells to tell them we'd be late. Anna Treadwell sounded nervous and worried on the phone.

Once we'd put twenty or thirty miles between us and the haunted crazy-house, Stacey and I stopped at a sketchy roadside grease pit called Uncle Roogey's Eatin' Place, which looked like a barn surrounded by a gravel parking lot and giant pine trees. We needed solid, heavy food and a chance to sit and shake out our nerves for a while. This local dive looked more promising than fast food.

The hostess, a gum-snapping girl of about fourteen, directed us to a booth with a wooden picnic-style table. Years of initials, hearts, crosses, and cryptic messages were carved into the surface. A ceiling fan revolved slowly above us. Drowsy, twangy country music played over the restaurant's tinny sound system, while billiard balls clacked in the next room.

"Ask me how much I don't want to go ghost-chasing tonight," Stacey said, settling into her wooden bench of a seat.

"I'm with you," I said.

"What do y'all want to drink?" Our waitress arrived, a middle-aged woman in apron who reeked of stale cigarettes.

"I'll have a beer," I said, and Stacey raised her eyebrows. I shrugged. "I need it."

"That sounds like a good idea. Me, too," Stacey said.

"We don't serve alcohol here," the waitress said, scowling at us just slightly. "The Lord forbids it."

"Sweet tea, I guess," I said, and Stacey seconded my order, looking disappointed.

"Y'all want some fried biscuits?"

"No, thank you!" Stacey said.

"They're free," the waitress added.

"Then we'll take them," I said.

They waitress walked off, leaving us with coffee-ringed paper menus to study.

"How do you do it?" Stacey asked me, her voice falling almost to a whisper.

"Eat fried biscuits? I don't know, I've never even heard of them."

"No, I mean what we just saw. How can you face things like that all the time? How do you deal with it? My skin's still crawling. I feel like I need to take a bath, and then burn the bathtub when I'm done."

"We don't deal with that kind of thing all the time," I said. "Most people hire us to help with homes or businesses. Ghosts in old, abandoned ruins don't bother people, unless someone tries to come in and renovate. A place like that old hospital is too huge, outdated, and rotten to renovate, so it's just going sit there as a ghost hive until someone tears it down."

"A ghost hive." Stacey shivered. She smiled as the waitress brought our mason jars full of iced tea, plus a chipped platter of crusty brown biscuits floating in gravy. They looked like they'd literally been dropped in a deep fryer, then drizzled with butter.

"Nothing could be as scary as these biscuits," I told Stacey when the waitress walked off. "They're the true abomination."

"I'm serious," Stacey said. "You don't get terrified? I didn't even know something like that place could exist. I don't know if I can handle this job, Ellie. Going right from one haunted place to another..."

"Listen, Stacey, Calvin hired you for a reason," I said.

"Because of all my ghost videos. That only happened by accident, though. At least the first one, in Colonial Park Cemetery. I was just trying to get some images for this class project..."

"But then you started deliberately looking for ghosts. It wasn't just an accident, Stacey. You were drawn to this. You chose to keep searching."

"Right, but I was just trying to capture images. I usually couldn't find anything, and even when I did get an image, it was fleeting, or barely there. They could be scary, but not *dangerous*. Not like something that could pick me up and bash me into a shelf."

"We told you it was dangerous," I said. "Some of them have strong psychokinetic energy. You've never heard of a ghost attacking anyone?"

"Of course I have! But you never know when a story's real, or embellished, or just plain made up," Stacey said. "Experiencing that for myself? It's too much."

"But you survived," I said. "I'm not going to lie. It's dangerous. Some of these entities are strong enough to kill you. That's why people need our help. People stuck with a haunting are desperate—usually they can't afford to leave their homes. There aren't many people who do what we do, Stacey, and when people need us, they really need us. And I think you have a talent for it."

"Really?" A little smile finally cracked through her pale, shocked expression.

"Sure," I said. Well, I wasn't sure, but she'd given me some reason to hope. "Any normal person would have taken off running out of that basement as soon as the ghosts began stalking us. You stayed and finished the job. So maybe Calvin was right about you."

"You say that like you disagreed with him," Stacey said. "Did you? Did he foist me on you against your will?"

Exactly. "Not exactly," I said. "I just worried about whether you could handle it."

"And what about now?"

"A little less worried." I gave her a tired smile, which was the best one I could manage. "Let's see how well the ghost trapping goes tonight."

Our waitress hovered nearby, staring at us like we were both crazy. I wondered how long she'd been listening.

I ordered some serious food: fried chicken, mashed potatoes, macaroni, green beans. Hey, I was really hungry, and I needed the calories for the night ahead.

Stacey annoyed me by ordering the salad after I'd set myself up for a pig-out, but she redeemed herself by adding a slice of pecan pie. Good girl.

Then it was time to go trap our ghost.

Chapter Thirteen

It was well past sunset by the time we reached the Treadwell home. Stacey and I had to stop at our homes to shower and change, because the asylum left us feeling nasty inside and out.

Anna answered the door, looking even more stressed than the last time I'd seen her. Lexa stood a little behind her, twisting her cloth doll, a deep frown etched into her face.

"Is everything okay?" I asked.

"We've had some trouble. Come on in." Anna moved aside to let us through the doorway.

Right away, I saw that the long wooden table had been pushed from the dining room into the hall, with one end shoved tight against the security door.

"She's mad," Lexa said. "She's trying to get us."

"What happened?" I asked.

"It started about an hour ago, when the sun went down," Anna said. "The door won't stay locked, and it just bangs open and closed. It doesn't happen if anyone's in the room, but the moment you step away..."

"I'm sorry," I said.

"Are you going to be able to take care of this or not?" Dale stomped down the stairs, buttoning his shirt over his pale, hairy stomach. He could have started buttoning a little earlier, if you ask me. "I'm not paying you a dime if we're still stuck with that ghost."

Dale seemed awfully eager to not pay us a dime, I thought. It wasn't the first time he'd said it.

"We're setting a trap tonight." I held up the tarnished silver necklace. "I think we found some good bait."

"That's her necklace," Lexa said, drawing puzzled looks from her parents.

"Exactly right, Lexa," I said. "We visited the old hospital where she used to live and dug it out."

"And that place was *haunted*," Stacey said. "I mean, really, really haunted."

"How does a ghost trap work?" Lexa asked.

"Step outside and I'll show you. You can come, too, Mr. and Mrs. Treadwell," I added. I just didn't want to explain the trap inside the house where Mercy's ghost might hear us. Mercy seemed at least partly aware of what was happening in the present.

"I want to see it!" Lexa bolted toward the door. Anna followed, then Dale, who gave Stacey and me a suspicious look, as though we were a couple of grifters running a scam. I'm used to that look.

We walked out to the driveway, and I opened a back door of the cargo van.

"This is a basic, standard pneumatic ghost trap," I said. Four traps stood upright in the unpainted wooden structure we use as a carrying case. I lifted one and held it out to my clients, and all three of them leaned forward, curious.

The trap was a cylinder, about two feet tall, resembling a large version of the clear plastic capsule that banks send through at the drive-up window. One end was sealed solid. I unlatched and removed the circular lid at the other end so they could look inside.

"It basically has three layers," I said. "The innermost is heavily leaded glass—we call that the 'ghost jar.' It's very difficult for ghosts to penetrate that material for some reason. Inside the glass are these wireless sensors that detect temperature and electromagnetic frequency, and they send their readings to my remote control—I'll show you that in a sec. If the inside of the jar grows cold, and the EM spikes at the same time, that's a strong sign that a ghost is inside.

"The middle layer is this copper mesh." I tapped the clear plastic exterior. The mesh could be seen through the plastic on the outside or through the glass on the inside—the trap was essentially transparent. "The mesh is charged by batteries at the bottom. It creates a second barrier, an electromagnetic wall to imprison the ghost. And the outer layer is just hard plastic to insulate the whole thing."

"Does that really work?" Dale asked, smirking at me. "It looks like something you stole off a bank teller."

"I've removed scores of ghosts with this kind of device," I replied. I loaded the trap into the stamper, which sort of resembled a four-foot microscope. A bottle of compressed gas was at the top, where the eyepiece of a microscope would be. I snapped the cylinder lid into a shaft below it, where the microscope's objective lenses would go. Then I locked the rest of the cylinder onto a little platform directly beneath the shaft. "When I press the button on the remote, the stamper slams the lid down onto the cylinder to seal the ghost inside. I can set it to automatically close when the sensors detect the temperature and EMF changes, but I prefer to operate it manually." I lifted the remote, which had a digital display screen and one big red button.

"That's pretty cool," Lexa whispered.

"I hope it works," Anna said. Dale snorted and shook his head.

"Carry it around front," Dale said. "I'm not hefting that dining table again tonight. I've got back problems."

"Can you make sure the front doors are unlocked, Mr. Treadwell?" Stacey asked.

Dale blew out a long, slow breath, as if her request was the most annoying thing he'd ever heard and unlocking the front doors was a nearly impossible task. Then he took out his keys.

Stacey and I picked up the stamper, a heavy and cumbersome piece of equipment, and lugged it together. We followed Dale through a path that had been recently hacked through the overgrown yard. Stepping stones were barely visible beneath a layer of stamped-down weeds. Dale carried my flashlight, and he wasn't all that considerate about lighting the path for us.

We reached the front steps, made of dark Georgia marble trimmed in brick.

"What the hell?" Dale asked. He stopped on the walkway, looking up at the double doors beneath the sharp, peaked overhang. One of them stood wide open. "I locked those doors this morning when you two left."

"Maybe Anna opened them?" I asked. "Or Lexa?"

"I doubt it. The girls won't go into the main house at all anymore. Just me and the workers."

"Maybe one of the workers—" I began.

"Probably. Freakin' slobs." Dale shook his head as he climbed the five steps. He pushed open the second door with a creak, then presented the pitch-black foyer with a sarcastic flourish, without stepping inside. "Here's your room, ladies."

Stacey and I lugged the stamper up the stairs and into the center of the foyer. Dale did not step inside with us, and actually pulled a pretty good vanishing act just after we walked past him. He was probably scared to enter the main house, too, and didn't want to hang around long enough to make his fear obvious.

Despite the open door and the hot June night outside, the interior of the vaulted foyer was still a little chilly. Stacey and I had cleaned it up after the failed mock funeral, including sliding the little end tables back against the wall where we'd found them, plus sweeping up an amazing amount of dust along with the shredded funeral flowers. The room still looked filthy, though, and smelled like rot.

We set up the stamper in the middle of the floor, then returned to the van a couple of times to haul in the rest of our gear. When we were done, we knocked on the side door again, because the family had returned inside the house.

"I think we're ready," I told Anna, while I stayed out on the covered side porch. "You may as well try to get some sleep."

"We can't watch you catch the ghost?" Lexa asked with a frown.

"Stacey will get it all on video," I said. "You can watch tomorrow."

"Okay." She was still frowning, but she looked a little relieved, too.

"Go get ready for bed, Lexa," Anna said. When the girl was gone, Anna asked us in a quieter voice: "Do you want us to unlock the security door in case you run into trouble? I could have Dale pull the table away."

"No, but thank you," I said. "Do what makes you feel safe. We'll be right by the front doors if we need a quick escape. I'm sure we'll be fine, anyway."

"All right." She seemed relieved. "Good luck."

As we walked away, I heard Anna lock the door behind us.

Back in the foyer, now lit by a few scattered electric lanterns, we set up for the night. We had our usual array of cameras, mostly pointed at the big stamper holding the cylindrical trap, the lid poised a foot above the open trap and ready to slam down at a moment's notice. We had a high-sensitivity microphone.

We also had a couple of sleeping bags, since there was no electricity to inflate my air mattress. The renovation workers were having trouble fixing up the wiring in the main house, though the power in the east wing seemed to work fine. We had a cooler with bottled water, sandwiches, and snacks.

"This is almost like camping," Stacey said.

"It's even worse than camping," I replied.

"We still have more than an hour until midnight. Let's take a look around this place." Stacey hopped to her feet.

"Seriously? After what happened at the asylum today, you want to go exploring a haunted mansion?" I have to admit, I was a little impressed.

"Do you think it's better to sit in the one room we *know* is haunted?" Stacey asked.

I couldn't argue with that. Our instruments weren't picking up any major electromagnetic activity, and we weren't seeing anything on the thermal or night vision cameras. Aside from the abnormally low temperature and the aggressive reek of decay, the room seemed quiet. I don't like to sit still for very long, anyway.

"Okay," I said. "As long as we're back before midnight. Bring your camera."

I strapped my heavy night vision goggles to my head, keeping them up on my forehead for now, and grabbed my flashlight. I double-checked my pocket to make sure the necklace was still there —we couldn't have the ghost coming by and scooping it up while we were gone. Active ghosts have a talent for making small objects disappear.

We started by looking around the main level. The spacious front parlor had a big bay window overgrown with vines on the outside. A decayed piano slumped in the corner, and a few crumbling books adorned the mostly empty bookshelves. A model sailing ship lay smashed on the floor among broken glass, as if it had once been inside a bottle. A mildewed sofa lay like a corpse under an even more mildewed sheet. The brick fireplace was cold and empty, full of ancient gray ashes.

"Nothing happening here," I said, checking my Mel Meter. "Let's keep going."

A heavy, abnormally wide sliding door stood closed in the north wall, opposite the giant bay window. Its unseen rollers screeched as Stacey heaved the door aside.

I pointed my flashlight into a dining room that dwarfed the one in the east wing. Layers of crown molding encircled the high ceiling. The fireplace was huge and gorgeous, made of large river stones and almost big enough to stand inside. Sideboards were mounted along one wall, opposite a row of tall, narrow windows that showed nothing but darkness outside. There was no furniture except for a single dining chair overturned by the door to the hallway, one leg broken as if the chair had tripped and fallen while attempting to escape.

Another sliding door led us toward a room at the back of the house, where we discovered a moth-eaten old wing chair poised by the small fireplace.

"Do you smell that?" Stacey sniffed the air, which had a slightly acrid odor. "It's very faint, but it's like old cigars?"

"This must have been the smoking room," I said. "You could imagine the men retreating here to drink and smoke after a dinner party. The ladies might have gone to the parlor instead."

"According to your friend from the historical society, they might have been smoking opium in here, too," Stacey said. "And those ladies were prostitutes, at least in the later years....These must have been some wild parties."

We crossed the central hallway to the kitchen, which had acres of countertop as well as a separate prep table. It was big enough to cook multi-course meals for a crowd of people. A discolored rectangle on the wall indicated where the refrigerator had been. A brown 1970s-style six-burner stove with a circular window in the oven door remained in the room, but you wouldn't want to eat any food that passed near it. Many of the cabinets had been bashed apart by vandals, and a disgusting black stain took up one entire side of the sink, the one underneath the rusty faucet.

"So gross," Stacey whispered, shining her light into the sink.

"The Treadwells really have their work cut out here," I said. "I hope they have a fortune to spend on renovation."

The first floor was creepy, but we didn't encounter any cold spots, banging doors, or headless horsemen, and our instruments indicated nothing at all. We found the back stairs, which ran above an empty room with washer and dryer hookups, and we climbed to the second floor. The stairs were narrow and steep, designed for servants rather than valued guests. My arms brushed the walls on either side of me, and I'm not exactly a broad-shouldered football player type.

I immediately did not like the second floor. The ceiling was much lower than the first floor, and the hallway felt cramped.

We looked into a couple of rooms, finding only debris. The rooms themselves were impressive, though, with high ceilings, dark timbers, marble accents, and tall windows trimmed in colored glass. The house had probably been elegant and attractive back in its long-lost prime.

Individual exterior locks had been added to most of the doors, probably during the mansion's boarding-house days after Captain Marsh died and his niece inherited the house.

There was no such lock on the bathroom door. Stacey wrinkled her nose at the cracked, dirty tiles and the open pipes where the sink and toilet had been. An oval-shaped porcelain soaking tub remained, its interior coated with black grime, as if a layer of mold had bloomed and died there ages ago.

"I guess the boarders shared the bathroom with each other," she said. "Ew. Lousy accommodations."

The next door was ajar, and I eased it open.

"Watch out!" I told Stacey. My flashlight showed rusty nails jutting out along the edge of the door, like a row of sharp teeth running from the top to the bottom. A few chunks of the door's edge were missing. They were still nailed to the door frame.

"I wonder why they nailed it shut," Stacey whispered.

I opened the door wider, and it let out a rusty creak. Unlike the other second-floor rooms we'd passed, this one was still partly furnished, with a sagging single bed topped with rotten old blankets. A cheap pine wardrobe stood closed in one shadowy corner, by the narrow, sharp-peaked window. The plain, ugly furniture looked out of place under the high ceiling with its intricate, hand-crafted crown molding depicting leaves and grapes.

"Ugh." Stacey covered her nose as she swooped her light around the room. "Smells like a possum died in here. And a skunk, too. Maybe it was a murder-suicide."

"It feels weird, too," I said. I was a little dizzy, and my stomach felt like it wanted to flip over. My Mel Meter detected nothing.

I clicked off my flashlight and slid my night vision goggles over my eyes. Every detail of the room stood out in stark green. I approached the wardrobe. The knobby, thick grains of cheap wood seemed to glow in sharp relief.

I hesitated, took a breath, then opened the wardrobe.

Inside hung several empty hangers and a patched, worn coat and frayed necktie from a man's suit. Whoever had owned it had lived in the forties or fifties, and had not been rich.

A thick layer of dust coated everything.

I lifted away my goggles and double-checked my meter. Nothing. I walked around the bed, then the tiny, bricked-up fireplace, and finally I circled the room. Despite my queasy feelings, I couldn't find anything.

I dropped to my knees and looked under the bed. What I found wasn't supernatural, but it was a little disturbing—a couple of broken syringes. I couldn't see any good reason to touch them or examine them further without wearing gloves, so I left them there.

"Why do you think they nailed this room closed?" Stacey whispered. She was lingering close to the door.

"No idea. Be careful on the way out."

We stepped past the door with its edge of crooked, rusty nails, then eased it shut.

The other rooms were similar to the first we'd seen, with beautiful high ceilings and arched, colored-glass windows whispering of the house's original glory, now coated in dust and grime. The walls were set at odd angles to each other, giving each room a unique shape.

The rooms were empty except for debris we didn't particularly want to inspect, plus an occasional chair, table, or bedframe. We found another bathroom, where the sink had been removed and the mirror above it smashed. We also found a second small bedroom that had been nailed shut and later pried open.

Looking inside that room, we found a decaying double bed with a rotten canopy. Lacy clothing hung in the closet, including an old-fashioned bustier and a scandalously cut red dress. We had the same uneasy feeling, but got no readings.

Back in the second-floor hall, I opened a slatted door, expecting to find a linen closet, but instead discovered a set of stairs to the third floor. It made the previous stairway look roomy by comparison. The stairs were steep and shallow, almost like a ladder.

"Should we check it out? They said the master suite is up there, right?" Stacey asked. There was apprehension in her voice, but a little excitement, too. I had to admit she was courageous. Maybe I was getting slightly less annoyed with Calvin for sticking me with a new apprentice to train. Maybe.

"There's no time," I said. "It's almost midnight. We need to go light up the trap."

Stacey looked both relieved and disappointed as I closed the door and walked back up the hallway.

Chapter Fourteen

We returned to the foyer by the wide front staircase. I gave the broken baluster on the second floor a sidelong glance—we didn't know for sure that Mercy had hung herself on that particular baluster, but I couldn't help imagining it.

Pale spots of electric lantern light glowed on the foyer floor. The room was at least ten degrees colder than all the others we'd visited. The EMF readings fluctuated up to 2.2 milligaus, then 2.3. It was the low end of the ghost-EM range, enough to indicate a residual or dormant haunting, at least.

"So, as far as we can tell, she usually begins in this room, then steps through that door and down the hall." I opened the door to the hallway, where Stacey's thermal camera had caught the cold spirit emerging from the foyer.

I was thrown off for a moment. Apparently Dale had been working hard today—or more likely, his contractors had been working hard while he stood around with a beer giving them unwanted advice, as he'd done with the roofers.

Fresh, unpainted drywall lined both sides of the hall, giving it the appearance of something freshly built. That meant they'd finished removing the rotten old paneling and updating the wiring, but I didn't want to throw a switch and test it out. Instead, I dropped my night goggles over my eyes.

"Let's cut her off," I told Stacey. I grabbed a hammer and a couple of nails from the portable workbench set up near the locked security door.

We returned to the lobby, where I closed the hallway door and began nailing it to the door frame.

"Whoa!" Stacey said. "Won't the Treadwells get upset about that?"

"Not as upset as they'll be if we don't get rid of their ghost." I hammered in the third and final nail, then tested the door. It was sealed tight.

"You're the boss." Stacey shrugged and checked her watch. "Three minutes to midnight."

"Let's light it up." I walked over to the big pneumatic stamper and reached into the cylindrical trap. The lid was already loaded into the stamper, ready to slam down and seal the trap at a moment's notice.

I dropped the tarnished silver necklace at the bottom of the cylinder, next to an unlit white candle mounted on a little tack. Two more tacks were built inside the cylindrical trap, one halfway up, one near the top. A white candle was mounted on each.

"Want to do the honors?" I opened my toolbox and held out a box of kitchen matches.

"Seriously?" Stacey's eyes glowed like a girl receiving a pony for her birthday. "Can I?"

"Can you handle striking a match?" I asked solemnly, resisting my urge to snicker at her eagerness.

"I can." She said it back with the same solemn tone, and I laughed.

Stacey ignited a long match, then reached it into the trap and lit the three candles. I walked around the room, gathering up and switching off our electric lanterns. I left them by our "campsite" with our sleeping bags.

"Now what?" Stacey asked.

"Blow out your match and sit down." I dropped into a cross-legged position on my sleeping bag.

"I feel like I should say something."

I laughed. "You're not casting a spell. Ghosts can feed on the heat of candles. You're just setting out food for it."

"So why did we need the necklace?" Stacey sat down beside me and clicked off her flashlight, leaving the candles as the only light source in the room.

"To really draw her interest. In a bad pinch, you can try using candles and nothing else, but it's so much easier if you have something else to attract the ghost. Now stay quiet and watch."

We watched the three candles burning inside the transparent cylinder. The copper mesh didn't obscure the view any more than a screen door blocks your view of the driveway. The leaded glass, though, distorted and magnified the flickering flames.

I returned my night vision goggles to my toolbox and strapped on my thermal goggles instead, leaving them on my forehead in case we needed them. This ghost, for whatever reason, showed up on thermal much better than night vision.

"Hey, when do I get my own thermal goggles?" Stacey whispered.

"They're expensive. Maybe after your, um, probationary period."

"I didn't know I had a probationary period."

"Sh," I said. "It's after midnight now. Watch for ghosts."

We kept our eyes on the array of camera display screens. On the thermal camera, the candles showed up as glowing red and yellow spots in an otherwise blue-tinged room. On Stacey's laptop, we could see soundwaves captured by the high-sensitivity microphone, which could monitor above and below the normal range of human hearing.

I laid my Mel Meter and the remote control for the trap side by side on the floor in front of me, so I could see whether the sensors in the trap showed a lower temperature or higher EMF signature than the room around me.

Then we waited.

The big house lay silent around us, the three flickering candles casting huge, shifting shadows all around the walls, especially where the light shone through the sculptured balusters of the staircase and the second-floor walkway.

After a minute, I heard a creak, and then another. It could have been nothing.

Another creak. Stacey looked at me.

Then a single footstep on the front stairs. Just one, but clear as a drumbeat.

"Did you hear—" Stacey began.

"Sh!" I slid my thermals down over my eyes and looked toward the staircase. A flick of deep purple appeared and vanished at the foot of the stairs.

My viewpoint became more blue, and I could feel the room turning colder around me. More tiny motes of deep-cold purple appeared in the air below the broken baluster, several feet above the three glowing red spots inside the trap. They blinked in and out of visibility. More and more of them began to appear, though, until I was looking at a swirling cloud of freezing cold maybe a foot across.

"Ellie!" Stacey whispered. "The thermal camera—"

I put a finger over her lips, while her eyes were bugging out. We couldn't risk scaring away the ghost.

The fine purple mist drifted downward and backward under the walkway, as if a light breeze were blowing it to the hallway door. I tensed, ready to see Mercy's reaction when she found it nailed shut.

The mist hovered there, becoming denser, vaguely beginning to suggest the shape of a woman. Then every particle of it froze at once.

A bang sounded from the door, as if someone had knocked on it angrily.

There was a second bang. Then the mist became animated again, condensing more into a clear woman-shape.

The readout graph spiked on the audio app—the high-sensitivity microphone had picked up something, though I hadn't heard a sound.

The woman-shape flowed toward the door to the front parlor instead, which I'd closed but not locked or barricaded in any way. She moved so fast that she blurred back into a cloud shape.

She had totally ignored our trap.

"Uh-oh," I whispered, hopping to my feet and picking up the remote control. "I think she's trying to find another way around."

I ran to the trap, carefully reached past the burning candles, and drew out the necklace.

The ghost reached the parlor door, and it swung open with a squeak.

"Holy cow," Stacey whispered. She grasped her flashlight, but fortunately didn't turn it on. She couldn't see the ghost except when it was on camera, near the trap, so the rusty sound of the opening door had surprised her and made her jump a little. "Holy cow, holy cow..."

"Mercy," I said, stepping slowly toward the ghost, the way you might deal with a spooked horse. "Mercy Cutledge. Can you hear me?"

The purple mist seemed to hesitate for a moment. Then it condensed again into a woman-shape, facing me from the open parlor door.

We regarded each other for a moment, though I could just barely discern the general area of her face.

When she spoke to me, I didn't so much hear the word as *feel* it stabbing deep into my brain like the tip of an icicle.

Leave. The word bored into my head a second time, making me wince. *Leave.*

"Why do you want us to leave, Mercy?" I asked.

She tilted toward me—her whole body at once, as though she were stiff as a board from her head to her feet—and drifted a little closer. She seemed to be examining me. It was an uncomfortable feeling for me, a sense of growing dread.

Then she began to dissolve into mist, the mass of her floating back toward the parlor door, tendrils of her reaching back into the dark parlor. I was losing her, as if she'd decided I was of no further interest.

"Mercy." I spoke calmly but firmly, as if I had some kind of unquestionable authority. I held up the silver teardrop. "Is this your necklace, Mercy? I found it for you."

The mass of purple mist hesitated, then drifted my way again.

"Ellie," Stacey whispered. "Ellie, I can see her. She's manifesting."

I raised my thermal goggles and parked them on my forehead. With my own eyes, I could see a wispy, transparent image of Mercy floating towards me, the hollow holes of her eyes fixated on the necklace dangling from my fingers. Her dark dress faded into nothingness somewhere around her hips, and her legs remained altogether invisible. She seemed to be wading through the air toward me.

Her face wore a blank expression at first...then contorted into extreme anger. Ghosts' facial expressions aren't limited by minor details like the boundaries of skin and muscle. They are pure energy and emotion. Sometimes they can give you a look that goes beyond the extremes of what living human faces can manage.

That was the kind of look Mercy gave me now, her eyes turning into triangular slashes that made me think of a jack-o'-lantern, the kind that's carved with the intent to scare rather than amuse. Her mouth, too, deformed into a huge angry frown that slashed down either side of her chin while also baring her teeth *and* snarling.

She darted toward me, and I braced myself—she was fast and filled with rage. Her voice rang in my head, just a raw, wordless screech.

Then she vanished.

After a few seconds, Stacey whispered, "What happened?"

"I'm not sure." I drew the thermals back on, looking around the room. It was all still unnaturally cold, tinged with blue, but I couldn't find the dense mass of cold purple anywhere. "Oh, no. I hope she didn't pop over to the east wing to haunt Lexa again."

"Without using a door?" Stacey asked.

"Ghosts don't need doors. Sometimes they think they do, or they do it out of habit, or they just like to scare everyone with a nice slam--"

She hit me all at once, from every side—a heavy, icy cold weight that sent me sprawling on my back, hard enough to knock the wind out of me and rattle the hardwood floorboards when I landed.

The ghost trap remote skittered out of my hand, away into the deep shadows below the walkway. I closed my fingers tighter around the necklace.

"Ellie! Are you okay?" Stacey ran toward me, slicing up the darkness with her tactical flashlight.

"Lights out!" I managed to gasp, though I could barely breathe. It wasn't just getting my lungs hammered to the floor. The frigid air now seemed much too thick, choking me as if I'd swallowed about a yard of thick, scratchy flannel. The ghost was pushing in on me from all sides.

I felt the necklace bite into my fingers like a cutting wire as Mercy tried to reclaim it.

"What do I do?" Stacey asked, standing over me with her flashlight extinguished, her face full of anguish in the sputtering candlelit.

"Take it," I forced myself to croak, waving the necklace at her.

Stacey squatted beside me as I lay choking on the floor. She took my hand, then slipped her fingers under the necklace. I made sure she had a tight grasp on it before I opened my hand and let it go.

She ran to the trap and held the necklace above the glowing candles.

The ghost stayed on top of me—all around me, really—keeping me pressed to the floor while I fought to breathe.

"Hey, ghost lady!" Stacey shouted, waving the necklace. "Is this what you're looking for?"

The pressure on me continued, so Stacey clicked on her flashlight and jabbed the beam into the space above me, where the darkness seemed to absorb the light. Not a bad move this time. I doubted any flashlight would chase the ghost away at this point—Mercy seemed pretty determined to get her property back.

The pressure finally eased, and I felt the cold mass rush away toward Stacey.

I pushed myself to my feet, gratefully taking a few deep breaths. Then I ran into the dim area under the walkway, where I'd last seen my remote bouncing away.

I drew my own flashlight to help me search. The night vision goggles would have been extremely useful at this moment, but unfortunately those were across the large room in my toolbox, and I didn't have time to grab them.

Stacey lowered the necklace into the trap, and then the ghost struck her, an invisible force sweeping her off her feet and knocking her to the ground. She cried out in surprise and pain.

The necklace clinked against the lead-glass bottom of the trap.

A moment later, the first candle, the one near the opening at the top, snuffed out. Then the second, halfway down. It looked like Mercy was inside the trap, but I wasn't able to close it.

I fought back panic as I searched for the remote. I finally found it in one dusty, cobwebbed corner and snatched it up.

When I turned around, the final candle had been snuffed out, and the necklace itself was rising quickly toward the top of the trap, curling and twisting in the air like a levitating snake.

There was no point checking the readouts on the remote—the ghost was definitely in there. I slammed my thumb down on the red button.

The stamper hissed as its piston arm drove down, slamming the lid into place. The necklace slapped against it, then tumbled downward and landed on the bottom of the cylinder, draped over the blown-out candle.

On my remote, the temperature and EMF readouts turned blank. This meant the battery pack at the bottom of the trap had electrified the layer of copper mesh, creating a charged field around the leaded glass jar nested inside. Ghosts couldn't pass through it, and neither could the wireless signals from my sensors within the trap.

"Are you all right?" I asked Stacey, helping her up from the floor.

"Couldn't feel better if I tried," Stacey said, but her shaky voice didn't match her words. "Did we get her?"

"I'm pretty sure we did."

Stacey and I leaned close to the trap to peer through the side.

"It looks empty," Stacey whispered.

"That's normal. You can't always see--"

A face appeared on the glass, so suddenly there was an audible slap even through the thick inner layer of glass and the hard plastic shell on the outside. Stacey and I jumped back.

It was Mercy, a simple image of her face painted in frost, with holes for her eyes and her distended, angry frown. Her hollow eyes seemed to regard us for a moment, and then the whole face faded, like a blast of condensation melting away from a window.

"Okay." Stacey's voice was still shaky. "I'd say we got her."

And that, more or less, is how you trap a ghost.

Chapter Fifteen

As soon as we were done, I texted Anna to tell her about it. It was approaching one in the morning, but Stacey and I had no particular desire to spend the rest of the night camped out in the old foyer, even though the room felt much warmer, lighter, and less oppressive. If Anna was asleep, she'd wake up in the morning with an explanation on her phone about what had happened and why we were gone.

Anna was still awake, it turned out. She and Dale met us in the east wing kitchen, Anna in a cashmere bathrobe, Dale unapologetically dressed in an old tank t-shirt and boxer shorts, which wasn't the prettiest sight in the world.

We sat at the kitchen table, our clients glancing between the empty-looking glass that we'd set out like a centerpiece and Stacey's laptop, where they watched our struggle to capture the ghost. Anna was pale, her hand covering her mouth, shaking her head.

"That looks terrifying," she whispered.

"I don't see anything." Dale flicked his finger against the clear plastic shell of the trap. "Kind of looks like an emperor's new clothes situation to me."

"You shouldn't have any more trouble with her," I said. "Your doors will stay closed at night now."

"They'd better," Dale grumbled. "What's this going to cost me?"

"We'll send you an invoice in a few days," I told him. "That'll be long enough for you to see that Mercy is gone."

"Lexa will be so happy," Anna said. "I feel relieved. Thank you so much."

Dale tilted the ghost trap back and forth, frowning, as if trying to shake up the ghost. He froze when a tendril of pale mist flickered inside, visible only for a few seconds before vanishing. He looked up at me with a bleach-white face, and I wondered what he'd seen from his angle.

It must have been more than a glimpse of white vapor, because he let go of the trap and leaned away from it.

"Get it out of here," he whispered. "I don't want to see it anymore."

"No problem." I stood, and Stacey stood with me. "We'll just gather up our things and go."

"Good." Dale walked to the refrigerator and cracked open a can of beer. "Sooner the better."

"What will you do with...the ghost?" Anna asked as I lifted the trap from the table. It was labeled with red tape and black marker—MERCY CUTLEDGE, plus the current date.

"We have a disposal method," I said. "She'll be very far from here. We've never had a recurrence of the same ghost after removing it. You can rest easy."

"It was so nice to meet all of you," Stacey said. "Tell Lexa we said bye. Such a sweet girl."

"I will." Anna gave a weary smile.

Dale chugged down at least half his beer, then stared coldly at us. I understood. He hadn't wanted to believe his house was haunted—he was more comfortable with the idea that his wife and daughter were going crazy. Now that it was over, he wanted us to get the heck of out his life so he could get back to pretending none of it had happened. Some people just find denial more attractive than adjusting their beliefs to new information.

I hadn't mentioned the single word we'd caught on the high-sensitivity microphone. It was the one thing Mercy had said to us. After cleaning up the audio, Stacey had determined that word to be *murder*.

We cleared out as fast as we could, though it took several trips to the van. It was close to two in the morning by the time we backed the cargo van out of the driveway. Mercy's trap was in the rack behind us, alongside the empty traps.

"We did it!" Stacey looked elated rather than tired. "We actually got one."

"It's a good feeling, isn't it?"

"Think of how much better their lives will be from now on." Stacey had a warm little smile on her face. "I think I love this job. I knew I would, but knowing that I *really* helped people, especially that little girl..." She shook her head. "I could use a drink, what do you think?"

"I could use about fifty hours of sleep," I replied.

We drove out to the office, where I parked the van inside the garage door in the back. I told Stacey to go on home, and she looked reluctant as she walked to her green Ford Escape hybrid SUV, a vehicle that made her feel environmentally friendly when she was hauling her kayak out to some national park. Stacey was brimming with excitement, and I guessed it would be a long time before she slept.

It was Stacey's first successful ghost grab, and maybe I should have celebrated with her, but I was worn down from the extremely long day.

I went to my little cubicle at one side of the workshop, where I forced myself to type out quick notes about all we'd done that day. Later, I would flesh it out into a full report to send along with the invoice. Clients like to see something for their money besides an apparently empty glass jar.

"Ellie," a voice said, making me jump. I turned to see Calvin, who'd crept up behind me as quietly as a ninja, despite his wheelchair. "How did it go?"

"We got her. Clients happy, money on the way." I hoped.

"And Stacey?"

"She did a decent job." I gave a quick recount of how she'd handled the asylum, plus the ghost in the Treadwell house.

"Sounds more than decent."

"She's good," I admitted. "She needs more training, but she's got the stomach for it. Maybe the brains, too. We'll see."

"It's almost as if I knew what I was doing when I hired her."

"She's not bad." I shrugged. I was actually a little more enthusiastic about Stacey's performance, but I knew where this conversation was going, and I didn't want to encourage Calvin too much.

"You've been avoiding me. I'm assuming it has to do with the psychic," Calvin said.

"We don't need a psychic. We just wrapped up the case without one. I think Stacey is enough."

"Technically, you're my employee," Calvin said. "I haven't died yet."

"Don't talk like that!"

"As long as you work for me, I expect you to listen," he said.

I slumped in my office chair. "Okay. What do you want?"

"You already know."

"All right." I sighed. "Next job, if it looks like a real haunting...we'll bring in your psychic guy and let him look around. Fair enough?"

"Fair enough." Calvin nodded. He looked exhausted and old, almost elderly.

"I need to go home and sleep. You should do the same," I said.

"Later. I've got some paperwork here. You go on."

He turned and wheeled away. I wondered if something in particular was bothering him tonight. Calvin was an insomniac at the best of times, but now he looked worried. Maybe it was just the strain of turning the field work over to me and a new girl. He wanted to retire, but I didn't think he seemed cut out for the crossword-and-shuffleboard lifestyle.

I finished up, drove home, refreshed Bandit's food and water, then sprawled across my bed, watching the slow rotation of my ceiling fan. It was hot in my apartment, especially as summer approached, and the window unit sucked electricity like a black hole, so I kept it on low to save money.

The rough day led to bad dreams, as they often did.

In this one, I was a kid again, in my childhood home, which was filled with smoke and heat. My long-lost dog, a golden retriever named Frank, was leading me through the fire. I kept my hand on his furry back, because the smoke burned my eyes and I could barely see him.

We descended the stairs, toward the enormous flames devouring the first floor of my house. As we reached the last step, the man appeared in front of us, cutting off our escape.

He was handsome, like movie-star handsome, with a long mop

of blond hair and chiseled features, his face clean-shaven. He wore a sable frock coat with a matching silk cravat and a fire-red vest, as though he'd just stepped out of the middle of the nineteenth century.

The only unnatural detail was his eyes. The irises were red, like his vest—but not *glowing* red or anything so dramatic. It was as if red were a perfectly normal eye color.

His grin was sly, almost a leer as he looked me over.

"You belong to me," he said, his voice a mellow, deep sound over the crackling wood of burning furniture and walls. "You will not forget me."

He opened his left hand, and a gout of flame erupted from it, like a magic trick.

"Come with me," he said. "We belong together."

Then the jet of flame swelled and billowed toward me, engulfing me and the dog before racing up the stairs toward my parents' room. I prayed my parents had already escaped the burning house.

I woke with a start in my bed, disoriented and confused until I remembered when and where I was—an adult woman now, living alone in a small brick loft lined with hex symbols.

Bandit gave a concerned yowl and bonked his head against my chin. I petted the cat and began to cry. I sobbed softly until I fell asleep again. This time, it was mercifully dark and dreamless.

Chapter Sixteen

The next day was a Friday, and Stacey and I rode out to a potential client's home, an old brick townhouse on Oglethorpe Street. We traced the groaning, moaning sounds in their walls to a portion of the basement ceiling that had begun to sag, putting heavy pressure on the water pipes. Plumbing and electrical problems are a common source of false alarms from the ghost-happy sorts.

We called it an early afternoon, since I didn't particularly feel like typing up the Treadwell report yet. I could do that at home, anyway.

I had a pretty great plan for the evening, which was to walk down to Gallery Cafe, order an iced thai coffee, and sit out at one of the little tables looking across the street at Chippewa Park. I would catch up on some work reading, specifically the last two issues of the *International Journal of Psychical Studies*.

The journal had been published for more than a hundred years, beginning as a niche periodical for professors sharing their research into telekinesis, hauntings, and Spiritualist activities like seances and automatic writing.

Over time, the academic community of parapsychologists grew smaller and smaller—sometime in the seventies and eighties, embarrassed university administrators began pulling funding from ghost and ESP research—so the journal had evolved to appeal to a more promising market of lay people ranging from ghost-hunting hobbyists to UFO conspiracy theorists. The digital edition pulses with ads for bottled genies, ghost-detecting powder, and zombie survival gear.

Reading the journal today requires a little bit of sorting wheat from chaff—okay, a *lot* of sorting wheat from chaff—but it's still the only place that publishes serious research into spectral activity. Right alongside the latest Bigfoot sighting, of course.

I began to read about a team who had investigated an allegedly haunted castle in England, but I ended up reading an unauthorized biography of Chrissie Hynde of the Pretenders. Hey, I can't work all the time.

Saturday was not a day off. In fact, I made Stacey meet me at the office at six a.m., which was unnecessarily early—I was sort of hazing the new kid, I guess. It all backfired when I realized it meant I had to be at work early, too.

We went to work moving the heavier equipment, like the stamper, out of the van to save gasoline on our long upcoming trip. We took out the cameras so they wouldn't be unnecessarily jostled on the road. All we left inside was the array of built-in monitors and the trap rack, which had been emptied except for the one holding Mercy.

Our destination was about two hundred miles away, westward across the broad, sun-drenched coastal plain, far from modern civilization. I drove us out of Savannah and into the pine forests of the hinterlands.

"You forgot to tell me where we're going," Stacey said.

"Goodwell."

"What's that? A town?"

"It's a really lively place," I said. "Maybe we'll grab lunch at a trendy new spot."

"But you said we were doing ghost disposal."

"If there's time." I pressed the accelerator and turned on the radio.

The view alongside the highway for the next three hours went like this: trees, cows, cotton, pecan and peach groves, cows, tobacco, corn, hay, cows, cow pastures, and cows. The view was sprinkled with old barns and tin-roofed sheds, the occasional lone, scorched chimney in a field, and some cows. Many of the towns were gas-station hamlets with a couple of whitewashed storefronts, though the really bustling places featured a Hardee's or a Dairy Queen.

Amateur mistake: I'd forgotten my MP3 player for the van, so we were stuck with plain old radio. This was not easy when Stacey thought modern country was the bee's pajamas, and half the stations in the area played nothing but. Far too much Taylor Swift was heard that day.

"So how did you get into this work?" Stacey asked, when I'd turned down the radio to mouse-whisper volume. Unfortunately, by removing the music, I'd opened the floodgates for conversation instead, and it seemed she was going to lead with some personal questions.

"I saw a ghost when I was fifteen," I told her.

"Really?" Her eyes brightened. "What kind?"

"A dangerous kind."

"Where?"

"At my house. My parents' house." I looked out the window. A pair of horses, one black and one brown, grazed near a pond in a field bright with wildflowers.

"What happened? Did you get rid of it?"

"Sort of. It's trapped now, anyway. Look, Stacey!" I pointed out the window as another pasture rolled into view. "Cows!"

I guess she took my not-so-subtle hint to change the subject, because she started filling me in on the latest *Project Runway* instead.

We turned off onto semi-scenic Route 230 through Unadilla, another town where the storefronts were empty and only the churches appeared to still be in business. That was the last town we would see.

The roads grew progressively worse, bumpy and full of potholes. By the time we reached Goodwell, there were weeds growing up through the streets.

If Goodwell ever had a sign announcing itself and welcoming folks to town, it's been gone for years, maybe fallen over and devoured by weeds along the roadside somewhere. It was a town that had grown up by a mill on the Flint River. The mill itself was now just a roofless, asymmetrical stone ruin.

I stopped at the central crossroads in town, among a handful of boarded-up brick buildings. The gas station was so old that the pumps were mechanical rather than digital, and high grass had grown up all around them. A railroad track ran through town, but given the size of the pines sprouting between the rails, it was obvious nothing had come down the track in years, probably decades.

"There's nothing here," Stacey said, looking around at the dilapidated little town.

"Almost nothing." I smiled and pulled around the corner. The old white church was crumbling, with pieces of its outer wall rotten away to reveal the timber bones beneath.

Behind the church lay the graveyard, enclosed by a waist-high brick fence with a wrought-iron gate. Rows of oaks with spreading canopies cast shadows over tall weeds and wildflowers, among which you could spot an occasional little granite gravestone, if you looked hard enough.

I parked next to the gate and stepped out of the van.

"Why are we way out here?" Stacey hopped out and glanced around. The empty town lay silent in every direction, a few of the buildings already half-eaten by kudzu vines. "This is kind of creepy, Ellie."

"I'll tell you why," I said, opening the back door of the van. "The graveyard has a good, sturdy brick wall and a gate that should remain standing for a long time. Want to grab the trap for me?"

Stacey lifted the trap out of the rack, and I slammed the door. She winced. The slam was startlingly loud in the quiet town, and few crows squawked and flew off from a nearby roof.

We walked to the cemetery's front gate, and I heard a distant rumble. The day had grown overcast, and low, ominous gray clouds filled the sky.

I thumbed through my keys to find the one marked Master Lock, and I slid it into the gleaming padlock holding the gate closed.

"Wait, how do you have a key?" Stacey asked.

"Who do you think put the new lock on there?" I pushed the gate, and it squealed open. I led Stacey into the shadowy graveyard, along weed-choked traces of gravel that used to be a path. Saplings, thorns, and other brush had sprouted among rows of headstones. "I think I'm the only one who ever comes out here. I certainly hope so."

"Do you bring all your captured ghosts here?"

"It's ideal," I said. "An abandoned cemetery in an isolated ghost town. The nearest town is twenty miles from here. It's a perfect wildlife sanctuary for ghosts." I stepped under the heavy, leafy arms of an old oak tree. A bench was barely visible beneath it. I pushed aside some thorny brambles growing around it.

Another ghost trap lay open among the weeds under the bench, its lid lying beside it. I picked it up. Written in black marker on a slice of red tape at the top was the name SAMUEL BRASWELL.

"Did that ghost escape from his trap?" Stacey asked.

"Nope. The ghosts we bring here get released."

"Seriously? Is that safe?"

"Remember, we're dealing with conscious beings here, or at least semiconscious ones. They usually can't escape the lead-glass jar at the center of the trap. Unless they're very dangerous, it's cruel to lock them in a trap forever. They could be stuck for centuries, or even longer." I tapped the empty trap I'd retrieved. "Mr. Braswell here was a dirty old ghost—he liked to rummage through women's underwear and sock drawers, or show up nude in their mirrors. Can you imagine stepping out of your shower to see a transparent, saggy old man watching you from the medicine cabinet?"

"And he's out running around?" Stacey cast a worried look at the deep shadows of the graveyard, which only grew gloomier as the heavy clouds darkened overhead.

"He wasn't violent. He never attacked anybody, never even touched anybody. As long as they aren't violent, we can release them here. Graveyards like this—an abandoned graveyard in a ghost town—have some kind of, I don't know, emotional or spiritual gravity that keeps them here. We don't know why it works, exactly, but it works."

"You don't think Mercy is dangerous?" She looked uncertainly at the sealed trap in her hands. "She attacked us!"

"Only when I deliberately taunted her. She hadn't attacked Lexa or anyone else. She acted like she was just trying to scare them away, being territorial about the house. Even when she attacked me, she didn't do any permanent damage. She's not a biter or a scratcher, or..." I hesitated, then I said it. "Or a burner."

"A burner? Is that what it sounds like?"

"Yeah. A lot of the ghosts you'll encounter have some level of psychokinetic ability. They can throw glasses or slam doors. If they can do that, they can also physically attack people. On a rare occasion, you might be unlucky enough to meet a *pyrokinetic* ghost instead, one who can start fires. Usually, those are ghosts who died in fires themselves."

"It sounds like you've met one."

"I have." Ready for a subject change, I put Samuel the Dirtball's empty trap down on the bench and took Mercy's trap in my hands. I popped open the panel on top with my thumbnail. Inside was a little mechanical dial with numbers at the edges. I cranked it to 2, then tossed it under the bench where the other trap had been. "In two hours, a cartridge of gas is going to fire and blow open the lid. You want to be out of here before it opens, because the confused ghost might glom onto you. That's the only ride out of this cemetery."

Leaves rustled around us. The wind was picking up, and the air smelled like rain.

"So that's it? We can leave now?" Stacey asked. The graveyard seemed to be making her uncomfortable, but I understood. I definitely wouldn't want to be there after sunset, when so many of the spirits I'd captured began to stir. They'd probably react like convicts who'd found their arresting officer wandering around the prison.

"We can leave." I picked up the empty trap and examined it. We'd have to check it for water damage, but it looked reusable.

Calvin called us on the drive home.

"Ellie," he said, "I just got off the phone with Anna Treadwell. She's very upset."

"Why? I haven't even sent their bill yet."

"She says things have taken a turn for the worse, and I mean *much* worse, Ellie. Noises all over the house, screaming, destruction of property."

"I definitely trapped Mercy," I said, looking at the trap with a sinking feeling. "They must have another ghost. A house that old—"

"You'd better get over there now."

"We're three hours away!"

"You can do it in two. Fix this, Ellie." He hung up on me.

I hate it when an open-and-shut case fails to shut.

"Let's get moving," I said, which was just in time anyway, because the clouds had begun to spill a light rain, and it didn't look like it would stay light for long.

"What's wrong?" Stacey asked, while I stomped down the gravel path to the gate. "You look like somebody kicked you in the stomach."

"We have to go back to the Treadwell house," I said. "It was more haunted than we realized."

Chapter Seventeen

It rained and rained the entire way home, pounding on the roof of the van and sloshing down the windshield too fast for the aged wipers. Visibility was poor, but fortunately we were traveling a highway through the middle of nowhere, which makes for pretty light traffic.

The storm surrounded us all the way to Savannah, unfortunately, where it was dark as night even though it was afternoon, and raging rapids flooded the gutters.

When we reached the Treadwell home, Anna opened the door, looking tense, like a woman who'd just stepped out of a shouting match.

"You made it worse!" Dale shouted, entering the hallway behind her before she could say a word. He had an open beer in his hand, and from the slurred sound of his voice, it wasn't his first. His sixth or seventh, maybe. "It's all worse!"

Down the hall, Lexa sat on the steps, peering around the corner at us.

"What happened?" I asked, looking at Anna instead of her husband.

"The house was quiet after you left Thursday night," Anna said.

"Peaceful. But on Friday, the workers were here late finishing the hallway, and then--"

"All hell broke loose!" Dale shouted, sagging and bumping his hip on the dining room table as he leaned against it. The table was blocking the security door again. He set his beer down and heaved the table to one side of the hall, audibly scratching up the hardwood. His beer can toppled over in the process, spilling foamy brew all over the tabletop.

Dale didn't appear to notice. Rather than clean up his beer, he staggered toward the security door and grasped the heavy deadbolt. Lexa watched him from the stairs nearby, saying nothing.

"Dale, don't open that!" Anna shouted, but he ignored her. I heard the rusty scream of the lock, and then Dale pulled the door open, but the hallway into the main house was too dark for me to see anything. I didn't want to go running over there until I knew what was happening.

"What happened when the workers were here Friday night?" I asked Anna.

"You may as well see for yourself." She gestured toward the doorway, and walked alongside me as I went. "They were just packing up—they're supposed to come back Monday and start on the kitchen, but I don't think they will. Just as they were leaving, they said every door in the hallway slammed shut, like something wanted to trap them inside. I heard it, too. Loud bangs that shook the house, just like after that fake funeral."

"Yeah," Dale said as we approached him. He glared at me. "*Just* like that."

"They had to force a door open to escape," Anna said.

"Hey, Lexa!" Stacey did a big smile-and-wave, still trying to charm the little girl.

"Hey." Lexa looked at her sandals, as if trying to dodge attention.

"After the doors slammed...this happened." Anna led me through the doorway.

The hallway, which had been on its way to a new, modern look last time we'd been here, now resembled a bomb-cratered war zone. Holes the size of bowling balls dented both walls, and the new molding and a portion of the ceiling had been cracked and shattered.

"They said the holes just appeared one after the other, like something was making footprints on the walls," Anna whispered.

"Something huge and invisible that didn't care about gravity. They ran out of here. I only got the story later, over the phone."

"So much for your ghost trap." Dale slumped against the door. His face said he wanted to punch my lights out, but his swaying stance said he was more likely to barf all over me. Neither option appealed.

"We did remove Mercy Cutledge from your home," I said. "It's possible that, in doing so, we awoke something else. A house like this has layers of history." I didn't exactly want to go into Captain Marsh and his love of whiskey, opium, and prostitutes—not with Lexa close by, listening in on every word.

"Yeah," Dale snorted. "Now you sound like this mechanic I knew back in Chicago. Go in for a lube job, he'll always just happen to find you need a new transmission or some expensive work like that. Like clockwork." Dale tried to punctuate this with another swig of beer, and looked surprised to discover he was no longer holding one. He wandered off into the kitchen.

"There's more," Anna said. "After they left, we heard things from the main house. Banging, crashing, yelling. Off and on all night. This morning, I found the medicine cabinet in our master bath was shattered. I walked in there in my bare feet and almost cut myself up. The sink was full of glass and pills. It looked like somebody had opened and dumped out every pill bottle, from the aspirin to Dale's prescription back medicine. All mixed in with little bits of glass. I had to throw it all away."

"I'm sorry," I said. "That sounds terrifying."

"We're still pretty shaken up."

"Have you had any more trouble with this door?" I stepped one foot back over the threshold of the security door so I could glance over at Lexa, too.

"No, but we've had it barricaded," Anna said. "The bolt did stay in place all night, I guess. It didn't keep them from demolishing my bathroom, though, did it?"

"We're dealing with a different ghost now," I said. "It might not care about that door at all."

"The other lady's gone," Lexa said softly, nodding. "These new things are worse."

"Have you seen another ghost, Lexa?" Stacey asked.

Lexa shook her head. "But I've heard them. And they're worse than the lady. They're scarier."

"Has anything else happened over here in the east wing?" I asked Anna. "Or has everything else been in the main house?"

"It's hard to say where all the sounds are coming from. It seems like they're mostly over there, but I can't be sure." Anna shivered. "The voices are the most disturbing. You can't make out the words, but they sound like people talking to each other."

"What about the main house? Was anything else damaged over there?"

"I wouldn't know. We haven't really gone exploring. The problems we already have are overwhelming. I'm scared to see what happens next," Anna said.

"We'll go exploring for you. Stacey, let's grab some gear." I gestured for Stacey to follow me out to the van.

"Can you get rid of the new ghost, too?" Lexa asked as we walked past.

"I'm sure we can," I told her. "We just have to learn more about it."

"We'll take care of it," Stacey said. She extended her hand toward Lexa. "Hey, cheer up! Give me five."

Lexa reluctantly slapped Stacey's hand. Stacey winked at her and gave her a thumbs-up, but Lexa didn't seem comforted by Stacey's attempts to lighten things up.

We didn't have much in the van, since we'd unloaded it that morning. Our tactical flashlights were there, and so was my toolbox, so I grabbed my Mel Meter night vision goggles and handed the thermal ones to Stacey.

"My own goggles! Finally!" Stacey said.

"Hey, I'm just sharing," I told her. "Be careful with my stuff."

Soon, we were stepping through the security door again, into the freshly wrecked hallway of the main house. My instruments showed a lower temperature and higher EMF activity, enough to indicate a background haunting. I could feel it, too, like cold spiders crawling under my skin.

I did not want to walk any deeper into that house, but I put on my bravest face. I'd also put on my leather jacket, because it looked like this new ghost liked to get destructive.

We did a room-by-room check, but most of the first-floor rooms looked as we remembered, though the air felt dark and heavy. We did not go down into the cellar—after the asylum basement, we wanted to avoid dark underground places as long as we could. We didn't have to say anything out loud. It took no more than a look between Stacey and me to agree on avoiding it for now.

We reached the foyer last, and found sawdust and broken chunks of wood scattered on the floor just below the walkway.

Stacey turned her flashlight beam to the second-floor walkway above us.

"Whoa, looks like somebody came through with a chainsaw," Stacey said.

Where there had been a single broken baluster, now several of them lay shattered, and the railing they supported was broken into pieces.

"Let's get a closer look," I said, and Stacey followed me up the stairs. I avoided using the railing just to be safe, though the portion of it alongside the stairway didn't seem damaged. Only the balusters along the second-floor walkway were destroyed.

"What a mess," Stacey said. The broken baluster pieces lay everywhere. It would have been easy for an unsuspecting person to trip over them and topple through the broken railing to the first floor.

On the second floor, the temperatures were lower and the EMF readings were high, two to three milligaus, a strong sign of a haunting.

The first thing we noticed was that the doors with rows of rusty nails stood wide open, making me think of Venus flytraps waiting to snap shut on an unsuspecting victim. Stacey and I had been careful to close them on our last visit, and the Treadwells said none of them had been up here since then. It was possible some of the workers had come upstairs, but it sounded like they'd been focused on the first floor.

Inside the rooms, furniture had been moved and closet doors had been thrown wide open. This was most obvious in the room with the broken syringes, where the single bed had slid from the corner to the center of the room and come to a halt in a diagonal position. In the other room that had previously been nailed closed, hangers and rotten dresses had left the closet and were scattered all over the floor, and the old blankets had been stripped from the bed and left in a tangled heap on the floor.

It looked as if some mischievous entity had run through the second floor, gleefully throwing everything into disarray, but we didn't find any major structural damage.

"I think the spirit just wants to destroy the new work, the remodeling," I said.

"Then it's probably going to hit the east wing much harder," Stacey said. "The family needs to watch out."

We reached the slatted door that opened onto the steep, dim staircase to the third floor. That door was flanked by closets on either side. We checked them both, but they held nothing beyond cobwebs and empty shelves littered with dead spiders.

"Who goes first?" Stacey whispered, shining her light up into the darkness and spiderwebs of the third floor.

"I'll do it." I clicked off my flashlight and slid my night vision goggles over my eyes. I started up the stairs, using my hands for balance. It really was more like a ladder than a staircase.

The steps creaked under my weight as I climbed up. The night vision showed me where I was going in lurid shades of glowing green. Unfortunately, it showed me a world of trundling palmetto bugs and spiders lurking in their webs. I used my unlit flashlight to clear a path for Stacey.

"How does it look?" she whispered.

"Fine. A little icky."

The stairs flattened out into a weird landing halfway up to the third floor. Weird because it was sort of like a short, narrow hallway. To my right, another steep staircase continued at a right angle to the first. To my left, the hallway extended a few feet and hit a dead end. An old end table sat there, with a vase of long-dead flowers parked on top.

"Where are you going?" Stacey whispered behind me.

"Just looking." I knocked on the dead-end wall. It sounded solid to me. I turned to start up the second flight, which was as narrow and unfriendly as the first, and possibly even steeper.

They led up to a rectangular trap door in the ceiling, as big as your average interior doorway but turned on its side. I took a breath, then pushed it open. If any inhuman things crouched in the darkness above, waiting to eat my face, then the loud rusty hinges of the trap door alerted them that I'd arrived.

The third floor had originally been nothing but the sprawling master suite. It was smaller than the second, and it had more furniture and bric-a-brac, but less graffiti, as if vandals hadn't made their way up here over the years, or something had made them leave fast.

To one side of us, we found a large, round den with wide steps spiraling away to the second floor. We were in one of the house's turrets, and narrow windows looked down on us from high above. Old furniture was pushed against one wall and draped in sheets. The large, attractive central fireplace, built to resemble a thick tree growing up through the middle of the room, had been plugged with bricks.

We checked a smaller room that might have originally been an office or other side room, but now it looked like a storage room. Antique lamps and odds and ends of furniture were crammed inside. An external lock had been added to the door, so this had probably been turned into a separate bedroom during the boarding-house years.

When we opened the door to the former master bedroom, Stacey and I both cringed and stepped back a little. The smell of rot was overpowering.

It was cold, just sixty degrees, and the EMF reading spiked up to 4.1.

The room was immense, with a very high, round ceiling, clearly the house's biggest turret, the underside painted with the remnants of a flaking mural that looked like something from ancient Greece, horned fauns chasing blushing nymphs. Or it could have been goat demons eating little girls. The painting was pretty deteriorated.

The room was still partially furnished, with a king-size canopied bed and a wing chair and a desk by the fireplace, plus an old armoire near the closet. Dark mold grew up along the posters of the bed, all over the sheets, and a huge, roughly circular patch grew on the ceiling above the bed. Runners of mold ran across the ceiling and down the closed double doors of the closet.

"Ew." Stacey pinched her nose against the stink. "This is going to take somebody a long time to clean up."

"I wonder if the roof's leaking," I said. "I thought the roofers were done, though."

"They need to recheck their work." Stacey walked to the picture window overlooking the front yard, then turned to the bathroom. "It's pretty foul in here, too."

"More mold?"

"No, just a grimy tub and a toilet and sink that haven't been cleaned in forever. Marble tiles, though, and some nice colored-glass windows. It was pretty luxurious in its day." Stacey shook her head.

"That day is now long gone."

"Can you have a look with your thermal?" I asked Stacey.

"Sure." Stacey dropped her goggles and looked over the bedroom. "The cold is everywhere, but there's a particularly cold spot over the bed. The closet looks extra cold, too."

Great. I walked over to the double doors and eased them open. I had a bad feeling about it, but there was nothing inside except more mold and the ever-present spiderwebs.

"Empty," I said. As I turned my back, though, I heard something. It was like a male voice, unnaturally deep, but I couldn't make out the words it said. It lasted about three seconds. I looked in the closet again. "Did you hear that, Stacey?"

"Hear what?" She joined me. "It's cold in there, but I don't see any obvious shapes or a center to it..."

Something heavy crashed downstairs. Voices rose through the floorboards—a shouting, angry-sounding man with a deep voice like the one I'd just heard from the closet. A woman screamed, and then her scream broke into cackling laughter.

We ran to the stairs, with me in the lead. I hesitated before stepping through to the second-floor hallway, because I heard a couple of voices nearby. They were distorted, but it sounded like a fast-paced conversation between two women. Stacey took my hand and squeezed it, letting me know she heard it, too.

The voices passed by, and I glimpsed some movement in my night vision, but nothing very clear. They were like ripples in the air.

I stepped out of the doorway to watch them ripple down the hall and disappear.

We looked into doorways, trying to find the source of the crash. In the broken-syringe room, the bed had moved again, and was now shoved against the window. I barely had time to notice that, though.

A figure knelt on the floor, transparent but thinly visible in night vision. He was a scrawny, shirtless man, with track marks all over his arms and at least a dozen syringes stabbed deep into his back, his shoulders, and his arms and legs.

As he became more visible, I realized he was *licking* at the two broken syringes on the floor, as though desperate to get something out of them.

"Stacey, are you seeing anything?" I whispered.

"Major cold spot on the floor by the wall." Stacey pointed at the same figure I was seeing. "It's starting to get clearer..."

In my night vision view, the transparent green man stopped his licking and looked up at us. I couldn't see much of his face, but a needle was stuck through his abnormally long tongue.

He vanished. That either meant he was gone, retreating into the gray zone where ghosts go when we can't find them, or he was coming for us.

Unfortunately, it turned out to be the latter.

I felt a rush of cold wind, then an impact on my breastbone that sent me tumbling across the hallway. Stacey screamed as something pushed her against the wall, then upward along it.

I lifted off my goggles while clicking my flashlight on. I stabbed the intense white beam at the empty air in front of Stacey.

There was an irritated hissing sound, along with a partial apparition. I could see one side of his face, plus a bit of his forearm and the hand pinning Stacey against the wall. A syringe was stabbed through his wrist like a crucifixion nail.

The half-face turned to me, glaring at the light with its dark, empty eye socket.

I wished I'd been prepared for more than a quick look-see around the house.

"Leave her alone!" I shouted, because there's nothing more intimidating than a girl with thick glasses armed with a flashlight.

A second, transparent hand materialized and lashed out at me. The syringe embedded in its wrist scraped along the sleeve of my jacket. Thanks, leather.

It turned back to Stacey, lifting her higher on the wall. She kicked out at it with her tennis shoes, but there was nothing solid to kick. This is why fighting with a ghost is totally unfair.

Then, naturally, she screamed: "Ellie! Help me!"

I didn't have my iPod, or I would have shoved some "Ode to Joy" down his creepy maw. I didn't have anything I needed.

I ran back into the room where we'd found him, and I carefully picked up the broken pieces of syringe, trying not to stick myself with the needle or broken glass. That way, I'd be less likely to pick up some weird disease and die.

"Hey, did you want these?" I held out the pieces of syringe. The pale half-face turned to me, and the half of its mouth I could see plunged into a wide-open frown, as if expressing horror. One of the hands reached for me.

I turned and flung all the pieces down the hall. This brought a faint, startled cry from the ghost, who dropped Stacey to the floor, began to chase the pieces of its syringe, then vanished.

I barely noticed all of this, because I was looking at the shadowy woman at the end of the hall. She was so solid that I initially thought I was looking at Anna. The woman watched as the broken bits of syringe landed at her feet and scattered.

She was a small, mousy woman with dark hair, wearing a high-collared white dress that did not belong in this century. She looked up at me, then vanished.

I recognized her from the old photograph—Eugenia Marsh, Captain Marsh's wife, who had died in 1901.

I couldn't dwell on this, though, because I had to turn around and check on Stacey. She was recovering, or at least rising unsteadily onto her feet while rubbing her throat.

"Are you okay?" I asked.

"It got me here." She showed me a red scratch near her collar bone. It looked like it had been drawn with a needle. "Can we go yet, or...?"

"We can go," I said. "We're not hanging around here without our equipment. We need to figure out what's going on." I looked back toward Eugenia Marsh, but she was gone. The syringe's needle rolled back and forth on the floor, as though someone were trying to pick it up but couldn't quite manage it. Our junkie ghost, I guessed.

We walked the other way, moving carefully around the shattered balusters, and hurried down the stairs.

Voices echoed from the second-story hall after we left. It sounded like they were arguing with each other.

Chapter Eighteen

"You have a multiple haunting," I told Anna and Dale Treadwell. Stacey and I sat on the couch in their living room. Anna sat in the matching loveseat, while Dale occupied his usual recliner. Lexa had been sent up to her room. A golf game was muted on the television. "We encountered at least three, possibly four ghosts upstairs. And a presence in the master bedroom. How long has that mold been there?"

"Mold?" Dale sat up in his recliner. "Where?"

I told them what we'd seen.

"Roofers probably screwed it up," he said, shaking his head and looking grim. It was an expensive problem. "I'm calling those half-wits first thing, when we're done here."

"What kind of ghosts?" Anna asked.

"Some were just voices," I said. "Women. There was a man who looked like a heroin addict..." Anna grew pale as I recounted the attack, some of which had been caught on Stacey's handheld camera. Stacey had dropped it when the thing grabbed her, which unfortunately had left it pointed at a baseboard the whole time. "The other, I think, may have been Eugenia Marsh, the captain's wife. I'll look at her picture again to check."

"Can you capture all these ghosts?" Anna asked, and Dale rolled his eyes and swigged his beer. Being drunk seemed to numb him to the seriousness of their situation. Or else he was just unhappy with the quality and speed of our service.

"It will take some time and research," I replied. "The problem is that this was a boarding-house for about thirty years, and a lot of these ghosts might be transients, people who were just passing through town. That makes them hard to identify, and it's much easier to trap a ghost if you know something about who they were in life. That's why we captured Mercy so easily. Anyway, we'll comb through the police records and obituaries again to see what we can find, but that'll take a while." I was disheartened to think of how much more time it would take to clear the place out, ghost by ghost.

"How long is a while?" Dale asked.

"As soon as we can, Mr. Treadwell. We'll dig into the research today. I'd like to set up another observation for this evening, with every camera we have watching every corner of the house. There's so much going on, I need some kind of overview of what's happening here. We'll watch the house all night and see what we can find. I promise you, we'll get rid of these things as fast as humanly possible."

Neither of them looked particularly pleased by what I was saying. I couldn't really blame them.

A high-pitched scream sounded from upstairs.

"Lexa!" Anna was on her feet immediately, followed by Stacey and me. Dale was half-rolling, half-leaning out of his chair when we left the room.

By the time I made it upstairs, Anna was already carrying Lexa out of the hallway bathroom, wrapped in a large towel. Anna had moved with superhuman speed, the way mothers can when their children are threatened.

Lexa was bawling and sobbing, her face pressed against her mother's neck.

"What's wrong?" Anna asked. "Lexa, what happened?"

"It got me," Lexa said. "I was just taking a bath, and it grabbed me. It hurt."

"Where?" Anna asked.

"My leg." Lexa raised her red, crying face, then lifted the edge of her towel. Three red scratch-like marks ran from her lower thigh to her calf, and they were growing darker and redder by the second.

"Did you see what grabbed you, Lexa?" I asked.

"No. I only heard it." She lay her cheek on her mother's shoulder. "It was a man. He laughed when he did it."

I walked past them into the bathroom. The bath was full, and an issue of *Seventeen* magazine lay on the tile floor beside it. I saw bottles of liquid soap and shampoos that had toppled over into the bath, but nothing else out of the ordinary. The room wasn't especially cold. Whatever had attacked her didn't seem to be in the room anymore.

When I stepped out, Dale had arrived, and was sort of trying to comfort his daughter by patting her on the shoulder. Stacey was trying reassure the girl, too, but I don't think she was making much progress.

"I don't understand," Dale said, shaking his head.

"Mr. and Mrs. Treadwell, you may want to spend the night somewhere else until we can fix this," I said.

"We don't have anywhere to go," Dale said.

"We can find a hotel," Anna told him.

"That's expensive. For how many days?" Dale looked at me.

"I can't say for sure, but we'll be as quick as we can."

"It's too much money." Dale shook his head, and Anna gave him a look so sharp and angry I'm surprised it didn't leave welts on his face.

"We're going to a hotel," Anna insisted. She carried her daughter into her room. "Come on, Lexa, let's pack our bags."

Dale watched them go, then turned to look at me. I expected him to make some more remarks about how much all of this was costing him, but now I saw sadness in his eyes and droopy frown.

"Listen, my severance package..." he began, then shook his head and start over. "Most of what we've got is tied up in this house. I lost my job, and Anna wanted to do this, so...what I'm saying is, we can't afford to move. We can't afford for this bed and breakfast idea of hers to fail. We'll be busted."

He looked helpless, almost like a child. I thought of their luxury cars and the pricey designer clothes Lexa wore. This was a family accustomed to easy prosperity, not ready for the rug to be pulled out from under them. Dale had a sad, anxious look, a man worried about failing to provide for and protect his family.

"I'm sorry." I patted him on the arm. "We'll take care of the ghosts. We will. You just take care of your wife and daughter, okay?"

He nodded, sniffling a little.

There wasn't much else Stacey and I could do without our gear, so we left soon after that. Dale gave us keys to the front and side doors in case he and his family were gone when we returned.

We drove back to the office, pulled in through the garage door at the back, and started loading gear. It wasn't exactly pleasant to unload the whole thing that morning only to reload it in the afternoon. My arms ached.

As we were getting started, Calvin wheeled out of his office. A young man walked beside him, with dark hair and those glasses with the black hipster frames. He was somewhere around my age. He looked kind of cute, actually. I hoped he was a new client.

"Ellie, Stacey, meet Jacob Weiss," Calvin said.

"Nice to meet you, Mr. Weiss," I said in my best meeting-a-client voice. I held out my hand and he shook it. "How can we help you today?"

"I'm, uh..." He shifted awkwardly on his feet and looked at Calvin.

"Jacob is the psychic I've been telling you about," Calvin said. "I called him in to assist on the Treadwell case."

I wanted to punch or kick something, or maybe just scream and tear at my hair, dramatic stuff like that. Calvin had sprung the psychic on me like this because he knew I was too polite to complain about it right in front of the guy. I hate Calvin sometimes.

I wanted to protest that we didn't need any help, but it was kind of hard to make that case at the moment, with everything going wrong.

"The Treadwells have a multiple haunting," I said.

"Let's talk in my office," Calvin said. "Psychics aren't supposed to get advance information."

Sounded good to me. No reason to feed the supposed psychic a bunch of info he could just regurgitate later.

When the door was closed to Calvin's office—a place lined with bookshelves crammed full of bundled clippings, file folders, and other paper randomness, plus overflowing cork billboards, like those serial-killer nests you see in movies where the killer collects all the evidence of his crimes—I said, "We don't need a psychic. Things aren't that desperate yet."

"Just tell me what happened today."

I quickly recounted what we'd seen at the house.

"It sounds like you could use a little extra help," Calvin said. "Just take him on your observation tonight. He can't hurt anything."

"He can get in the way."

"You're a pro, you can handle it," Calvin said.

I sighed. "Whatever. Do you still have that OxyContin prescription?" I knew he'd been taking it for pain at one point.

"I do, but I try to avoid using it. Why?"

"Got a couple extra for me?"

"Has the case got you down that badly?" Calvin had an amused smile.

"No, it's bait for the junkie ghost. He seemed like the most dangerous one there—I'll bet he's the one that smashed apart Anna's medicine cabinet. It would be nice if we could remove him, at least, while we try to figure out the rest."

"All righty." Calvin opened a desk drawer and rummaged through it, then found a brown medicine bottle and handed me a pair of pills. "Don't take 'em all in one place."

"Ha." I turned my back on him and walked out the office door.

"You," I said to Jacob, who stood with his hands in his pockets, like a kid waiting for instructions. "Help me load up the van. Stacey, I want you to read through all the information we have on the Treadwell house."

"I already did that," she complained.

"Do it again. But first, call up the former owners of the house and see if anyone will talk to you."

"I already did *that*, too. Nobody called me back."

"Try again."

"Why don't any of them want to talk, anyway? I don't get it," Stacey said.

"That's normal. Most people who encounter a haunting want to forget about it. Plus, there's the guilt."

"Guilt?" Stacey asked.

"Imagine you've bought a house," Calvin said, "And later discovered it was inhabited by a dangerous or scary ghost. Now all you want to do is sell the house and escape the situation. Will you tell potential buyers about the ghost?"

"I see what you mean." Stacey shook her head and walked over to my cubicle, where there was a land line and stacks of photocopied information from the library and Historical Association, plus files sent over by Calvin's friends at the police department.

Jacob and I loaded all the equipment that would fit into the van—cameras, microphones, traps, the stamper, and other gear. I spoke to him very little beyond giving instructions, since I didn't really want him there in the first place. If he didn't like my cold attitude and wanted to leave, that would be great with me.

But the goofball just kept smiling while he worked, as if eager to help lift the heavy stuff. I had to admit it was convenient to have a guy on hand for the van-loading portion of the afternoon.

As we were finishing up, Stacey ran over, more or less hopping on the balls of her feet. I'd been vaguely aware of her voice as she used the phone at my desk. I knew from experience that calling former property owners to ask them about a ghost was typically a lot like throwing yourself against a brick wall again and again. The mansion had gone through a number of buyers over the past few decades, so she'd had a lot of calls to make.

"What are you so thrilled about?" I asked her.

"I got one!" Stacey beamed. "She's willing to talk. The staff never gave her my last message, I guess."

"Who is it?"

"Guess."

"Do I have to?"

"Aw, no fun." She raised her eyebrows. "Louisa Marsh. She said she'll tell us whatever we want to know if we go see her."

"Captain Marsh's grand-niece?" I asked.

"Technically, her father was Captain Marsh's grand-nephew," Stacey said. "I don't know if that makes her the great-grand-niece or what, but she's willing to chat."

"Good work, Stacey!" I said. It was a nice break. If we were going to speak with one former owner of the house, we couldn't do better than Louisa, who had lived there for thirty years. "When?"

"I set it up for tomorrow afternoon. She insisted we speak to her in person, though. It's kind of a drive, but..." Stacey shrugged.

"No, that's great." I slammed the back door of the van. "And we're all done here."

"So, do we go to the haunted house now?" Jacob asked.

"No, we don't go right now," I said. "What kind of experience do you even have, Jacob?"

"I've been training with Hattie Gardener. She lives off the coast of South Carolina, on one of the Gullah islands."

"She's a good woman and a strong psychic," Calvin said. "She doesn't travel much anymore, though."

"Okay. Well, Stacey and I have had a long day, so we're taking a dinner break," I told him. "You can drive separately and meet us at the Treadwell house later. There's no extra room in the van, anyway."

"Whatever you want," he said. He looked nervous.

I told Calvin good-bye, then Stacey and I drove away.

"He seems nice," Stacey said. "You don't like him, though, do you?"

"It's not even him. I don't like Calvin springing things on me. And I don't like working with psychics."

"Why not?"

I took a breath. "Well, there are three kinds of psychics: those who are genuine, those who are fake—some of them don't *know* they're fake, though—and the ones who are kind of in between. They may have some abilities, but they aren't reliable. In the modern world, we have good scientific tools for finding ghosts. We don't need to call in the witch doctors."

Stacey nodded, taking that in. "So you don't think he'll help us?"

"I think he'll get in the way. That's one reason I wanted him to drive himself there. We'll let him do whatever he wants so I can tell Calvin we cooperated. Then we send him home before the real work begins."

"All right. Where are we eating? I'm starving."

Chapter Nineteen

When we arrived at the Treadwell house, it was almost dusk. The family was gone.

Anna had left us a note wishing us luck, and Lexa had signed it, too. Nice girl. I hoped we could make her house safe for her.

When Jacob arrived, we led him in through the front doors instead of the side door. As far as he could see, the house might well be uninhabited, especially when his first sight of the interior was the graffiti-covered foyer with the shattered second-floor balustrade.

He, Stacey, and I each carried an armload of equipment. Stacey would be setting up cameras while Jacob toured the house gathering his psychic impressions, or at least making stuff up.

"Okay, that's weird," he said, just a few paces inside the hallway. "There's like a fading echo in here. There's really no spirits in this room, but there was something here."

Stacey made wide-eyes at me. *Lucky guess*, I mouthed with my back to him.

Stacey gave an exaggerated shrug.

"Set something up in here," I told her. "Just one camera."

"Thermal or night?"

"Surprise me."

"So, hey, Jacob," Stacey said, while assembling a thermal on its tripod, "How did you get into being a psychic? Was it just always a thing for you?"

Great. Stacey was going to make small talk, totally wrecking my cold-shoulder approach to making Psychic Boy choose not to work with us.

"Hattie says I had to be born with it," Jacob replied. He was strolling the edges of the room, taking in the doorways, the rotten windows, the profane juvenile-delinquent scrawl painted on the walls. "She says I must have learned to close the door as a boy, but I don't remember anything like that. Maybe I closed the door *and* blocked it out. My father definitely wouldn't have believed me if I'd started talking about ghosts."

I waited near the parlor door, my arms crossed. Stacey seemed to be taking her time.

"So what happened?"

"There was a plane crash about a year ago," he said. "I didn't die. Five of us lived. Just five. When I woke up in the middle of the Alps, still buckled into my seat, you know, I saw a crowd of people standing around me, talking. Then I saw their bodies all over the snow." Jacob shook his head. "I've been putting up with the spirits ever since. It's not what I wanted. I'm an accountant, I'm supposed to be studying for my CPA exam, not...whatever we're doing here."

"That's terrible!" Stacey looked up at him and stopped working. "Were any of your family or friends on the plane?"

He shook his head. "I was flying alone. I was going to meet some friends in Italy, but I had a layover in Berlin, and the plane from Berlin to Rome went down in the mountains."

"Wait, I remember that on the news. Only like five people..." Stacey trailed off. "I'm sorry. That's terrible."

"Yeah, I'm really sorry to hear that," I said.

"I wouldn't mind if we stopped talking about it," Jacob said, and she nodded.

We walked through the parlor and into the dining room, while Jacob kind of mumbled and nodded to himself. I held a digital voice recorder in one hand to take notes for me, and a flashlight in the other because it was already very dark inside the house.

Jacob raised his head, and his ears perked up like an alert dog's. He ran the rest of the way across the dining room, then rolled aside the door to the smoking room.

"Right here," he said, walking into the middle of it. "I can hear music, maybe a scratchy phonograph...men are talking. They're drinking, smoking, playing cards, dice...the dice are made of elephant ivory, he's very proud of that..." Jacob closed his eyes.

"Who's very proud?" I asked.

"The man at the center. Huge man, with a huge beard. They're all his guests. The men are inebriated, and there are women, too, but not their wives...they're more like. Oh. Wow." Jacob removed his glasses and rubbed his eyes. "I didn't know it was going to be that kind of party."

"What do you see?" I asked.

"Yeah, describe it in detail," Stacey added, with a wicked grin.

"They're prostitutes. No other reason they'd be doing *that* with these fat old men." Jacob's eyes opened again. He strolled by the fireplace, with its elaborate scrollwork, still nodding to himself. "Yeah. I can smell the smoke, the perfume...can't you smell it?"

"Not personally." I nodded at Stacey to set up a night vision camera here.

Jacob had another strong reaction when we walked through the kitchen. He grabbed his stomach, nearly doubling over, and winced in pain.

"Jacob?" Stacey put her stuff down and ran over to put an arm around him. I hurried over.

"What happened?" I asked.

"Ugh. A woman, with a pain in her stomach. I think it killed her. I think she died here. Or she started to die here, and finished up there, in the master bedroom." He pointed toward the ceiling. "They carried her up there. The servants or whatever."

"She died in the house? Do you know her name?" I asked.

"No idea. A small woman, dark hair...very religious..."

I nodded. It sounded like Eugenia Marsh. Stacey set up another camera.

As we approached the second floor up the steep back stairs, Jacob make a sickened noise and put his hands to his head.

"What now?" Stacey asked.

"It's really bad up here," he said. "We should be careful."

"True." Stacey nodded, looking at me. She really wanted him to be a genuine psychic, I guess, or wanted me to believe it. I was still waiting and seeing, though.

"Okay. We can do this." Jacob took a deep breath, then

continued up to the second-floor hallway, as though it took a great effort. We stayed close to him. I was a little better prepared for ghost attacks this time.

He paced back and forth in the hall, shaking his head and laughing a little.

"Oh, no," he finally said. "It's crazy. They're going in and out, flickering in and out of sight..." He clapped his hands. "Okay. Here's what we've got: I see a couple of drifter types, one of them's like a hobo from the 1920s...the next guy, he's a drug addict, bad, to the point that he hasn't let go of it even in death. But he can't get a fix, because he's dead. He's kind of a 1940s or 1950s guy, and he wears that kind of suit and fedora that everybody wore, even though he's basically homeless and he commits petty robberies...these guys aren't really from here, they're just passing through, only they're not, because they got caught here."

"Caught by what?" I asked.

Jacob raised a finger, telling me to be quiet. He certainly acted more commanding when he was being psychic. "You've got another big thug guy, his throat's cut...oh, and hookers, hookers, hookers. At least three of them, but they didn't know each other in life. They're from different times. Like one is kind of in a fringed-out flapper-style dress, and the other is in these, like, hot pants from the Seventies...yeah. There are a few different people here."

"Why are they here?" I asked. "What do they want?"

"They're...stuck. Oh, yeah. Something's holding them here, and it's not just trapping them. It can kind of control them, it has power over them. They're prisoners, though. They don't want to be here."

"What's holding them?"

"I can't..." He closed his eyes. "They don't want to talk about it. They're all shrinking away, back into the walls...they're running away from me." He looked at me again. "Well, they didn't like that."

He walked along, pointed to occasional rooms and saying "bad...bad...bad..." These included the two with the rows of nails in the doors. "They've all got a story. None of them expected to stay here when they came. It was like a net...a spiderweb, to catch stray people. Most of these weren't so bad in life, but now they're twisted and violent, they're under the spell of the house."

"Is there a way to free them?" I asked.

"I don't know."

We returned downstairs for more cameras, then took Jacob up to the third floor.

"Yeah, it's thick up here, isn't it? And cold," he said. "Some of the oldest ones stay up here. They barely look like people anymore, they're shriveled..."

Jacob stopped just inside the master bedroom, looking at the mold-encrusted bed, then up at the giant patch of dark mold on the ceiling high above it.

"This is that woman again, from the kitchen," he said. "She's defiant. The mold is her way of crying out, reaching out. She resists him more than the others, but she's tied here, too, by the same kind of...I want to say it's almost like a rope, a black rope anchoring each spirit to the darkness below." Jacob's head snapped around and he looked at me with a cold, solemn expression. "Does this house have a basement?"

"Yeah," I said. I didn't want to go down there.

After grabbing two more cameras, the three of us returned to the wine cellar door by the kitchen. We pushed it open. Rough-hewn steps led into the rock-lined darkness below.

"Who wants to go first?" Stacey asked, trying to make it sound funny, but it didn't. That cellar was creepy by anyone's standards.

"Let's get in and out fast." I started down the stairs, widening the lens on my flashlight so it changed from a narrow beam into a flood. This kind of made it a worse offensive weapon, as far as chasing ghosts away, but a better defensive one. Like a shield of light.

Each one of those rough old stairs just had to creak beneath me as I stepped on it. Every single one.

The cellar was unnaturally cool at the top of the steps, but felt like a deep freezer by the time I reached the bottom. My breath plumed out in front of me. I swear, if we could learn to harness and domesticate ghosts, we could save a ton on air conditioning, especially down here in the Deep South.

I wished I had my trusty Mel Meter or at least some kind of EMF meter with me, but I'd left that in my toolbox out in the foyer. I didn't want to give our supposed psychic any clues. I had to admit, though—he was hitting pretty close to home, as far as I could tell.

The walls were rocks held together with a massive amount of cement. It felt like the oldest part of the house, the one that probably hadn't been altered much since the original construction. No 1970s stovetops here, though there was an old wood-burning furnace, obviously long abandoned. Rusty tools, sheeted furniture, and crates and boxes filled the room, leaving only a few twisty paths through the clutter. A huge built-in floor-to-ceiling wine rack held nothing but dust and spiderwebs. The floor was paved with concrete and more river rocks.

I felt ill. Stacey didn't look too happy, either, but Jacob looked far worse, like he'd contracted a disease and was about to keel over dead.

"It was down here," he said. "But not exactly *here*. I can't explain. Is there a door? Another room?" Jacob sprang from his sickly slump and dashed along the walls, searching with his flashlight.

"Don't get too far away," I warned him. "I'll help you look."

As far as we could find, though, the cellar was a single large room. We even checked behind precarious heaps of boxes to see if any sort of passageway had been concealed over the years.

"I don't get it." Jacob kicked at the floor. "Maybe all the stuff was taken away, and that's why..."

"What stuff?" Stacey touched his shoulder, leaning in toward him. She was dangerously close to flirting with him, actually.

"He killed them," Jacob said. He squeezed Stacey's hand. "He brought them down here...somewhere right around here. It was a ritual thing, black magic. He thought killing them would extend his own life. The thing is...when he died, he didn't *stop* the killing. There was a supply of people drifting through, and sometimes he would wake up and take one for his collection. Because he controls all the other ghosts." Jacob's eyes were bugging out, and he was sweating.

"Stop!" Stacey screamed. She drew her hand back from him. "Stop, I can see it!"

"I'm sorry," he whispered.

"It was horrible," Stacey said, looking at me. "The migrant workers, the addicts and petty thieves, the prostitutes...people he thought nobody would miss. People he thought were no better than animals."

"Who?" I asked. "Who was he?"

Jacob shook his head. "Whatever he looked like in life, he's become so twisted and mutated. Now he's more like a festering tumor. That's how I see him. And all the other ghosts are stuck to him."

"Was it Captain Marsh?" I asked. "The man with the big beard you saw upstairs?"

"Could be," Jacob said. "He could be one of those guys from

the smoking room, yeah, but he got into something dark...or something dark got into him." He stiffened. "We need to get out of here."

"Why?" I asked.

"We just do. It could get ugly."

"All right. Stacey, are those cameras ready?"

She nodded. She'd placed tripods with thermal and night vision, spacing them far enough apart that if one were to fall down, it wouldn't collide with the other. We would monitor them from the van outside.

We hurried upstairs. Stacey and I had been more or less unconsciously avoiding the basement throughout our investigation, and now I understood why. It was extremely creepy down there, and we'd both felt it. Maybe it was the center of everything happening in the house.

Jacob helped me carry the heavy stamper upstairs to the room where we'd found the broken syringes. I crushed up an OxyContin pill with the steel ridges that protruded in front of my flashlight lens, then dumped the powder into the ghost trap. I lit the three candles as an additional lure.

I set it to automatic—a ten-degree drop in temperature plus an EM spike would make it seal the trap, though I could still activate it with the remote if I wanted.

Then we walked back to the foyer, toward the front doors.

Jacob hesitated, tilting his head as though picking up a signal.

"The darkness that's here," he said. "It's welling up. Something was holding it down for a long time, but now it's been unleashed, and it's growing. The monsters will be coming out of the walls soon. I don't know who your clients are or what their plans are, but they should probably just tear this place down."

"Well, thanks for your advice," I said, after waiting to make sure he was finished. "And thanks for coming out. Have a safe drive home, all right?"

"You're not staying here, are you?" he asked.

"Not inside the house."

"Promise me you won't go in there," Jacob said. "Nobody should go in there, especially at night. Okay?"

"We promise." Stacey patted his arm. "Thanks."

Outside, where night had fully fallen now, Jacob pulled away in his fairly new gray Hyundai, the car of ultra-sensible people.

"I thought he was kind of amazing," Stacey said.

"He was okay," I said. "Let's get in the van. We still have work to do."

"Don't you ever get a chance to sleep?" she asked.

"Sure. In between cases."

She trudged after me to the van.

Chapter Twenty

The array of monitors in our van is built behind the driver and shotgun seats. Two narrow, very uncomfortable bunks fold down from the walls, which is convenient for overnight trips, but you don't want to sleep on them unless you have absolutely no other choice. More comfortable options would include a park bench with a newspaper blanket, or a bed of slightly rusty nails.

They were good enough for now, though. We dropped them and sat down to watch the dozen small monitors, some of which periodically flipped viewpoints among cameras throughout the house.

"Do you think what he said is true?" Stacey asked. "Somebody was doing weird occult murders down in that basement?"

"I'd need more evidence than a psychic's word," I said.

"He was right about other stuff."

"Maybe." I settled back on my camping pillow.

The house was quiet for a while, but then things began to happen. First it was just small things—a door slowly swinging open or shut, a creak or a footstep, a cough. Then came the voices, here and there, murmuring too low to make out. Then a shout, a scream, and a loud crash that had no physical cause we could see.

"That poor little girl, Lexa," Stacey whispered. "Lying awake at night, hearing this from her bed."

I nodded.

A thermal camera in the second-floor hall caught the shape of an icy cold woman walk past, then vanish. Our night vision cameras showed suggestions of people moving in some of the rooms on the second and third floor, but they faded quickly.

"That's a lot of activity," I said after a couple of hours. "I don't know if I've ever seen a house this active."

Then two screens turned black.

"What were those?" I asked.

"Uh," Stacey said. "Yeah. Those were the cameras in the cellar."

"What happened? Did something knock them over?"

"Not that I saw. They just turned off."

"Okay." I stood up and stretched my legs. "Let's go check it out."

"Seriously? I thought you said it was too dangerous. That's why you're out here with me."

"Yep. And that's why we're bringing the ghost cannon." I knelt on the floor, reached under my bunk, and unsnapped the latches on something that roughly resembled a big black tuba case. "You said you wanted to see it in action."

"Yeah, but...maybe not right now, okay?" Stacey said. "Do we really have to go in there? The house is obviously crawling with ghosts."

"The basement might hold the key to everything," I replied. "And something's happening down there. I want to check it out. We need to fix those cameras."

"Ugh," Stacey said. "All right. As long as we bring the ghost cannon."

I lifted it out of its case. It looked like a big round cylinder of a stage light with a carrying handle on top. The battery pack was so heavy I had to strap it to my back. I couldn't hook the batteries to my belt if I wanted to keep my pants on for more than two seconds, which I typically do in most situations.

We closed up the van and walked through the front doors of the house. I used my regular flashlight, as did Stacey, because I didn't want to burn the house down with the cannon.

We crossed the dark lobby and entered the main hallway, heading for the kitchen and the wine cellar. Voices echoed from the floors above. Quick footsteps banged overhead, as if someone were running, then stopped abruptly.

I kept moving, slowed considerably by the heavy weapon I'd chosen to bring.

Here are several reasons you should never use a ghost cannon. First, they're painfully heavy and unwieldy. Second, they're unreliable. Third, even when they're working, they suck a lot of power and don't last long. Fourth, they get hot enough to burn your hand after a couple of minutes. Fifth, they're a major fire hazard—the intense blast of light can ignite anything dry and flammable, like paper, wood, and other materials commonly found in old haunted houses.

There's only one good reason to use a ghost cannon, and that's because you absolutely have no other choice. While a powerful flashlight beam of a few thousand lumens can startle a difficult ghost and confuse or annoy it into leaving you alone, it will never stop the real monsters when they're determined to attack you.

For guaranteed safety—for a minute or two, at least, until it overheats or the battery pack runs dry—you want a specially designed light that can cast more than a million lumens. That's the ghost cannon. Created as an offensive weapon against the most difficult ghosts, it can save your life, provided it doesn't kill you first. It puts out the kind of light and heat normally associated with the big searchlights that the military use to watch the skies, or Vegas hotel owners use to draw attention to their skyscrapers.

That's what I was lugging to the basement with us.

Stacey pushed open the wine cellar door.

The cellar air was freezing cold and much heavier now. I felt like things were watching me from the shadows, but my flashlight revealed nothing, as if the things melted back into corners and walls just before the beam hit them.

"They're dead," Stacey said.

"Who?" I asked, feeling anxious.

"These cameras." She'd walked a few feet ahead of me to check them. "Like something drained the batteries. I can't even get them to turn on."

There's the downside of using electronic equipment. While most ghosts can feed on fire, or even ambient heat in the air, more sophisticated ghosts learn to suck energy out of batteries. We'd just fed a little snack to whatever dark thing dwelled in the cellar.

Above us, the cellar door slammed shut, making us both jump.

Footsteps creaked on the stairs. It sounded like more than one person, like a group walking in slow single file.

I shined my flashlight up to the steps, but I didn't see any apparitions.

I did see the steps *themselves* move, each one bending and squeaking again and again, as if a parade of unseen shoes pressed down on the old wood.

My heart was banging hard in my chest. I managed not to scream.

"What do we do?" Stacey whispered.

"Finish changing the batteries," I said. I was prickly and sweaty all over, despite the deathly cold of the cellar. I knew I was surrounded by invisible monsters.

I moved closer to her, holding my flashlight on the camera so she could use both hands.

A low murmuring of voices swirled in the cold air around me, encircling me.

"Leave us alone," I said, trying to sound commanding rather than terrified. I'm not sure it worked. "I'm warning all of you. Get back."

The murmuring grew louder. Shapes formed in the air around me, like simple, transparent faces stretched into exaggerated frowns.

They moved in on us.

"Stacey?" I asked.

"Almost done. Sorry, my hand keeps shaking." She slid the new battery into place with an audible click.

As if this were some kind of signal, the ghosts charged us, grabbing at my hair, my sleeves, my legs. Stacey screamed, so she was probably experiencing the same thing.

I turned on the ghost cannon.

The scorching-white beam threw the ghosts into full relief. I saw the menagerie Jacob had talked about, the transient-looking men and the scantily clad women. A few crawled on the floor like worms, their ghostly forms severely decayed. All of them were grabbing at us.

A sound like a scream echoed through the room, and it didn't come from Stacey. The ghosts scattered, retreating into walls or just vanishing where they stood. I could feel the heat of the cannon throbbing against my leg and arm.

"What did you see?" I asked. "How many?"

"How should I know?" Stacey whispered.

"Think."

"Eight? Ten? Way too many, let's get out of here."

"Did you see anyone that looked like Captain Marsh?"

"I don't think so. Hey, I didn't know there would be a pop quiz afterward. Let's talk about it somewhere outside this house, okay?"

"You're sure those cameras are working?" I asked.

"They're working! Can we please go?"

We walked up the stairs, Stacey in the lead, with me walking sideways and swinging the ghost cannon back and forth, flooding the cellar with blinding light. I hadn't seen anybody who looked like Captain Marsh, either, but they'd scattered quickly.

The cellar door at the top of the stairs was stuck. Stacey kicked it until it popped open.

We hurried back across the kitchen. The remnants of the cabinet doors banged open and shut as we passed, which only made us put on speed.

We made it out the front doors. The hot, humid night air felt like a warm bath after the freezing basement.

"That was too much," Stacey whispered, shaking her head.

I switched off the ghost cannon as we walked toward the van. I remote-unlocked the van with the key fob, and Stacey opened the back door. She groaned as she looked inside.

"It's like the house is kidding," she said.

I walked up beside her. She was looking at the monitors.

Despite the fresh batteries in the cameras, both of those in the basement had turned dark again.

Chapter Twenty-One

For the rest of the night, our monitors picked up apparitions, sounds, voices, and occasional moving objects. The wardrobe door in the syringe room opened and closed. We had a pile of evidence to show the house was haunted, but that wasn't going to help our clients much. They needed the specters gone, permanently.

As dawn broke, we shut down our gear—Stacey could power down the cameras remotely so we didn't have to go back inside. We went into town and treated ourselves to breakfast at Clary's Cafe on Abercorn Street, where I had sourdough bread French toast stuffed with strawberries. I felt like I deserved a leisurely, carb-filled breakfast under the outdoor awning. I'd been awake for more than twenty-four hours.

That's why our next move was to go home and sleep. I skipped returning to the office for our cars and instead dropped Stacey at her apartment, several blocks from the College of Art and Design campus, then I drove to my place and crashed hard on my bed.

I awoke at noon and went to retrieve her. We had a two-hour drive south to Waycross to meet with Captain Marsh's only living relative, Louisa. Did I mention this job involves a lot of driving? Whether you're going to check out a haunted beach resort in Florida, or tracking down people who lived in a haunted house years and years ago, you're spending a lot of time on the road. I brought my MP3 player this time, so there was a little less Taylor Swift, a little more Runaways.

Louisa Marsh lived in a nursing home in downtown Waycross, a five-story institutional building whose front entrance was framed in big concrete blocks with peeling remnants of green paint. The place looked depressing before we even stepped inside.

The staff directed us to the recreation room on the fourth floor, where a couple of old men drowsily played chess at a table, a few other residents sat alone drowsing in front of newspapers, and a few more drowsed in front of a *Press Your Luck* rerun on the TV. A guy with a checkered suit and big muttonchop sideburns kept saying "No whammies, no whammies!"

We found the eighty-year-old woman gazing out a narrow window at the dingy streets below, dust dancing around her in the yellow light. She seemed lost in thought, and the nurse had to say her name a few times to get her attention.

The woman was small and wiry, wearing a fuzzy pink bathrobe with moth holes all over it. Her hands were gnarled with arthritis. Her eyes were small and pale, sunken deep in a wrinkled face. She looked frail and moved slowly.

"Ms. Marsh, I'm Stacey Ray Tolbert," Stacey said. "I spoke to you on the phone yesterday. About the house?" Stacey added, when the woman just gave her a puzzled look.

"Oh, of course, dear." Louisa's voice was weak and shaky. "You want to buy the house. Where's your husband?"

"I'm not married, Ms. Marsh," Stacey said. "Still shopping for that, you might say."

"Good." Louisa gave a small nod. "I've seen too many women ruined by marriage. Never went for it, myself. I like my independence. I like to spend all morning in the bath if I want, or eat two pieces of peach cobbler all by myself, without worrying what some man will think."

"That sounds like a smart approach, ma'am," Stacey said.

I pulled over a couple of plastic chairs so we could sit down.

"Ms. Marsh," I said, "There may be some confusion. We're not here about buying the house. In fact, you already sold the house in 1985."

"Oh, my." Louisa touched her fingers to her mouth. "I believe you're right."

"My name is Ellie Jordan, and I'm a detective." I handed her an Eckhart Investigations card, but she didn't look at it. "Stacey is a detective, too."

"Oh, like Angela Lansbury!" Louisa smiled.

"Yes, ma'am," I said. "We're investigating a case that involves the history of your house. We were hoping you could tell us about it."

"Where to begin?" Louisa shook her head. "I did love that house dearly."

"Did you ever meet Captain Marsh himself?" I asked.

"Oh, yes. Uncle Gustus. My parents did not think much of him—he was a wild sort, you understand, who liked to have some parties for gentlemen, and there was always gossip. Still, my father believed the old man had money hidden somewhere, and we were his closest relatives, so we went to visit. Holidays, Uncle's birthday, and so on. Then you'd never know how much my parents disapproved of him. Uncle Gustus would bounce me on his lap and dangle a few idle comments about his will, like waving a string in front of a cat. My parents were the cat, you see." She laughed, then coughed, and I smiled. The woman was much more spry when discussing the past than the present, fortunately.

"I didn't care for him when I was a girl," Louisa continued. "He was scary, with that giant beard and deep voice. Even his laugh was scary to me. He would make me sit with him, and he'd pet my leg like this." She passed her hand over her knee a few times, which made me think of the strange claw marks on Lexa's leg.

"Did he ever...hurt you?" I asked, trying to put this issue of child abuse as delicately as possible.

"Not so much. And true to his word, he remembered us in his will—me, anyway! He left everything to me, which made my parents livid." Louisa chuckled. "He must have known what they said about him in private, or guessed it. Oh, there wasn't much money after all. He'd sold most of his land to pay his gambling debts. It was mostly just that big, lovely old house.

"My parents insisted I should sell it, but I had my own troubles with them. I wanted to get away. I was twenty years old, and having my own house looked like a world of freedom to me. So I didn't sell it. I moved in, but it was in such a state that I couldn't afford the repairs. That's when I started renting out rooms."

"And this was 1954? 1955?" I asked.

"Around then, I'm sure. When you've seen so many years, child, they all begin to melt together in your memories. President Eisenhower was in office, I can tell you that."

"So you inherited the house, and you ran it as a boarding house," I said. "What can you tell us about those years?"

"I can certainly tell you the house drew in all kinds of odd strangers from the road," Louisa said. "Maybe because it was always being repaired, maybe because there were warehouses and such around. It wasn't in the pretty part of town, not at all. We had dockworkers and such coming to stay, and working women, you know. My uncle probably enjoyed that."

"You mean he enjoyed it after he died?" I asked, a little confused.

"Well...yes." She fidgeted nervously and asked for water, which Stacey ran to fetch for her. Stacey returned with a large paper cup, and Louisa took a tiny sip.

"Did you encounter any ghosts during your time there? Any evidence the house might have been haunted?" I asked.

She sighed. "Yes, the house was haunted. I would occasionally see people walking around, and they would just disappear. Or you'd hear voices, or things falling down when nobody was in the room. The first I saw was my uncle himself. I was dusting the games room, or the smoking room they called it, when I began to smell something burning. I thought the house was on fire! I just about ran out of there screaming, but then I saw Uncle Gustus, sitting in his old wing chair by the fire, smoking one of those big, smelly cigars he loved so much. He was just watching me clean."

"Oh, gosh. Were you scared?" Stacey asked.

"A little, of course. Not as much as you might think. Remember, I didn't hate Gustus anymore. I was grateful to him for leaving me everything, for setting me free of my parents. I can't begin to say how much I appreciated that. So I just looked back at him, and after a little while, he faded away."

"Did you ever see him again?" I asked.

"Lots of times. Sometimes he spoke to me, told me I was always his favorite. Sometimes I'd feel him playing with my hair, or touching me on the knee. And I'd greet him like a friend. I wasn't scared of him, or any of the others, because I knew he'd keep me safe from them."

"The others?" I repeated. "Other ghosts?"

"Oh my, yes, here and there...they'd make themselves known. Some of them were as restless as a flea-bitten dog, but they never did me any harm."

"Did you wall off the east wing of the house to protect yourself from the ghosts?" I asked, taking a guess.

"Oh, dear, not the ghosts," she said. "The boarders! You've never seen such ill-bred, profane, uncultured men. The women were just as bad. Drunks, loud, behaving like animals. I carved out the east wing to give myself a little peace."

"That must have been dangerous," I said, "A woman running the place alone, with those kinds of boarders."

"Oh, yes. But I wasn't alone much. I always had a handyman or two to keep the house running—that place was always trying to fall apart. They would help me with the rough ones, too. Some of those boys loved to fight, so they didn't mind when one of the renters gave them the opportunity." Louisa chuckled a little to herself.

"Can you name some of the men who worked for you over the years?" I had my pen and pad out, ready to jot down more potential witnesses. I needed any insight into the house I could get.

"Oh, yes, but most of them have passed on. The last two were the best. Buck Kilkenny and Dabney Newton. Those boys could fix anything—including men who refused to pay rent, if you get my meaning. I'm sorry, but it was rough times, and rough folks, too."

"I understand." I jotted down their names.

"I called them my rousties," she added. "It's a word from the circus people. A roustabout, actually, someone who does all the odd jobs around the circus."

"Do you know if Buck and Dabney still live in Savannah?" I asked.

"I wouldn't know, child. They were alive last I heard, that's all I can say. Buck and Dabney..." Her eyes grew a little misty. "They were the ones who found that crazy woman's body."

"Really? Mercy Cutledge?" I asked.

"Oh, yes."

"What can you tell us about her?"

"There isn't much to say, is there? She was a...well, an escort, I suppose they call it now. She entertained men at my uncle's parties for a time, then she snapped and murdered my uncle. Stabbed him in his bed! Such horrifying news. Such a crazed woman. When I heard they were letting her out of that hospital, I just..." She shook her head.

"How did you react?" I asked.

"Well, I thought she would come after me next! The world these days..." Louisa shook her head. "Some people felt sorry for her, but I never did. She was a *murderer*."

"I understand," I said. "So the ghosts didn't scare you at all?"

"Not after I got used to them. Honestly, the house was always full of strangers coming and going. The ghosts weren't nearly so dangerous as the living."

That didn't exactly match my experience with her house, but she seemed to mean it.

"Did anything change after Mercy died there?" I asked.

"It got kind of quiet," Louisa said. "I'm not sure if I saw my uncle again after that. I didn't live there too much longer myself. The city came along and said I had to get it up to code or stop renting rooms. I couldn't afford to turn it into a modern hotel, so I had to put it up for sale. I was sad to move out, but the place felt different, anyway."

"Different how?" I asked.

"Silent. Not so lively. Like the ghosts were old and tired, and they didn't show up so often." Louisa shrugged. "You probably think I'm crazy, but after so long, they almost felt like family. Well, one of them *was* family." She smiled a little. "Uncle Gustus used to comfort me with his presence. After that crazy woman hung herself, I just felt alone in that house. So I lived in an apartment for a time, down on East Broad Street, but it never felt like home. And this place..." She looked around. "To be honest, I don't remember moving here at all."

I thought over what she'd said, then asked for the names of anyone else who had worked at the boarding house, other handymen she'd employed over the years. I asked about people who had died there. She remembered a few violent deaths and overdoses, but nobody she'd known personally, nobody whose name she could recall after all this time. "I just let the police handle all of that," she said.

I saved the most difficult questions for the end.

"Ms. Marsh," I said, "To your knowledge, did your Uncle Augustus have any interest in the occult?"

"The occult?" She blinked, as if startled by the question. "What do you mean?"

"Black magic, sorcery, that sort of thing," I replied.

"Oh...*goodness*." She shook her head. "Where would you get an idea like that?"

"We've heard it from a couple of people," I said.

"Who? The crazy woman?" Louisa chuckled. "Uncle Gustus was not a religious man. He liked his drinking, his gambling, and his women. Most people disapproved of him. But you listen to me right now." She tapped her fingers on the arm of her chair, leaning toward me a little. "He had no interest in God, nor in the Devil, neither. He was only interested in pleasure—sinful pleasures, some would say. But that's the limit of it. Don't believe anyone who tells you different. And don't go around saying that about him. He doesn't deserve to be remembered like that."

I doubted she would like my next question, either—but sometimes you have to be direct.

"Did Augustus ever murder anyone?" I asked.

"Who have you been talking to?" Louisa looked deeply offended. Her face flushed, and her hand crumpled into a fist on her chair arm. "I don't think I want to speak to you women anymore."

"It's just a follow-up to something we heard," I said. "I'm very sorry if it upset you, it's really not a big--"

"I'd like you both to leave now."

"Can I just ask one or two more questions?"

"Absolutely not!" Louisa was turning red. "Do I need to call an orderly to throw you out? Because I don't mind doing that at all."

"That won't be necessary, Ms. Marsh." I stood up. "If you want to talk more about your house, or your uncle, please call me. My number's on the card."

She looked out the window and didn't reply.

"Well, that wasn't much help, was it?" Stacey asked a few minutes later, as we walked down the concrete front steps of the nursing home. "Or was it?"

"I have some hope for follow-up interviews," I said. "I want to talk to some of the people who worked there."

"I feel sorry for her, though," Stacey said. "It sounded like she had a weird, lonely life, and now I guess her mind is slipping."

I just nodded.

I made Stacey drive the van home. As soon as we were on the road, I called Anna Treadwell to update her: we'd observed a number of ghosts in her house, we'd set a trap for the dangerous one we'd encountered, we'd interviewed Louisa Marsh. I reluctantly added "brought out a psychic" to our list of concrete actions, since I needed to pad it out a little. The only accomplishment they really wanted to hear of course, was "got rid of the ghosts." I wished I could have said that.

"When do you think we can move back?" Anna asked. They were staying at the Econo Lodge by the airport, which told me everything about their dwindling family budget.

"Soon," I told her. "We're working day and night."

She didn't sound reassured.

I called Calvin to give him the names of Louisa Marsh's employees over the years. Maybe he could turn up something, or put in a call to the police department. It was Sunday afternoon, so if we were lucky, somebody would have time to talk to a retired homicide detective.

As it turned out, we were a little bit lucky.

Chapter Twenty-Two

Buck Kilkenny and Dabney Newton were two names known pretty well to the Savannah police department. Their record of petty theft and drug offenses didn't make them particularly memorable, but they also owned a scummy dive bar by the interstate over in Port Wentworth, just a few miles inland from Savannah and part of its metro area. Interestingly, that place was called Roustie's. Calvin's police contacts advised us to stay away, but I'm not great at taking advice.

We pulled into the parking lot of the bar, which looked like a repurposed Pizza Hut, with brick walls and a flaking red roof. A few motorcycles sat outside, along with more than one dingy pick-up truck decorated with the Confederate flag. The bar looked like a place where meth-addicted rats went to die.

"You know, it's weird," Stacey said as she parked the van. "Louisa's story didn't totally match the original police report from 1982."

"Which part?"

"I've read that thing a few times, and it doesn't mention Buck and Dabney at all, or any maintenance guys discovering the body. It just sounded like Louisa walked out there one morning and found

Mercy hanging from the baluster."

"That could be important," I said.

"Maybe." Stacey shrugged. "Her memories seemed pretty fuzzy to me."

"She wasn't too clear about the present, but her recall of the past seemed pretty crisp to me. I'm glad you mentioned that before we talked to these guys."

"Hey, that's what a good assistant ghost trapper is for, right?" Stacey forced a smile. She had a distracted look on her face, like something was bothering her. I wondered what was on her mind, but I didn't feel like having a heart to heart in the parking lot at Roustie's, where a biker might puke on our tires at any moment.

We stepped inside. Though it was late Sunday afternoon, there was already a scattered crowd. Acrid cigarette smoke hung in a permanent yellow fog over the room. There were a few glowing neon beer signs, a couple of pool tables, some tables and chairs you wouldn't really want to touch. A bar took up one corner of the place, with a small empty stage beside it.

The clientele was what you'd expect from the cars outside, a mix of bikers and big old boys with meshback caps. There were a couple of women among the bikers, hard-looking types in their forties.

We drew a few glances, especially Stacey. I didn't linger near the door but strode directly across the place toward the bar. I didn't know what Buck or Dabney looked like, so I addressed myself to the bartender, a man in his fifties with a heavy salt and pepper mustache and a serious beer gut. His t-shirt featured a cartoony old man on a fishing boat. The rag tied onto his head featured flaming skulls firing missiles out of their mouths.

"What'll it be, ladies?" the man asked. I assumed the question was directed at Stacey's chest, because that was where he was looking. He leaned on the counter toward us.

"I kind of wouldn't mind a mojito," Stacey said, and I cut her a look. She pouted at me. "What? Okay, a sweet tea."

"Only sweetie we got in here is *you*, darlin'." The bartender punctuated this slice of wit with another big grin at her shirt.

"We need to speak with Buck Kilkenny or Dabney Newton," I said. "Are either of them in today?"

"Whoa, girl got serious." The man straightened up and backed away, eyeing us suspiciously. "You cops or what?"

"P.I.," I told him. "It's nothing serious. Just some background research for a client."

"What kinda research?"

"I would have to speak to Buck or Dabney about that," I said.

"I got to say, y'all ain't too good at being P.I.'s, cause one of them fellers is standing right in front of you, and you didn't even know it. Buck Kilkenny." He held out a fairly dirty hand with fingernails chewed into dangerous little points. I shook it with a polite smile.

"Nice to meet you, Mr. Kilkenny," I said. I gave him my card. "I'm Ellie Jordan, and this is Stacey Ray Tolbert. Our agency actually specializes in the paranormal."

"What's that?"

"We trap and remove ghosts from haunted houses," Stacey said.

"Oh! Heck, yeah, I've heard of y'all." He glanced at the Eckhart Investigations card with renewed interest. "Yeah, must be a good trade, lots of dead folks in this city. What can I do for you pretty ladies? You sure you don't want a drink? I can put it on the house, since I'm the house." He winked at Stacey.

"I wouldn't mind a bottled water, if you have one," I said.

"Got a water glass." He grabbed a tall, badly spotted glass from the overhead rack and filled it with water using a little hose.

"Thank you," I said, though I had no intent of drinking it. The whole place was filthy, okay? I was pretty sure my jeans would make a peeling sound when I climbed off the sticky barstool. "We're looking at a very haunted house right now—the Marsh house. Louisa Marsh told us you and Dabney used to work there."

"Oh, yeah, back when we was pretty much dumb kids." He lit a cigarette and poured himself a whiskey, asking with gestures whether we wanted one. Stacey and I shook our heads. "Hell, I guess I was twenty-five, twenty-six...Dabney and I knew each other since high school, he was a year ahead of me. We always ran around together. Yeah, Ms. Marsh paid us pretty good to try to keep that old heap from falling apart. I'm surprised they haven't tore it down yet."

"It's still there," I said. "How many years would you say you worked there, Buck?"

"Hell, how I would I know? It was a lot of partying in them days, a lot of Friday nights...I'd say four or five years, off and on."

"What kind of work did you do for her?"

"Just about everything. Fixing windows, painting, patching the roof...you name it."

"Ms. Marsh told me you also did some security work," I said.

"Aw, yeah. When somebody got out of hand—starting fights, or trashing the house, wouldn't pay, wouldn't leave, whatever—we'd clear 'em out for her. Why you asking about that?"

"Just getting a complete picture. Now, here's the big question: did you ever experience anything unusual in the house?"

"You mean like a ghost?"

"Exactly."

"Bet your ass! Especially early in the morning, or when night was coming on. Sometimes we'd come in and our tools would be moved around, or just plain missing. Sometimes you'd think you saw somebody walking into a room, but the room would be empty. Heck, sometimes the *door* was still closed, and you couldn't figure out where they went."

"Anything else?"

"The voices," Buck said. "You might hear one talking at you, and there'd be nobody there. Sometimes it sounded like a big man. One time there was a woman, I never will forget. I was changing out the lights up there in the second-floor hall, and the voice says right in my ear, 'Come on, sugar, let's have a drink.' Like she was hitting on me. Thing was, nobody was there in the hall, and plus I was way up on that ladder, so how's anybody gonna talk right into my ear, anyway?"

"Did that scare you?" I asked.

"Well, yeah, but not enough to start turning down Ms. Marsh's money. Heck, Dabney got it worse. He one time felt some guy's hands grab him and shake him, like he was mad. That was late, late at night, later than I ever worked." Buck sipped his whiskey, glanced around, and grinned. He lowered his voice and said, "Dabney spent a whole night or two there with Ms. Marsh, if you get my meaning. She was about twenty years older than us, and I don't think she was *that* much of a looker, but she picked him, anyway." He shrugged. "That's how it goes. But I don't think that ghost liked him spending the night with her. It's the main reason Dabney stopped doing it, that ghost."

"That's really interesting," I said, returning his conspiratorial grin. He knocked back the rest of the whiskey.

"What's going on out here?" A tall, thin, acne-scarred man about Buck's age walked out from the door behind the bar area, wearing a black wife beater shirt and an old cap with the logo of the Sand Gnats, our city's minor league baseball team. He scowled at Buck.

"You ain't drinking at the bar again, are you?"

"Nope." Buck moved to hide his whiskey glass with his body. "Just entertaining these pretty girls, Dabney."

"And you ain't run 'em off yet?" Dabney looked us over, smiling around the toothpick grasped in his teeth. "Hoo-wee. Y'all from out of town?"

"No, sir," I said.

"They's private detectives," Buck told him. This knocked the leering grin right off Dabney's face.

"What do they want?" Dabney approached us, looking as suspicious as Buck had.

"We're just doing some background on a house that may be haunted," I said, passing him a business card. "The old Marsh place. We've already spoken with Louisa Marsh, and Buck was just telling us about some ghostly encounters you may have had while working there."

"He was, was he?" Dabney asked. "Buck, go check the deep fryer in the kitchen. It's busted again."

"But I wanted to keep talkin'--" Buck threw a desperate look at Stacey.

"I bet you did. Now go fix it up."

Buck sighed and walked back through the door. Dabney watched him with his arms crossed, then turned back to us.

"Now what do the two of you want?" he asked.

"We were wondering if you'd ever experienced anything supernatural at the Marsh house," I told him.

"Like what?"

"Anything. Tools moved out of place, voices, apparitions...maybe something grabbing you or scratching you," I said.

"If I did, I don't see how it would be any business of yours," Dabney said.

"We're trying to remove the ghosts for our clients," I explained. "They're the new owners of the house."

"New owners, huh? Sounds like somebody had a big pile of money to burn. That place won't stay put together no matter what you do to it."

"Do you have any idea why?"

"Just an old place, that's all. Falling to pieces."

"Are you saying you never encountered a ghost while working

there?" I asked.

"I ain't gonna sit here and tell you gossip about Ms. Marsh or her family, or none of that," Dabney said. "It's disrespectful to her."

"Ms. Marsh didn't mind telling us about it earlier today," I said.

"Then I guess you already heard what there is to say."

"She said there were ghosts, including her uncle, Captain Marsh."

"I won't say there was nothing there." Dabney found Buck's whiskey glass and scowled. "You'd hear bumps in the night, stuff like that."

"Did you ever spend the whole night there?" I asked.

"What are you saying?" Dabney narrowed his eyes at me.

"Just asking."

"I don't have anything to tell you," Dabney said. "I see you're not drinking, so you may as well clear out."

"All right. Thanks for your time." I slid off the stool—just as predicted, the seat of my jeans peeled away with a gross slurping sound. Stacey did the same. We started to leave, and then I turned back. "Just one more quick question, Mr. Newton. Did you ever meet Mercy Cutledge?"

"Why you asking about her?"

"She may be the one haunting the house."

"Huh." Dabney scratched his chin, as if putting together his answer very carefully. "Well, she killed that old man before I was even born. The only time I seen her, she was already a corpse. So I guess, no, I'd say I didn't know her at all."

"Did you and Buck find her body in the foyer of the house?"

"Me?" He looked taken aback. "Naw. Buck and I came in late that morning—long night before, probably. We did a lot of late nights in them days, drinking and carrying on. The police got there before we ever did."

"Okay, that fits the police report," I said. "Thanks for your time, sir."

He rinsed out Buck's whiskey glass and rubbed it with a yellowed, crusty towel while he watched us walk out the door.

"That was pleasant," Stacey said, shuddering as we left the dim bar for the low orange sunshine outside. "So it sounds like Ms. Marsh remembered things wrong, huh?"

"It sounds like it." I climbed into the driver's side this time. "Let's go get the house ready before sunset. I don't want to be in there after dark."

Stacey was very quiet as I started the engine. She had that same distant, distracted look on her face.

"Is something wrong?" I asked her.

Something was.

Chapter Twenty-Three

"I don't know if I can do this anymore," Stacey said, while I headed east. The Marsh house, on the west side of Savannah, was only a few miles from Roustie's, so we had plenty of time before dark.

"Do what?"

"All of it. This work. I've been attacked by ghosts again and again just in the past few days. Twice in the Marsh house, not to mention that asylum basement..." She shivered at the memory. "I'm gonna lose my mind if this keeps up. I can't handle it. I'm having nightmares, Ellie. Crazy, crazy nightmares."

"It's not always like this," I said. "But occasionally it gets dangerous. The nightmares are normal, too. You get used to them."

"Just thinking about going inside that house one more..." Stacey shook her head. "Maybe my mom's right, and I need to move back to Alabama. Figure my life out. Things like that."

"Must be nice," I said.

"What?"

"To feel like you have that option." I took a long look at her, then I stepped on the gas, charging down the interstate.

"Hey, our exit's coming up," Stacey said.

"We're making a detour."

"Uh, do we have time for that?" she asked, looking at the wide orange sun sinking behind us.

"Unless there's an unexpected Sunday-night traffic jam, I think we'll be okay." I drove us south into the suburban sprawl, where Savannah's historic squares, parks, mansions, and churches give way to a more typical land of strip malls and subdivisions.

Anticipation knotted up my stomach as we drove down a tree-lined side road and turned into a neighborhood. The sign read RIVERSIDE POINT, though the neighborhood was at least a mile from the nearest river. It was surreal—I hadn't been back in at least a year, maybe more.

"Where are we going?" Stacey asked, checking the time on her phone. She looked antsy. I understood. We had a couple of chores to do inside the Marsh house before dark fell.

The neighborhood was an older one, the architecture ranging from 1950's bungalows to those asymmetrical 1970's houses with the high roofs and weird angles. The place mostly looked like I remembered, except for some taller trees, a few gardens that had been rearranged or removed, a couple of houses painted different colors. Several of the yards were overgrown and badly kept. They hadn't been like that ten years earlier, or my dad would surely have griped about it.

I parked on the side of a road, in a gap between two houses. No house stood there, just a wooden fence with a couple of KEEP OUT signs.

"Where are we?" Stacey asked again.

"This is where I grew up." I climbed out of the van and motioned for her to join me.

The fence was five feet high, so we could just look over it. I stood on my tiptoes for a better view.

Enclosed within the fence was a misshapen hump of red Georgia earth, with scattered weeds growing here and there. There weren't nearly as many weeds or wildflowers as there should have been in an open, sunlit lot like this. There was too much death in the soil.

"Was something here?" Stacey asked.

"There have been six houses here over the years," I said. "The first was a plantation house, when this was all farmland. It burned down. The last one was my house. It burned down, too, when I was fifteen. Every house built on this spot has been destroyed by fire."

"Whoa, all six of them?" Stacey shook her head, looking at the empty lot. "Was it one of those pyromaniac ghosts you were talking about?"

"Pyrokinetic. Well, I guess pyromaniac isn't wrong, either. In 1841, a family lived in the house here—wife, husband, three kids. The wife, a pretty woman named Elizabeth Sutton, grew kind of bored with her marriage, I guess. Her husband was much older than her. She had an affair with another man, an extremely handsome man named Anton Clay. He was a rich young merchant in the cotton trade. He had plenty of female admirers, but he wanted Elizabeth.

"Eventually, Anton pressured her to leave her husband and family to run away with him. Elizabeth refused and broke off the affair. Anton didn't like that at all. In fact, he kind of snapped."

"What happened?" Stacey asked.

"He came to the house very late one night, while everyone was asleep. He broke in and set the entire place on fire. Everybody died—Elizabeth, her husband, her small children, three slaves, and Anton himself."

"How terrible," Stacey whispered. "Those poor kids!"

"Since then, every house built here has burned down, with no clear cause of the fire. I guess nobody has come along to risk building a seventh one yet. But eventually they will."

"Were you hurt in the fire?" Stacey asked. "Or your family?"

"I would've died if my dog hadn't woken me up." I smiled a little, but there was no real joy in it. My heart was hurting. "Sweet little Frank. You know how golden retrievers always look like they're smiling? Anyway, he jumped on my bed and woke me up, and my room was full of smoke.

"The dog led me out. I couldn't even see him most of the time, there was so much smoke, and the upstairs hall was full of fire, just billowing up and out, a wall of flames. He managed to steer me downstairs and out of the house. Good dog. The best." I was tearing up already, and I wiped my eyes on my sleeve. "On the way out, I saw him."

"Who?"

I took a breath. "Anton Clay, I found out later. The guy was truly handsome, I mean he could be a movie star or something. You could see why a bored young wife would have an affair with this guy. His eyes were powerful, and sharp like they could cut you into pieces with a glance. In life, they were blue, but when I see them, they're fire red. He was dressed in a cravat, vest, and an old, old-fashioned coat, like he belonged a hundred and fifty years in the past. Which he did.

"I didn't know who he was back then, of course. He held out his hand, and he said something like 'Come with me. We belong together.' And I mean, in the middle of everything, I was so startled to see him there, surrounded by my burning living room. He should have been on fire, where he was standing, but his coat wasn't even singed. And his eyes and voice kind of hypnotized me, making me stay where I was. I probably would have stood right there and let the fire take me if Frank hadn't barked and nipped at my hand.

"I got going again, toward the door. When I looked back, the man was gone, but the fire was welling up toward me like it meant to get me before I could escape.

"Frank and I made it outside just before that wave of fire swept out the front door and spread out across my porch, which was all made of wood and went up fast." I shook my head. I wasn't even looking at Stacey, just staring at the desolate hump of land in front of me.

"Was your family okay?"

"My parents both died that night."

"Oh, my God, Ellie." Stacey moved close, putting her arms around me. I couldn't help resisting at first—force of habit, I guess. Then I let myself sort of half-hug her, and that much contact made me start crying. I wrapped both my arms around her, feeling broken and helpless and stupid all at once.

"I was the only one left," I whispered. "I never even saw Frank again after that night. One of the firefighters took him to a vet, but he'd breathed a ton of smoke and he had burns all over him. The vet put him to sleep, the same night he saved my life. I didn't even get to say good-bye to any of them, not my parents, not even the dog. It just happened too fast." A sob hitched in my chest, but I fought it, not wanting to totally break down in front of her. "My parents were good people. They didn't deserve to die like that. I miss them so much."

We held each other while I cried and tried to get myself together.

In case you're wondering, this was not at all how I'd meant things to go. I'd believed I could keep up a solid, stoic front, but I'd been wrong.

After a minute, I stepped back and wiped my eyes.

"They put me in the hospital overnight, for some first-degree burns. I was truly in shock, I couldn't process what had happened. My whole life, the people I loved the most, were gone, all vanished into smoke.

"A police detective came to visit me the next day. He was kind of a heavyset older guy, just starting to go gray. He asked me about what I'd seen, and I told him everything, even about the nineteenth-century man and how he'd kind of cast a spell over me. I was just like a robot, spitting out information, not caring whether I made any sense or whether anyone thought I was crazy.

"So this detective tells me about the history of the place. He'd been researching it. He's the one who told me about the five earlier houses that burned down in the same spot, and later, when he'd studied it more, sent me the story of Anton Clay. By then I was living with my aunt in Virginia, which felt like a million miles from home.

"I stayed in touch with that detective. I kept sending letters asking for more information. He would reply with just quick little notes if he didn't have anything new to tell me. He eventually retired from the force and started a private detective agency specializing in ghosts..."

"Mr. Eckhart," Stacey said.

"That's how I met him. All I wanted to do was the same work he was doing, getting rid of the bad ghosts so they couldn't hurt anyone. I particularly wanted to learn how to destroy *that* ghost." I pointed to the center of the empty lot where my house and my parents should have been. "So I moved back to Savannah for college, and I insisted Calvin train me on the side. He really didn't want to, but I didn't leave him much choice. It was either take me as his apprentice or deal with me camping out by his office all day."

"Did you get rid of the pyro ghost?" Stacey asked, following my gaze. "Is he gone now?"

"The thing is, we can't really kill ghosts. They're already dead. Sometimes you get lucky and convince one to move on peacefully, but sometimes you have to trap and remove them. The really nasty, violent ghosts don't go to the refuge cemetery in Goodwell, where we took Mercy. For the truly evil ones, we bury them in a different cemetery. We bury the whole trap with the ghost still inside. That's literally the best we can do."

"So that's what we would do if we trapped that heroin-addict ghost that attacked me, right?" Stacey touched her breastbone, where the needle scratch was still visible. She'd been treating it with Neosporin. "Just bury the trap?"

"Right."

"But wouldn't the batteries run out eventually? The ones that power the electrical field around the jar?"

"Eventually, after several years," I said. "But the combination of the lead-glass ghost jar, and all the cemetery earth around it, will pretty much pin the ghost into place forever, as long as nobody disturbs the buried trap."

"Sounds hellish."

"Violent ghosts shouldn't be so violent, then. It's their own fault." I looked her directly in the eyes now. "The dead are not our concern. We're here to protect the *living*. We stand on the border between the world of light and the darkness beyond, and there aren't very many of us. The world is teeming with the dead.

"So, when I say it must be nice to have the option of going back to your parents and thinking over what you'd like to do with your life, that's what I mean," I told her. "This is what I do. This is what I am. And if I don't, who will?"

Stacey nodded slowly, a thoughtful look on her face.

"I know you got into this because you thought it was neat to capture images of ghosts with your cameras," I said. "And you're good at that, and we need that. But you're also strong. You don't run from danger, and you wouldn't ditch me if things got too hot."

"I wouldn't," she said.

"You don't just have the talent for this, you have the nerve and the guts. I've seen it. And I'll admit, Stacey, I didn't want Calvin to hire you, but I'm glad he did. It was the right call. I want you beside me in this, protecting the living against the dead. I need you. I can't do it alone."

There. That's the stuff I'd actually meant to say, more or less. We looked at each for a moment.

"So are you with me?" I asked.

She hesitated, then nodded slowly. "Yeah. Yeah, Ellie, I'm with you. Partners?" She stuck out a hand.

"Don't be silly. You're the new kid, and I'm totally in charge." I shook her hand. "But, yeah, eventually. Partners. Now let's go kick some supernatural ass."

Stacey grinned.

Driving away, I resisted the urge to look back. Once before, visiting alone, I'd see Anton inside the fence. He was no longer handsome, tailored, and spit-polished, but charred, his entire body a smoldering black wreck, except for his intense red eyes. Those had stared at me out of the charcoal skull-mask of his face, and I knew he was waiting for me.

Chapter Twenty-Four

Our side trip did put us off schedule, so when we arrived at the Marsh/Treadwell house, we had less than twenty-five minutes until sunset. We had to get in and out of there fast. Our chores included changing out camera batteries and manually switching on the cameras themselves. They never had much trouble shutting down remotely, but there were always a few stubborn ones that had to be turned back on by hand. With a house so ghost-infested, it was better to turn them all on before dark rather than risk having to run inside at night.

"Let's split up to save time," I told Stacey as we walked into the foyer. It was funny how the foyer had once seemed the center of the haunting, but now felt like the safest room in the house—though that wasn't saying much.

"Isn't that what they always say in a horror movie? Right before somebody gets killed?" Stacey asked.

"Usually, yeah. So hurry."

We divided up the first floor, switching out battery packs and turning on cameras. I took the second floor, while Stacey climbed on up to third. I really can't say who had the worst of that, but we agreed to meet in the kitchen and go down to the cellar together. Nobody was going in that place alone, even if the sun was still up.

The sun didn't reach down into that darkness, anyway. The cellar had no windows.

I made my rounds on the second floor, changing out camera batteries and double-checking that the cameras themselves were working. In the junkie's room, the trap remained wide open, waiting for a ghost to spring it. The crushed-up pill powder was still in the bottom, but the candles had burned down to nubs and gone out before we'd left that morning.

I reloaded it with three fresh candles and lit them up. As I did that, I heard a clear footstep in the hall.

"Almost done, Stacey." I turned, but nobody was there.

"What's that?" Stacey's voice crackled over my headset.

"Were you just out in the hall?" I asked.

"Nope, still up on three. This mold is spreading fast. The whole inside of the closet is coated with it now."

"Okay. I think the ghosts are starting to move around. I'll meet you downstairs."

A minute later, I descended the steep, narrow back staircase and walked through the laundry area into the kitchen.

Then I froze. A woman stood there, looking out the densely overgrown bay window. It was not Stacey, nor anybody else from this century, given the high, stiff lace of her dress that totally concealed her neck. The dress was dark and long, almost puritanical with its starched-straight lines.

She was smallish, with dark hair and thin lips. It took a moment for me to recognize her.

"Mrs. Marsh?" I said, turning down the volume on my headset so Stacey wouldn't distract me. "Eugenia Marsh?"

The woman turned slowly. The fabric of her dress did not move at all. It was as though she hovered just above the floor, pivoting in midair. She held a bone-white teacup on a saucer in one hand, and her turning didn't seem to disturb it at all.

She looked right at me, her eyes staring into mine—she was definitely a conscious entity, not a residual recording.

It seemed like she was about to speak, but she didn't. Instead, she raised her teacup to her mouth, took a sip, then placed it back on the saucer.

She looked at me for another moment, and then her lips turned black. Veins of black rose on her face, spreading out from her mouth across her nose, her cheeks, her chin. Some of them ran down into the collar of her dress. Two pulsing black veins grew upward toward her eyes, turning them solid black.

The flesh on her hands and face crumbled. Her dark hair shriveled and turned pale gray.

Then she crashed to the floor. By the time she landed on the scuffed, dirty old tiles, she wasn't much more than a skeleton in a dress. I watched her melt away into the tiles, feeling more than a little disturbed.

"Ellie, what's up?" Stacey dashed into the room, out of breath, waving her phone. "I couldn't hear you. What happened?"

"I just ran into Eugenia Marsh," I said. "We'd better get out of here. The ghosts are stirring."

The sun was already out of sight when Stacey and I stepped out through the front doors.

We sat out in the van that night, watching the monitors. It was similar to the previous night—lots of footsteps, voices, doors swinging open or shut. A chair slid a foot or so in one of the rooms. A few half-formed, quick-fading apparitions passed the night vision cameras. The thermals picked up moving cold spots that appeared and disappeared.

This time, Stacey and I napped in shifts, taking turns watching the array of screens and listening to the speakers. This worked pretty well for a few hours. The only downside was that I slept on one of those narrow, hard drop-down bunks.

She woke me up about three in the morning, shaking my shoulder and babbling excitedly.

"What?" I grumbled, opening my eyes. I was still half-lost in a dream where I'd been drowning in a giant bowl of Lucky Charms. Don't ask for more details.

"He sprung the trap!" Stacey said. "Junkie guy, I'm guessing."

"Really?" I sat up, more awake now, and looked at the monitor. The broken-syringe room, as viewed in green-on-green night vision, showed the stamper arm fully depressed, the cylindrical trap sealed tight. "Finally, some progress. Did you see it happen?"

"Yeah, just now. I was about to review it on thermal."

"Do that," I said, rubbing my eyes.

Stacey punched keys on her laptop. A thermal video image of the room appeared on the monitor, and she backed it up a few minutes.

"There," she said, pointing to a wispy deep-blue mist that drifted around the three bright red spots of the trap's candles. It moved slowly, as though being cautious.

One tendril of pale blue finally extended into the trap. It snuffed out each candle as it passed, sucking out the energy.

By the time the shape reached the broken syringe at the bottom, the cylindrical shape of the trap was filled with dark blue. The ghost was inside, investigating the powdered opioids.

The trap's sensors obviously picked up on it, because the stamper arm slammed down, sealing the lid.

"Got it!" Stacey said, beaming.

"Wait." I looked closer. "There's no cold spot inside that trap. It's completely ambient temperature." I couldn't double-check the sensors within the trap, of course, because the EM field blocked their little wireless broadcasts.

"I don't get it."

"Back it up and run it very slowly."

"Okay..." She frowned as she used her mouse.

In slow motion, the arm of the stamper began to fall. Just before the lid sealed the trap, something appeared on the screen beside it. It was just a thin line, like a wire, and it was solid black on the thermal, which meant it was probably cold enough to burn your fingers.

In an instant, the thin line yanked the entire dark-blue mass out of the trap like a fish on a hook. It hauled the ghost away through the floor.

Then the trap sealed.

"What was that?" Stacey asked.

"Looks like someone had a tight grasp on Mr. Junkie," I said. "And he wasn't willing to let go."

"So...does that mean our traps are worthless now?"

"For this case, maybe. We'll have to reset the trap to know for sure."

"You want to go in there again?" She glanced at the case holding the ghost cannon.

"Not tonight," I said. "It's not worth it. We're going to have to figure out a new approach. Let me know if anything else happens."

I lay back on my hard little bunk, thinking it over. I mainly thought about Eugenia. From what Jacob had said, her little manifestation to me must have taken a lot of effort and energy.

I thought about what she might have been telling me, and what it might mean for our case.

Chapter Twenty-Five

About an hour after sunrise, I parked my old Camaro outside my apartment. I went in through the exterior door I shared with other tenants, then up the stairs to my place, where I was ready to crash, or maybe just sit and read for a while.

I stopped outside my door, because it was open.

It wasn't wide open, just an inch or two, but I was fairly certain I hadn't left it that way. I also hadn't smashed the lock and door handle on the way out.

In this situation, the smart thing to do is walk away and call the police. You don't want to make decisions based on impatience, exhaustion, or anger at having your home violated.

Unfortunately, I was feeling impatient, exhausted, and the early red twinges of anger. I drew the stun gun—now concealed in my purse, because I don't go around wearing my utility belt in public—and kicked my door to make it swing wide open. It was a good, solid front kick. My kickboxing classes finally paid off a little, yay.

"Who's in there?" I shouted. "The cops are coming now, but if you want to run, I'll give you a head start."

There was no reply. Nothing moved in there...not even my cat.

"Hello?" I stepped inside, holding my stun gun high. I had

enough stress and problems in my life already. If I encountered a burglar, I'd be happy to take out my frustrations on him.

If he'd hurt my cat, I would probably zap him in the eyeballs.

I pounced into my little studio apartment, ready for a fight. Nothing stirred, so I probably looked a little ridiculous. Better ridiculous than sorry.

The apartment was trashed—the bed askew, the mattress thrown against the wall and slashed open, furniture moved, drawers pulled out, clothes scattered everywhere. It looked like they'd searched the place, then grown bored and started smashing dishes and glasses in my kitchen nook, then broken my poor, ancient TV set. The hex signs and dreamcatchers had been ripped from my walls, and someone had painted LEAVE TOWN in big red letters, along with what might have been an attempt at a skull and crossbones. They'd used red paint for added effect.

"If someone's here, you have five seconds to get out, or I'm going to start shooting." So I didn't have a real gun, big deal. He didn't know that, whoever he was.

I stalked through the apartment, checking the only places a person could hide—the kitchen pantry, the closet, under my bed. Nothing. I glanced out at the tiny balcony, but it was empty and the door was still locked.

Something rustled behind me. I spun around, holding out my stun gun, ready to pump somebody full of voltage.

"Mrow?" Bandit poked his head out from under the sofa. He looked around cautiously, as if emerging from a bomb shelter into an uncertain world.

"Bandit!" I scooped him up and hugged him, and he gave me a little purr and tucked his head under my chin. He must have been scared, because Bandit isn't usually much of a cuddler. "What happened? Did anyone hurt you?" I checked him for cuts and injuries, but it looked like he'd been wise enough to keep out of the way while they ransacked my apartment.

I placed him on the couch and looked again at the threatening graffiti on my wall. Either some long-lost enemy had emerged from my past in search of revenge, or this was related to my current case. Only a handful of non-dead people had any interest in what I was doing, so I thought the identity of the vandals was fairly obvious.

That was like the puzzle piece that reveals the whole picture. Suddenly, I understood the entire case and what we needed to do.

I took out my phone.

"Don't you usually sleep during daylight hours?" Calvin asked when he answered.

"Mercy Cutledge wasn't crazy, and she didn't kill herself," I said.

"That's a new development. I'll celebrate by continuing to drink my coffee."

"Can you give me the psychic guy's number? We'll need his help."

"So you *do* like working with Jacob?"

"I'll let you know after tonight."

When I called Jacob, I said, "We need your help again."

"Who is this?" he asked.

"I thought you were psychic," I replied.

"Ellie?"

"*Yes.* Save my number in your phone. You need to come with Stacey and me today."

"Yeah, slight problem with that," Jacob said. "I'm employed. I'm already walking into work."

"You're an early bird."

"You gotta be, if you want to eat worms," he said. "Sorry, my boss won't let me off. They stuck me with a senior partner who's a real...well, he's very determined to exceed his clients' expectations in a time-efficient manner." The sudden shift in his voice told me he'd probably crossed paths with some co-workers at the accounting firm. "I can't just step out. He doesn't even know about my...hobbies."

"Okay, one sec." On my phone, I pulled up the weather channel. "Can you get out by five?"

"Sure, if I want people to think I'm a slacker."

"This is serious. We have to be able to depend on you, Jacob."

"Six-thirty," he said.

"Too late. Can't you bring a computer and work on the way? It's a long drive."

"A long drive where?"

I finally talked him into it.

Chapter Twenty-Six

To save time, we picked up Jacob right from work, a tall block of a building with its black-glass windows overlooking the fountains and gardens of Johnson Square. He was on his phone, speaking rapidly to a client, a laptop case in one hand. He nodded at me as he climbed into the back of the van and sat in the bucket seat we'd had to plunk into place for him—the rear seats were usually gone to make room for gear.

He didn't finish his call until we'd reached the western edge of town.

"Mind if I compile some financial statements back here?" he asked.

"Compile whatever you like," I replied.

Once again, we made the three-hour drive to the ghost town of Goodwell. Stacey parked us right by the cemetery gate. I looked out at the overgrown graves. The sun was already below the horizon, the sky turning purple. The moon was full.

"Should I grab a trap?" Stacey asked.

"We just want to talk with Mercy and see what she can tell us. I don't think taking her prisoner is a good first step." I unlocked the cemetery gate and pushed it open. Voices seemed to whisper all around us. I tried to tell myself it was just the grass, weeds, and leaves blowing in the evening wind, but I doubted it. I kept my flashlight pointed at the ground, not wanting to startle any spirits away.

"Oh...wow." Jacob stopped a few paces inside the gate, and Stacey bumped into him from behind.

"What's with the roadblock?" she asked him.

"This place is pretty unusual," he said. "I'm feeling a lot of...loose spirits. That doesn't make any sense, but normally, in a graveyard like this, the ghosts are kind of rooted to their little spots, or hang close to them. Here, it's like a bunch of spirits who don't really belong."

"Sounds accurate." I walked to the bench under the sprawling oak and retrieved Mercy's trap. It had popped open just as programmed. If nothing else, we'd recovered one trap on this journey.

I pretended not to hear the footsteps, or to notice the feeling of being watched by unseen eyes, but chill bumps prickled all over my body. Invisible things began to touch me in a fairly unfriendly way, grabbing at my limbs. I felt one icy fingertip on my face and jerked away from it.

"They're all crowding around you," Jacob said. He held up a hand. "Wait, wait...they're all talking at once. Wow, they're really mad at you, Ellie. They're saying you took them from their homes and stuck them here."

"I did," she said. "They should have stopped harassing the living."

"They just got a lot louder."

"Can you find her or not?" I asked. There had been plenty of time on the drive over to tell Jacob about Mercy and show her picture to him.

"It's hard to...everybody be QUIET!" he shouted, as though he stood in the middle of a loud concert, or maybe the world's largest daycare center. All I could hear was leaves shuffling and sticks breaking. He pointed in the general direction of a tall, leaning obelisk. "You, right there. You're Mercy, aren't you?"

"You found her?" Stacey asked.

"She's furious. At you." Jacob pointed at me. "She looks ready to attack."

"Mercy, can you hear me?" I asked.

"She's nodding, and she's kind of stalking up on you," Jacob said.

I could feel the air growing cold and heavy around me, in a way that reminded me of the Treadwell house foyer when she was still haunting it. Probably the same temperature and EM reading, though I didn't have my instruments to check.

"Mercy, now that I understand better, I'm truly sorry I took you away," I said. "You were the one holding back the dangerous spirits, weren't you? You were trying to warn the living." I'd figured this much out after Louisa said a number of ghosts had inhabited the house, but most of the activity had ceased after Mercy's death in the foyer. "That's why you were the only one everybody saw. You were the guardian of the house, the protector of the living."

"I'd say she looks less angry now," Jacob whispered. "She's listening."

"Captain Marsh did murder people, just like you told the police. Occult, ritual murders. Jacob says Captain Marsh thought he could extend his life through black magic, which is pretty useful when your main hobbies are smoking, drinking, and consorting with prostitutes. All the other ghosts are his victims, aren't they? He's the one holding them all there."

"Wow, she's excited," Jacob said. "I almost can't focus on her. She's like a blur of energy. Ever seen the Tasmanian Devil in those old cartoons?"

"That's why you killed him, you found out what he was doing. But even stabbing him to death didn't stop him. He kept on killing people after he died," I said. "Because he *liked* it, I guess. He liked having all those ghosts to boss around. But his first murder was his own wife. He poisoned her because her constant praying and churching didn't fit the life he decided he wanted. You can't be practicing the dark arts in a house filled with prayer. And his niece, Louisa—she knew that old ghost was killing a boarder here and there, but she didn't care. She was on his side. Maybe because he left her the house. Do I have it about right?"

"She's nodding so fast her face is a blur," Jacob said. "It's kind of sick to watch."

"Mercy, we just need to ask you something," I said. "How did you hold all the ghosts back for so long? Tell us everything you can about Captain Marsh and how we can stop him."

Jacob looked at the empty space behind me for a minute, not

saying anything.

"Well?" I asked.

"She's clamming up," Jacob said. "I don't know, she just got quiet..."

"Anything you can tell us at all," I said. "We came a long way to speak to you."

"She..." Jacob shook his head. "She doesn't want to tell you anything. She doesn't trust you."

"Because I trapped her and took her away?"

"I would guess so. She...wait." Jacob squinted and tilted his head, as though struggling to hear. "She won't tell us, but she'll show us."

"Okay, show us," I said.

"Back at the house. She wants to come back with us." Jacob gave me an apologetic shrug.

"So...I *should* go grab a trap, then?" Stacey asked.

"Not a trap," Jacob said. "She wants to hitch a ride with somebody."

"Wait," Stacey said. "It sounds she like she wants somebody to invite her to possess them? Is that right?"

Jacob nodded.

"That's your department, Jacob," I said. "She can possess you."

"Uh, what?" Jacob asked, giving me a look that indicated he didn't quite agree with my plan there. "Possess me?"

"It falls under psychic stuff, if you ask me," I replied. "That's you."

"The girl's got a point," Stacey added, taking my side.

"I'm not..." Jacob looked at the empty space beside me again, then smiled wickedly. "It doesn't matter what I want. She doesn't want to possess me. She wants...you." Jacob pointed at me.

"Me? Why?"

"Because, like I said, she doesn't trust you. She wants to keep an eye on you."

"But she trusts you?" I asked Jacob. "She just met you."

"And I haven't imprisoned or kidnapped her, so I have that going for me," Jacob said. "Those are her terms—she possesses you, Ellie, and goes back to the house, or she won't help us. She's worried you'll betray her or use the information for some other purpose than exorcising Captain Marsh."

This didn't exactly appeal to me. Possession is typically

associated with nasty, twisted sorts of ghosts who want to use your body in ways that are violent, destructive, or just plain disgusting. Things I would rather do than get possessed by a ghost include eating a bucket of live leeches, swimming in piranha-filled waters while bleeding from a dozen cuts, and sticking my head into the mouth of a hungry, hungry hippo.

"What other purposes could there be?" I asked, desperate to change the course of the conversation.

"She thinks you might be working with Captain Marsh," Jacob said. "I mean, she had him trapped in his corner of the house, and you're the one who unleashed him, along with his host of captive spirits. Maybe you want to help him, or learn occult stuff from him. That's what she's afraid of."

I sighed. Time was wasting, and I didn't think Mercy would change her mind very soon. From her perspective, I was the enemy. Apparently she was a fan of the "keep your friends close, your enemies closer" philosophy—so close that she would actually be inside me.

"You know what?" I said. "We have to get moving. Just tell me what to do."

"You'll let her possess you?" Jacob asked.

"Yes! Let's just get it over with."

"I think all you have to do is invite her," Jacob said. "Out loud. State your intention clearly."

I took a deep breath, trying to steel myself against the danger I was allowing inside me.

"All right," I said. "Mercy, you can hop inside me for the ride back to the house. You cannot have control of me, though. And it's just for tonight. When we're done, you have to leave me in peace." I really had no idea whether my conditions were binding. I didn't exactly have a supernatural lawyer handy to review the terms of the contract. For all I knew, once she was in me, I would be her prisoner for life.

I felt the cold heaviness close in around me, just as when Mercy had attempted to rip the silver necklace from my fingers. For a moment, I couldn't breathe, and the world grew even darker. I shivered, thinking I would pass out.

If you've ever had an ice-cold snake slither into your head and coil down your spine, freezing your heart and guts, making the rest of your body turn as numb as a corpse, then you've had a somewhat milder experience than letting a ghost possess you. It was terrifying, sickening, and disturbing. I wanted to scream, vomit, and run away all at once.

Then she settled into me, filling my stomach with ice. I felt off-balance and cold, but I seemed to retain control of my mind—as far as I could tell, anyway.

I had my doubts once I heard myself speak through my Novocain-numb jaw.

"Let's go get that bastard," I said. The voice had a much deeper Southern accent than my own, and a bitter, frosty edge.

Stacey and Jacob shared a worried look. I turned away from them and stalked toward the van, impatient to confront the murderous monster lurking in the old mansion.

Chapter Twenty-Seven

I had Stacey drive us back to Savannah, since I wasn't sure whether it was safe for me to drive while under the influence of an angry ghost.

Cold fury built inside me, mile by mile, and I gripped my tactical flashlight like it was a shotgun and I was on the way to settle a backwoods family feud.

Mercy's memories flickered across my mind like half-remembered nightmares. At one point, I lost touch entirely with the world around me. I found myself fearfully descending rough-hewn plank stairs into a dark, freezing space framed by rock walls.

In the darkness, I saw a girl, maybe nineteen or twenty years old, lying on a mound of smooth river stones. I felt like I knew her. Her short dress had been cut open, and so had her arms and throat, as if someone had intentionally drained her blood. Strange symbols were carved all over her body. Her eyes were open and lifeless.

She was my friend. He'd killed my friend.

I started in my seat, back in the van now, the dream vanished.

"Ellie? Ellie?" Stacey was saying.

"What?" I snapped, rubbing my aching head.

"Okay, good," Stacey said. "You looked really tranced out for a minute there. You were even drooling."

"I was not!" I protested, before finding my chin and shirt slippery with my own slobber. How embarrassing. Fortunately, I had other things on my mind, so I wiped my mouth and glared at the road ahead. It was midnight, and we were almost to the house.

When we arrived, I jumped out of the car, opened the back of the van, and made sure my utility belt was fully loaded. Then I popped open the ghost cannon case, strapped the battery pack onto my back, and stomped toward the front door of the house. I hadn't said a word. I was completely focused on the job at hand.

"Uh, hey, Ellie?" Stacey said, jogging up beside me. "What's the plan here?"

"We go in and get him." My voice was a low growl, not entirely my own. Mercy's hate for Captain Augustus Marsh filled my body like cold fire.

"But the cannon just chases him away, right? Ellie, slow down!"

I leaped up the steps, despite the heavy and unwieldy ghost cannon in my hand. Mercy's ghost seemed to lend me supernatural strength, while also taking away control of my mind and body. I was more like a passenger along for the ride.

I unlocked the front doors. Apparently Mercy didn't feel like stopping to answer Stacey's question.

I stepped into the dark foyer. Despite the almost total lack of light, I could see fairly well, which I also credit to Mercy. Ghostvision. I didn't need my night vision goggles, or even my flashlight. I holstered the flashlight and hefted the cannon in both hands.

Stacey and Jacob followed me inside, standing behind me. I didn't say anything to them. I was too busy looking up at the row of shattered balusters. I snorted.

"That was his pathetic way of getting back at me," I said, but it wasn't really me. It was Mercy's voice. "Trying to dishonor my space. But I don't care about that at all."

"Where do we go now?" Stacey asked.

I hesitated, then led them down the hall, into the kitchen. I could hear voices above me, and for the first time they weren't distorted beyond audibility.

"They're back," someone said, a female.

"He's not going to like that," a male voice replied.

"We'll stop her," hissed another female.

I didn't care. I walked through the kitchen and threw open the rickety wooden door to the cellar. I looked down into the freezing darkness...then I hesitated, suddenly filled with doubt.

"Okay," Stacey sighed, pointing her flashlight into the darkness below. "If we have to. I just wish you'd tell us what's going on, Ellie—"

"This isn't right," I said. I spun, almost knocked Jacob over with the big ghost cannon, and dashed to the narrow back stairs. I jogged up, not looking back.

"Okay, wait!" Stacey ran up the steep stairs with me, while Jacob reluctantly followed.

The second-floor hallway was crowded with ghosts.

It was the gang I'd seen in the cellar two nights earlier, the drifters and prostitutes from across the decades, the transient people Captain Marsh had been able to kill without drawing too much interest from local authorities. I recognized Mr. Junkie, now in his 1940s fedora and patched coat, syringes planted all over his arms and back. A faceless blond woman wore the fringed red dress I'd found in one of the wardrobes. The seventies hooker girl in the hot pants lingered in a shadowy corner, smoking a phantom cigarette and watching us with hollow, empty eye sockets.

They fell silent and turned toward us. I hefted the ghost cannon.

"She's back," Mr. Junkie said.

I advanced, and the herd of ghosts drew back from me as one, retreating to their shadowy doorways, repelled as though they were water and I were a dense drop of oil flowing past.

I can't say whether they were driven back by me with my ghost cannon ready to fire, or by the presence of Mercy inside me, the formidable ghost who had made it her mission to keep them trapped and powerless all these years.

I felt a kind of kinship with Mercy then. We'd been doing the same job, protecting the living against the dead. We approached it from slightly different angles, of course.

"Stacey, the stairs," I said. She dashed ahead and opened the door to the very steep and narrow staircase that twisted its way up to the master suite.

"I don't mean to slow you down there," Jacob said, "But there's a bunch of spirits staring at you. I don't think they wish you well."

"I know," I said. I ran up the steep stairs, somehow keeping my balance while holding the hefty ghost cannon ahead of me.

I reached that weird hallway landing, where the stairs to the third floor led up to the right. To the left, the hallway extended a few feet and dead ended into nothing.

I turned left.

I ran up to the wall and smacked it hard with my fist, then I kicked it. I snarled in frustration—actually *snarled* like a wild animal. That had to be the angry ghost inside me. I set down the ghost cannon, drew my flashlight, and banged the butt end against the wall, trying once again to find a spot that rang hollow.

The raised steel ridges around my flashlight lens, designed to help SWAT raiders and soldiers break down windows and doors, swung dangerously close to my eyes again and again, but I didn't seem to care about hurting my face. Or Mercy didn't care, at least.

I knocked over the little antique table that decorated the dead-end hall, ignoring the vase on top as it crashed to the floor and shattered. Then I kicked low on the blank wall, still trying to find a hollow spot.

"Didn't we already check there?" Stacey asked, coming up behind me. "There's no hidden panels or anything."

"Because she walled over it," I growled. I holstered my flashlight and pointed at the ghost cannon on the floor beside me. "Stay here," I ordered her, meaning for her to watch over our most powerful piece of equipment.

"Stay here? Where are you going?" Stacey asked.

I didn't reply as I hurried past her, dodging around Jacob as he tried to join us.

"What's up?" he asked.

I didn't answer him, either. My ghost-haunted brain was entirely focused on the task at hand.

I dashed down the steep stairs three at a time, then ran through the kitchen into the first-floor hallway, aiming directly for the security door into the east wing.

It was locked, bolted on the other side, but this was no major obstacle for Mercy, who'd opened the door so many times in her attempts to make the Treadwell family move out, away from danger.

I pressed my hand against the door. I felt a portion of her flow out of me like cold smoke through my fingers. I heard the rasp and clack of the heavy bolt drawing aside.

The door creaked open.

I walked on through, to the closet where Dale and Anna stored their home-restoration tools. I decided the sledgehammer had a nice heft to it and would do nicely.

The second-floor ghosts eyeballed me again as I passed them on the way to the stairs, whispering among themselves, a sound like dry leaves scratching their way down the street in a gust of wind.

Captain Marsh clearly hadn't given them the order to attack me —not yet.

I stalked up the stairs, my lips peeled back into an insane grin. Inside me, Mercy was exultant.

"Whoa," Stacey said, when I reached her and Jacob. "Don't you think we should maybe call our clients before we bash apart their house?"

I wasn't looking at Stacey. I was looking at the fourth person on the landing, the small, dark-haired woman in the high lace collar whom Stacey could not see.

The ghost of Eugenia pointed to the blank wall I was about to demolish.

"Destroy him, Mercy," she said. "For both of us. For all of us."

I nodded.

"Can you see her?" Jacob asked me.

"Yes. She's okay. She won't hurt us."

"Maybe not, but I'm feeling some bad stuff creep toward us." Jacob pointed up the second flight of stairs, the one that ended in a trap door to the master suite.

I saw them pass right through the door, dark and rotten shapes crawling down the stairs on their hands and knees. Because of Mercy possessing me, I now understood that these were among Captain Marsh's earliest victims, people he'd killed in his first ritual sacrifices. There were about six of them, and they'd mostly been hobos and vagrants in life, but one had been from a fairly prominent local family, a personal enemy of Captain Marsh after some business deal gone sour. Now, as long-decayed ghosts, the rich man was indistinguishable from the homeless.

"The crawlers," Eugenia said. "My husband sends them to torment me. You must hurry."

I turned and swung the hammer, bashing a hole through the center of the dead-end wall.

The entire house seemed to rumble. The rotten crawlers slithered down the stairs, some of them crawling sideways on the stairwell walls.

"It's getting worse." Jacob pointed down the stairs to the second floor, where the ghosts had so far been content to watch and whisper. Now the entire crowd advanced up the stairs toward us, their faces twisted with rage and hate. Some of their faces had gone transparent, giving a ghostly view of the skulls beneath the pale skin. "They're all ganging up."

Every ghost in the house had come out, except for Captain Marsh himself, waiting down in his lair. Waiting for me.

Eugenia threw herself at the shadowy crawlers. One grappled with her, but the other five continued their relentless advance.

"Try to slow them down," I said. "Jacob, you get the ones from downstairs. Stacey, you get the crawlers."

Stacey swung her flashlight beam up the stairs. The crawling apparitions didn't scatter or vanish, but I could now see them in greater, more grisly detail.

"How do I slow them down?" Jacob asked. "Jabbing this flashlight at them?"

"That would be a good start, yes," I said. We'd given him one of our high-powered tactical flashlights for the mission, but I doubted they would slow this mob very much. "Stacey, music?"

"Oh, yep. Get back, crawlers! Last warning!" Stacey touched the iPod on her belt.

Taylor Swift's "We Are Never Ever Getting Back Together" blasted at about ninety decibels from Stacey's portable speaker on her belt. The timbers of the house seemed to vibrate around us. I have to admit, it seemed to give the ghosts some pause.

"Maybe something a little holier!" I shouted. Then I swung the sledgehammer again, bashing a second hole into the wall.

"Sorry," Stacey said, fumbling with her iPod while the ghosts recovered and began to advance on us again from both stairways, clearly ignoring Taylor Swift's firm rejection of pursuing any further relationship.

A relatively fast-paced Gregorian chant replaced the pop song. I had somewhat better hopes for that.

I didn't look back, though. I kept pounding the wall, punching four, five, six holes. Mercy urged me on with her spectral energy, swinging the hammer with the same righteous fury that had driven her to grab that butcher knife from the kitchen after finding her dead friend, the fury that had sent her up these same stairs to stab the murderous Captain Marsh in his sleep.

The wall splintered and cracked. I broke through plaster, masonry, studs, and joists. Chunks of wood piled up at my feet, and I swept them aside with the head of the hammer. Then I kept swinging, first high over my head, then low like the hammer was a massive golf club of destruction. I was bashing myself a new doorway.

"This isn't going to work much longer!" Stacey shouted. I turned to see the ghosts from above and below crowding into the hallway. "Ellie, I need to use the ghost cannon!"

"No," I said. "We have to save the full charge for *him*."

"Then I need a Plan B. You have one, right?"

"Um," I said. "Jacob, can't you, like, lash out at them with your psychic medium powers?"

"Not that I'm aware of!" Jacob was doing his best to stay between Stacey and the ghosts, while she was doing her best to stay on the front line and protect me while I hammered. I appreciated both of them, especially since their flashlights and music weren't doing much to hold back the horde.

"Just push out some intense emotion or something," I said. "Ghosts are all about drama and emotion."

"Would fear work?" he asked. "I've got plenty of that hanging around."

"Not fear! You'll start a feeding frenzy. Use anger or something."

"Like being angry at myself for being here?" Jacob asked.

"Think about...think about how it felt when you woke up in that plane crash," I said. "There had to be some big feelings there, right?"

"So you want me to throw months of intense suicidal depression at them?" Jacob asked.

"That would be perfect, thanks!" I turned back and began bashing the wall again, widening the crevice I'd carved out so far. I was beginning to see something beyond it.

Behind me, I heard Jacob take a few deep breaths, then let out a long sigh, like something buried deep in his gut had been set free. I took another swing at the wall, knocking aside a skeletal frame of wood. I could see where we were going now.

When I turned back, the ghostly horde had slowed greatly. Jacob faced them, clutching his hands to his head, grimacing as though in intense pain. He was protecting us for the moment, but it looked like it was hurting him pretty badly.

"Good, keep it up, Jacob," I said. I turned to look through the gaping, jagged hole I'd made.

On the other side was a door carved from dark ebony, which is pretty heavy, expensive stuff. The door handle was ornate, silver-plated, gripped in the teeth of a devilish gargoyle face.

"Here it is," I said. "We made it."

Then I slumped, as if my body had turned to rags, and Stacey had to catch me so I didn't crack my head against the wall. The sledgehammer crashed to the floor beside my feet.

Mercy's fury and energy had driven me on until that moment, powering me up like a shot of steroids, or a can of Popeye's spinach. Now I sensed she was exhausted. I could feel her deep in my gut, curled up in a depleted ball of energy. I didn't think I would get much more help from her tonight.

Now my arms and back ached from recklessly swinging the hammer, and blisters had formed on my fingers. Mercy had worn me out, too, and the job was just beginning.

"Are you okay?" Stacey whispered.

"I'm great," I panted, wiping sweat from my face. Weak-kneed, I approached the ebony door.

"What's that?" Stacey asked.

I reached a hand toward the silver gargoyle latch. I was definitely trembling, but I couldn't say whether it was from too much exertion or from the dark batch of fear boiling up in my belly.

Before I touched it, the silver gargoyle's jaw flexed with a sharp squeak. The black door swung open silently, revealing the darkness beyond.

As with the stairs into the wine cellar, these were rough planks of wood surrounded by rock walls. They descended into pitch blackness. Cold radiated from the darkness below, along with a kind of reverse wind, seeming to tug things toward it like a black hole. The air temperature plunged into deep-arctic range. I could feel my lips and nose chapping in the sudden freeze.

Marsh, the master ghost, had opened the door for me. He wanted me to come down and see him.

The fear that struck me then was profound and total, the kind of awful dread that starts deep inside the pit of your stomach and grows up your spine to blossom into a black bloom of total horror inside your skull. It wasn't the kind of fear that makes you run and scream. It was the kind that makes you die of fright, because you know the end has come.

I swallowed.

Down in the darkness, a deep voice gave a long, rumbling moan, as if in response to my gulping sound.

"He's there," I whispered.

I picked up the ghost canon and started toward the doorway, ducking under the remnants of the wall I'd bashed to pieces.

"Ellie?" Stacey asked, touching my arm.

"Stay with Jacob," I said. "Do not let any of those minions through this door."

"But, come on, you're not going by yourself--" Stacey looked into the horrible, freezing darkness below.

"Mercy is coming with me," I said, not mentioning that Mercy had more or less collapsed inside me and might not be heard from again. I still had some of the ghostvision going for me—I could see the horde coming to kill us all. I guess that was a good thing. I couldn't see in the dark anymore, though, so I drew my flashlight and clicked it on. "Cover my back. That's, like, an order. Seriously."

Stacey nodded and turned to face the ghosts, blasting them with a tactical flashlight in each hand while they trudged their way through the melancholy blue haze of Jacob's sadness. It looked like they were attempting to cross a swamp while wearing heavy boots. Jacob's hands covered his eyes, his teeth bared in pain.

I turned my attention to the evil waiting below, and I started down the stairs, the ghost cannon in one hand, my flashlight pointed ahead of me.

"Captain Marsh!" I said. When in doubt, act like you're in control. Showing fear to a ghost is like feeding a stray cat—once they get a taste, they'll never leave you alone. "I know you're down here. It's time for you to leave this house."

The stairwell did not immediately widen to give a view of the room below, as the wine cellar stairs did. The raw rock walls stayed narrow, brushing my shoulders every step of the way. I wondered how Captain Marsh, a man of some height and girth, had fit through here. I suppose he sucked in his gut.

My heart beat faster every step of the way. The stairs below me creaked and groaned under my weight—which isn't *that* much, people —and the whole rickety staircase structure felt much weaker than the one in the wine cellar. I was tense, waiting for it to collapse below me. Nobody had walked down these stairs in many years. They could easily have been rotten through, or even eaten by termites.

The cellar seemed completely silent. I hadn't heard the moaning sound again.

The walls finally flared out as I reached the bottom stair, but not by much. My flashlight found rock shelves built into the walls on either side, like stone bunk beds stacked three high. A skeleton in decomposed clothing lay on each one.

I'd walked into a crypt.

"Captain Marsh?" I said, shining my flashlight forward. Across the roughly oval-shaped room, opposite the stairway, a little alcove had been carved halfway up the wall. Its lower lip was framed by layer after layer of black-wax stalactites, as though countless black candles had been burned there over the years.

Inside the alcove squatted one of the ugliest pieces of art I'd ever seen, a black volcanic-rock sculpture of a rotund little humanoid with cloven hooves, a pot belly, and a flat face adorned with tusks and horns. It was about a foot tall. Its clawed hands were clasped as though in prayer, but its bugging black eyes looked straight ahead, and its neck was stiff and fully erect.

Below that, on the floor, lay something I'd seen in Mercy's memory: a mound of smooth river stones. She'd found the body of a friend there, another regular working girl at Captain Marsh's nonstop party.

Now a mold-encrusted hardwood coffin lay on top of the rocks, the lid closed.

That's him, Mercy whispered in my mind. *He told Louisa to move his body here.*

"Whose bodies are these, Captain Marsh?" I asked. "These are the people you killed when you were still alive, aren't they? You sacrificed them to that tiny little idol in the corner. Where'd you find that? One of your trips to New York? Or across the ocean?"

I could feel something watching me from all sides, but I couldn't see anything but shadows and skeletons. The presence was heavy in the air, which was beyond foul and hard to breathe. I tried not to think of how much corpse-dust I was sucking up with each breath.

"It's an ugly little thing, isn't it?" I asked, shining my flashlight onto the idol again. "It looks so wimpy, too. Couldn't protect you against one angry girl with a knife. Hey, a little bird told me that's you in there." I kicked the foot of the coffin, jostling the rotten wood.

The low moaning sounded again, all around me, a deep bass far below the normal range of the human voice. The cement-rock floor seemed to shudder, or maybe I was just losing my balance.

A shadow formed on the wall, right in the center of the glowing puddle of light cast by my flashlight. It swelled to swallow up most of the light, taking the shape of a larger-than-life man with an enormous beard, most of the head projected onto the ceiling.

There was nothing in front of me that would have cast such a shadow.

"You didn't like that, did you?" I asked. I kicked his coffin again, then again. Portions of the rotten lid cracked away and tumbled inside, and I glimpsed a skeletal arm in a rotting suit jacket.

He roared now, swelling out from the wall in three dimensions. He spread through the room like inky black smoke, engulfing the idol, his own casket, and the crypt bunks on either side of him.

The darkness billowed forward, diminishing my flashlight beam until it was no more useful than a paper match.

I holstered the flashlight.

I faced a wall of solid darkness, which had swollen to fill the entire back half of the cellar. Its surface pulsed and wavered organically, like the flesh of a massive, oily black tumor.

It bulged toward me.

"Okay, Augustus," I said. "I know you're a big, bad monster of a ghost, but right now I need you to get out of my way."

I put on my sunglasses, raised the ghost cannon, thumbed it to the highest possible setting, and pulled the trigger.

The underground crypt lit up like a dive bar at closing time. The cannon flooded the room with scalding hot light, and I could see every detail of the skeletons on their rocky bunks. The back half of the room remained dimmer, as though some kind of dark veil were drawn across it, but I could still see Marsh's rotting coffin and the idol in the wall beyond it.

An angry-sounding groan shook the room as the darkness seemed to retreat into the walls.

From my own experience, I had a pretty good idea that if we moved these bodies out of the house, we might knock out the haunting altogether, sending the restless spirits on their way to wherever they're supposed to go. We would start with Captain Marsh's remains.

"Hey, Stacey!" I shouted.

"What's up?" Stacey leaned through the doorway above, looking down at me while pointing her flashlights in the opposite direction. She looked pretty pale and terrified, which is the proper reaction to trying to stave off a horde of attacking ghosts.

"Give me a hand with this old corpse," I said.

"I knew you were going to say something awful," Stacey replied. She leaned out of sight, I assume to pass Jacob a flashlight, then started down the stairs holding her one remaining light, though she didn't need it at the moment. The room could not have been any brighter.

Then I heard something snap behind me. A scorching heat scalded my back, and I cried out in pain. The ghost cannon blew out like a candle, plunging the cellar back into darkness. I fiddled with the switch, but the big light-blaster was dead.

"What happened?" Stacey asked, shining her flashlight toward me.

"The battery pack malfunctioned," I said, grimacing in pain. "Marsh might have—watch out!"

I drew my regular flashlight and pointed it toward her. The crawlers were following Stacey into the cellar, scurrying like rotten spiders on the walls and low ceiling all around her.

"What is it?" Stacey asked.

"Get back! The crawlers are surrounding you."

"I don't see anything." Stacey shined her flashlight around, then reached for the thermal goggles on her forehead.

The crawlers slithered down the wall, into the stairs below her.

"Get off the stairs!" I shouted, but Stacey had no time to react.

The crawlers tore into the rickety old staircase, ripping away the railing, the steps, and the support beams all at once. The cracking of a hundred pieces of wood filled my ears, sounding weirdly like grease sizzling in a pan.

Stacey screamed as the staircase collapsed beneath her. She crashed down to the cellar floor in a storm of broken wood and rusty nails. I heard her cry in pain, then fall silent as a stout beam and a few chunks of railing and stairs crashed down on top of her. Her flashlight rolled away and thumped against the wall. The Gregorian chant ended abruptly, as though her iPod had cracked.

"Stacey!" I screamed, starting toward her.

Dark, cold laughter echoed all through the room. I can't say there was much mirth in it. I felt ill.

I turned to see the wall of pulsing, flowing darkness had returned, swelling even bigger, and I had to step back a few paces as it grew toward me. My flashlight beam didn't penetrate it at all.

I tried the ghost cannon again, but it didn't respond. If Marsh had sucked all the power out of the battery pack, then he'd only grown stronger while putting my best weapon out of service.

A bushel of my enemy's grain is worth twenty of my own, I thought. That's from the *Art of War* by Sun-Tzu, which is the sort of thing Calvin makes me read. I'd just given Marsh twenty bushels' worth, then.

I shivered as the darkness expanded and thickened. I tried desperately to think of what I could do to avoid getting killed in the next five seconds. If Marsh got me, I would become another of his slave ghosts, haunting and terrorizing anyone who tried to live in the house. He might even make me kill for him.

I wanted very badly to check on Stacey, but if I turned my back on Marsh's malevolent presence, it could mean death for both of us.

Placing the ghost cannon on the floor, I raised my flashlight toward the darkness again. That was when Marsh lashed out at me. Something huge and hard, like a giant's hand adorned with brass knuckles, smashed into me head-on, flinging me across the room.

I slammed into the rock shelves at one side of the crypt, banging my rib cage pretty hard, followed immediately by my head. Little bursts of light exploded behind my eyelids.

Then I tumbled and crashed to the rock floor, another hard impact that felt like a slap across my entire body. I shuddered in pain and tasted blood in my mouth.

Though I felt like I couldn't move, I forced myself up to my knees. I grasped the nearby rock shelf. In the darkness, my fingers bumped against an old thighbone.

"Don't touch me," a voice whispered in the air near my throbbing, spinning head.

The deep, almost subsonic laughter rumbled again, so deep and powerful it made my joints ache. I could barely hear it over the screaming pain in my head and ribs and back.

I pushed myself to my feet, but I wobbled and swayed, my balance still out of whack. I almost fell over, but then a hand grabbed me.

It felt deep-freezer cold *and* wet and squishy, an unnatural combination. In the light from Stacey's flashlight, and my own flashlight held loosely in my stunned and weakened fingers, I could see what was gripping me.

The wall of darkness had pushed close. From it had emerged the head, arms, and torso of Captain Marsh, but they didn't quite match the pictures taken of him when he was alive. He was made of dense darkness—it looked like he was carved entirely out of liquid petroleum, the surface of him flowing thick and slow. I could see every detail of his face, which looked like a monstrous version of his portraits, every detail gleaming and black, the beard stretching out from his face all the way back into the wall of darkness behind him, the liquid-black locks tangled and writhing like blind serpents.

His eyes, pure black like the rest of him, stared into mine. His mouth opened in an unnaturally large grin, like the jaws of a crocodile, the teeth widely spaced and sharpened into points.

Marsh pulled me toward him. I resisted with all my remaining strength, which wasn't much. I planted my feet on the floor and leaned back away from the horrible specter, while dark laughter burbled out of his maw. If he'd let me go, I would have fallen and smacked into the rock floor, but I guess he didn't know about judo and turning your opponent's strength against him.

I called out Stacey's name, but my voice was weak. She didn't respond. I couldn't see her, but as far as I could tell, she hadn't moved since the staircase collapsed around her.

I heard Jacob shouting in pain upstairs, but I couldn't help him, either.

The hideous shape of Captain Marsh gave me another hard pull, and I stumbled. I just barely managed to plant my feet again and resist getting drawn into the inky black wall.

His face grew larger, expanding to more than twice the natural size of a human head. His jaws spread open, and he laughed again.

"*Come to me,*" his black-oil mouth said. "*I'll make you eternal.*"

I didn't know how much longer I could hold out—his strength was massive, while my own was currently somewhere around the level of a kitten drowsy on too much warm milk.

I dragged my feet as far from him as I could, so I was leaning toward Marsh and the darkness from which he'd half-emerged. If he let go of me, I would fall right on my face, probably breaking my nose on that stone floor.

My grip tightened on my flashlight.

"Okay," I told him. "You murderer. You want me to come to

you? I'm on my way."

I pushed hard with both feet, leaping toward him while he yanked on my arm with all his force. His liquid-black jaw dropped in a wide open frown, and confusion wrinkled his forehead.

I flew right through him, into the blackness beyond. My guts turned instantly sour, and I was both nauseous and dizzy. The air was cold and thick as polluted water, almost impossible to breathe.

This was the belly of the beast.

I managed to land on my feet, only to stagger forward and trip over the rock mound at the center of the room. I crashed face first into Marsh's coffin, feeling the rotten lid rip beneath me like old paper.

Cold, sharp hands grabbed at my legs. At first I thought it was Marsh's skeleton seizing me, but there were too many hands for that. I heard a few male voices—they were panting, with a lusty sound I didn't like at all.

The crawlers, I realized. They'd taken out Stacey, and I was next.

I felt a frigid tongue lick the back of my neck. It felt like the rotten skin was sliding off, leaving a residue on my flesh.

I shouted and swung my flashlight at them, which didn't help much, but it got me moving again. I kicked, then pushed myself forward on my hands and knees. The crawlers grabbed at me everywhere, keeping me from standing. Between the thick, heavy pressure of the air and the grisly ghosts, I was barely able to move...but I *did* keep moving, inch by inch.

It was eerily silent now, like the dark depths of the ocean where no light has ever been. Even my own breathing was muffled.

Pulling myself across the rocky floor with my fingers, knees, and toes, I finally reached the wall. Hands grabbed my hair and ripped at my clothes. My jacket was torn away, and unseen claws and teeth sank into my arms, back, and neck.

Biters and scratchers. I detest them all.

I drew myself up the uneven rock wall. At least one of the crawlers was right on my back, his arms locked around my waist in a disgusting embrace, so I wasn't able to stand.

I didn't need to stand, though.

My hands scrabbled over a slick, crumbling surface. Years of accumulated black candle wax.

I managed to reach a little higher, and my hands closed around the base of the ugly little idol.

With an angry grunt, I pulled it out of its niche and brought it crashing to the ground. It slammed into the rock floor beside me.

The entire house shook now, as if a major earthquake had struck it from below. Dust and grit rained down all over me from the ceiling, and I thought I could hear timbers creaking and groaning in protest. The whole cellar roof was about to come crashing down on top of me, bringing the full weight of the house with it.

A deep snarl thundered and echoed through the room, making my eardrums pop. The thick, foul air rippled and splashed around me.

A swarm of tiny glowing orbs appeared in the darkness around me like luminescent fish. They quickly grew, taking the forms of the second-floor ghosts, the ones who weren't quite as decayed as the crawlers, like Mr. Junkie and the assorted prostitutes.

They all had a pale glow, their mouths downturned in exaggerated expressions of fury, their skulls still visible through their faces. By their glow, I could also see the dark crawlers on the floor around me.

The ghosts closed in around me like a pack of hungry hyenas, grabbing and slashing at me from all sides. I didn't have long to live.

I pressed one hand against the fallen statue to hold it in place. Then I raised the other, which still held my flashlight. The light was useless deep in this spiritual darkness, but those little raised steel ridges around the lens...those would work just fine. I hoped.

I brought the flashlight down as hard as I could and smashed into the bug-eyed face of the statue. I heard an audible cracking sound—I'd chipped it, at least.

Marsh's roar sounded again, and the cellar floor rumbled. Was that a trace of pain in his voice? I hoped so.

I smashed the idol's face a second time, then a third. The house was shaking and creaking, spilling more dust all over me, making me cough.

The next time I brought my flashlight down, there was a much louder crack. Half the idol's head broke away and hit the floor. The broken chunk of god-head looked like one of those big stone flakes cavemen used as knives and hand axes.

Marsh's voice howled again, and there was *definitely* pain in it this time.

The ghosts closest to me vanished, as though someone had grabbed them all and flung them aside.

In their place rose the black-oil head and torso of Marsh, emerging again from the darkness. Both his large hands plunged toward my throat. His face twisted in inhuman fury.

"Captain Augustus Oliver Marsh," I gasped, still choking on dust. "You are forever banished from this house."

I seized the broken flake of the idol's head. As Marsh's form reached me, I stabbed the sharp chunk of the idol directly into his oily black heart.

Marsh's face melted into an expression of horror. His freezing hands grabbed at mine, but I wasn't budging. I managed to slide the stone fragment in a little deeper.

"There," I whispered. "You believe in the power of this idol—now I turn it against you."

He gave a long, shrieking howl that rattled the skeletons on the walls, knocking one out of its bunk and onto the floor, where it smashed into pieces.

The heavy darkness shrouding the room began to lift and scatter like a thunderhead breaking apart. The horde of ghosts backed even farther away from me.

Marsh shrank away from me, too. The oily black surface of his skin ruptured, and the darkness shrank into patches all over him. Beneath that surface, he was a pale ghost like the others. He no longer seemed bigger and stronger than the rest.

He clutched his thick gray hair in his hands and let out a keening wail as he looked at the broken idol.

"Your power is gone," I said.

He looked at me with his transparent pale eyes going wide, his jaw dropping, his enormous beard drooping around his face like that of an elderly, defeated lion.

"No," his voice rasped. Then, pathetically, he pleaded, "Don't hurt me."

"It's not me you have to worry about," I replied.

Rustling, whispering voices rose all around us, like the last dead leaves of fall. The ghosts were closing in, some walking, some crawling—but not toward me this time.

Augustus Marsh, steamship captain, mass murderer, and part-time occultist, watched warily as they approached.

"Get back!" he ordered them. "I am still in command. Get back!"

"That's not exactly true anymore," I said. "You know it. And they can feel it."

The horde encircled him slowly, closing in around him. They still seemed hesitant to step too close.

"No!" he said, holding up one hand palm out. "I command you, I command..."

"You thought you'd live forever," I said. "But you're already dead. It's time to accept it."

The horde moved closer to him. One crawler, a badly rotten hobo ghost, was the first soul brave enough to reach out and grab Marsh. Marsh flinched and leaped back, right into the arms of more of his former captives.

Expressions of wrath twisted all their faces. As they pounced on him, I was reminded again of a pack of starving hyenas leaping on a carcass.

Apparently they'd taken it easy on me, maybe resisting Marsh's orders to stop us with whatever shred of individual will they'd had. While I couldn't see Marsh through the crowd, but I heard snapping, ripping, gnashing, and a lone voice screaming as they tore him apart. There was so much pain in it that I almost felt sorry for him, until I remembered he'd personally murdered every ghost in the room.

Well, almost every ghost. He hadn't killed Mercy himself, either when he was alive or when he was a murderous spirit.

Now I felt Mercy rising in me, glowing with the thrill of victory.

She didn't leave my body then, but that was okay. We still had unfinished business.

The swarm of ghosts began to swirl faster and faster. Marsh screamed as they ripped into his essence. They became a moaning, biting whirlwind of pale, misshapen faces and hands, no longer looking human at all.

They dragged Marsh down to the rocky floor, next to his own coffin.

I caught one last glimpse of him there, shriveled and bitten, whimpering as his freed prisoners tore away what little he had left.

Then they took him down through the floor, deep below the ground, hopefully all the way to Hell. I pointed my flashlight and watched the last curls of ghostly mist fade among the cemented rocks, making sure they were really gone.

Then the room was quiet. The temperature was already rising, from deep freeze to mildly cool.

"Stacey?" I ran over to the collapsed staircase, where she lay among broken heaps of wood and exposed rusty nails. She bled from her nose, she had several large bruises, and her eyes were closed.

I touched her shoulder and rubbed it gently, not wanting to disturb any injuries she might have sustained.

"Stacey? Stacey? Are you awake?"

"Ugh." She squinted her still-closed eyes. "I'd rather not be."

"Are you hurt?"

"What do you think?" Stacey asked.

"Where? Is anything specifically bad?"

"No, just..." Her eyes opened. "My arm. Oh, my freaking *arm*. I think it's broken."

"Which one?"

"The one I landed on," Stacey said. I moved my flashlight around and saw her left arm tucked and twisted beneath her. "Good thing I'm a righty," she added. Spunky girl.

"I'm sorry," a voice groaned above us. It sounded like another ghost. I pointed my light up there.

Jacob knelt in the doorway over the collapsed staircase, barely able to grasp his flashlight. The poor guy looked like someone had dunked him in gravy and thrown him into a pit of lions. His clothes were shredded, much like mine, and red scratches crisscrossed all the bared flesh, as well as his face and neck.

"I'm sorry," he said again. "I tried to hold them back, but..."

"Don't apologize," I told him. "We would have been dead ten minutes ago without you. You saved us. Are you hurt? Can you walk?"

"Only if I really have to," he said, then he slumped against the doorframe. "What do we do now?"

"I guess we'd better call an ambulance," I replied. I brushed my fingers across Stacey's head, kind of an attempt to comfort her. It was less awkward than it sounds. She gave me a pained smile.

"Don't forget the coroner," she added, glancing at the skeletons in the wall. "I wonder if funeral homes give discounts for mass murder."

Chapter Twenty-Eight

The next afternoon, Stacey and I sat at the dining room table in the east wing of the house, facing the Treadwell family, just as we had on our first visit. It was a sweltering June day outside, and golden summer light flooded the house. All the dark shadows had been chased away.

Jacob was back at work, where hopefully he had a good explanation for the numerous scratches on his hands and face. Attacked by a pack of feral cats who'd dragged him through thorn bushes, maybe. Anything was more believable than the truth. He hadn't exactly advertised his unwanted psychic-medium abilities around the accounting firm, since he did not want to get fired or sent on mental health leave.

All of us had stitches. Stacey had fractured her wrist, and the hospital had splinted it before releasing us early that morning.

It had been a busy day, with the police gathering reports about the dead bodies we'd found. The coroner's office was still at work in the main house, exhuming bodies from the crypt.

Now, Stacey and I finally had a chance to sit down with our clients.

I laid out the story for the Treadwells, leaving out some of the more scandalous or scary details for Lexa's benefit. Everything would be in my final written report...which, I suspected, they were no more likely to read than they were to watch the DVDs Stacey had prepared of ghostly apparitions and activity all over their home. Still, people liked to get a hefty package of stuff for their money.

"So the ghosts are definitely gone this time?" Dale asked. He wasn't drunk or cocky now. He seemed chastened and humbled by the experience. "They aren't going to come back?"

"They've all moved on," I said.

"Even from the crypt?" he asked, still looking worried.

"Definitely," I replied, and he got a reflective look on his face. I imagined Dale changing the newly-discovered room into some kind of man-cave, with a hideous couch and beer signs. The evil old idol might be replaced by a shrine to the Cubbies. I held back a laugh. "After last night, I'd say this is now probably the least haunted house in all of Savannah. Call us if you have any trouble, but I don't anticipate any. We can do a follow-up in a few weeks if you'd like."

"Then we can keep going with the renovations? The rooms will be safe to rent?" Anna asked.

"Yep, as soon as you clean up the mold and broken syringes, you can make this a really nice place," I said. "You'll probably find that the remodeling goes much faster and cheaper, with fewer problems than before. That's normal."

"Thank goodness," Anna said, sighing a little. She smiled at her husband, and he smiled back. It felt like ice breaking in the sunlight.

"What about Mercy?" Lexa asked. "Did she move on, too?"

"She's leaving the house with us," I said. I hadn't mentioned the part where I was possessed by Mercy's ghost. I could feel her inside me, restless.

"Can you thank her for me?" Lexa asked. "She was just trying to warn us about the bad ones. She was really a good ghost."

"She was, but she's ready to leave now," I said. "You don't have to worry about any ghosts anymore, Lexa. Good or bad."

Lexa nodded silently. She'd been through a lot.

As we left the house, stepping out onto the driveway shaded by oak and moss, Stacey took a last look at the sharp peaks and high roofs of the Gothic-style house.

"You know, once you get rid of the ghosts and spiders, it is a pretty nice mansion," she said. "I bet it will make a cute little hotel."

"Yeah. I think they'll be fine," I said. "I hope their check clears."

We drove away.

Chapter Twenty-Nine

"So, does that thing really have black magic or not?" Stacey asked.

We were at the office, in the basement. I was carefully sliding the two pieces of Captain Marsh's broken idol into a ghost trap. I sealed the lid.

"I have my doubts," I said. "The important thing is that Marsh himself believed in it. It was the focus of his powers."

"Yeah, but he killed those people to lengthen his own life, and that worked, right? I mean, he lived to be a hundred and six."

"Some people have longevity on their side." I placed the trap into a giant steel safe, eight feet tall, on a shelf alongside similar sealed traps. The one next to it held an old voodoo doll bristling with needles.

"If you don't believe in the occult stuff, why are you stashing that thing? Why not just toss it in the trash?" Stacey asked.

"It's Calvin's policy." I shoved the steel door shut. "Better safe than sorry."

"And keeping a vault full of supernatural bric-a-brac from old cases counts as safe?" she asked.

"Maybe not, but that's our job. We face the dangers so other people don't have to."

"Hey, you should put that on our business cards!" Stacey said.

A whirring and clanking sounded above. Calvin descended from the ceiling, caged inside the little industrial elevator that connects the three floors of the building. His bloodhound Hunter stood beside him, languidly wagging his tail. Hunter liked riding the elevator.

When it reached the floor, Calvin opened the cage door and rolled out. The dog stayed loyally at his side, but drifted in Stacey's direction, knowing she was good for a long scratch under the chin.

"Case closed?" Calvin asked, glancing at the safe door, and I nodded. "Good. That sounded like a tough one."

"It was," I agreed.

"What do you think of the psychic kid? Any good?"

"Better than expected," I said. "He helped us break the case, and he also held back a swarm of attacking ghosts. We may as well keep his number on file."

"Or maybe invite him out for lunch," Stacey suggested. I looked at her, and she blushed. "Or, you know. Coffee?"

"What about this one?" Calvin inclined his head toward Stacey. "Are we keeping her or throwing her back?"

I gave Stacey a long look.

"It's up to her," I finally said. "Personally, I'd like to keep her."

"I'd like to stay," Stacey said. "This work matters. And there's almost nobody willing to do it."

Calvin nodded. There wasn't much left to say, and only one thing left to do.

Chapter Thirty

I walked into Roustie's the next night, accompanied by Jacob and Stacey. They lingered near the front door while I walked up to the bar—I just wanted Dabney and Buck to see I wasn't alone. I didn't know how Jacob would fare in an all-out brawl with these people, but maybe he could make them all miserably depressed or something.

The bar hosted a much bigger crowd than it had on Sunday afternoon, and David Allen Coe played loud on the jukebox. As I approached the bar, Buck was entertaining a couple of hefty biker guys while pouring their drinks.

"...so the sign says, 'Liquor in the front, poker in the rear'!" Buck was shouting to be heard, or just shouting because he was drunk. The bikers laughed, and one of them pounded his fist on the bar as if he couldn't control himself. Then they asked for more drinks.

"Hi there, Buck," I said.

He looked up at me, and the drunken smile vanished from his face.

"Maybe you want to talk at the end of the bar?" I sat down a few stools away from the nearest customer, under the rack of drinking glasses and next to the cash register.

Buck stared at me, saying nothing. He clearly didn't know how to react, because he ran back to the kitchen door and shouted for Dabney. Dabney scowled when he saw me.

The two of them approached with fairly hostile looks on their faces. Buck muttered something to Dabney and pointed at my two friends by the door.

"Hi, boys," I said. "You two were such a big help with my investigation, I thought you'd be curious how the case turned out."

"Yeah, all right," Buck said, nodding rapidly until Dabney elbowed him to stop.

"First, I should remind you that I'm not the police," I said. "My job is to serve my clients, which is usually about removing the ghosts from their homes. It's not my job to dig up old criminal cases and prosecute them. Are we clear on that?"

The two of them just stared at me. Dabney narrowed his eyes a little, while Buck actually gulped, then poured himself a drink.

"I have to tell you," I said. "Captain Marsh—Louisa's great-uncle, you know—he was a real monster in life. He liked to murder passing strangers, rootless people, anybody the authorities wouldn't notice had gone missing. But after he died, he *really* became a monster. He kept on killing the same sorts of people. I think Louisa knew about it and helped him. She definitely covered up for him. She walled up the crypt under the house where the bodies of his victims were stored."

Dabney and Buck glanced at each other, Buck's jaw dropping open. They probably didn't know about that. It would have been done soon after Louisa took over the house, when Dabney and Buck were still children.

"So that gives you some idea of why the place was so haunted," I continued. "Just think about Louisa for a moment, living alone there, seeing nobody but strangers, while serving the murderous ghost of her dead uncle. Maybe she was just really grateful to him for leaving her the house. Maybe Louisa's a little twisted herself. You have to wonder whether she was crazy when she got there, or whether the house and that evil ghost made her that way.

"Anyway, when she heard her great-uncle's killer, Mercy, was being released, she decided she wanted Mercy dead. Maybe she was afraid for her own life, but I suspect Captain Marsh's ghost wanted it done. He wanted revenge, and he wanted Mercy to die right there in his house so he could torment her for years to come.

"There was one problem. Mercy wasn't some drifter staying at the house. She wasn't going to show up on her own. That's why Louisa sent you two to kidnap Mercy after she got out of the hospital. You brought her to the Marsh house, you put a noose around her neck, and you threw her over the railing."

"That ain't...hey, that ain't..." Buck tried to come up with something to say.

"Shut up, Buck," Dabney said. "You ain't got no proof of that, lady."

"Actually, I've heard it from the victim herself, Mercy," I said. "I work with ghosts, remember? But I figured it out before she told me. The two of you gave yourselves away by ransacking my apartment and threatening me. That's when I knew you had something to hide. Add together the inconsistencies between what Louisa told us a few days ago and what she told the police thirty years ago, and I pretty much figured it out."

"Dang it, Dabney, I told you we ought to leave her alone--" Buck began.

"Shut up!" Dabney actually slapped Buck across the face, and Buck cringed like a long-abused dog. Then Dabney turned to me. "Nothing you're saying could hold up in court."

"Hey, I told you, I'm not the police." I held up my hands defensively. "I'm not trying to put together a case for the prosecution here."

"Then what are you trying to do?" Dabney asked.

"I'm just getting to the part y'all don't know about," I said. "You see, Captain Marsh had power over almost every ghost in that house, because he'd personally killed them. When he was alive, he first poisoned his wife to get her out of his way, then he ritually sacrificed the others down in his cellar—the crypt cellar, the one y'all maybe didn't know about. He sacrificed them to this ugly little demon idol. Lord knows where he got it, but there it was, surrounded by old candles.

"Anyway, he didn't kill Mercy. You two did. In fact, Mercy had killed *him*. So, by the rules of that household, Mercy's ghost actually had power over Captain Marsh's ghost. She used it to stand against him, to protect the living against him and trap him down in his lair. For the longest time, Mercy was the only ghost anyone encountered there, and her only goal was to drive people away for their own safety.

"Now, Captain Marsh was a powerful ghost, so you can imagine how strong and powerful Mercy's ghost became, fighting against him all those years. Like a bodybuilder in heavy training, I guess. That's something to think about.

"When I take a ghost out of a house, I usually do a catch and release. I look for the proper place to let the ghost free. Mercy had a particular place in mind."

"Where'd she want to go?" Buck asked.

Behind them, a neon Michelob sign glowed brighter, then fizzled and died. The entire sign slipped off the wall and crashed to the floor.

"What was that?" Dabney jumped and turned to look.

"She wanted to come and stay with you two, her murderers," I said. "I can't imagine why, but I thought it would be nice to honor her last request, don't you?" I slid off my stool, my jeans peeling away from the sticky cushion. "So I've brought her here. Maybe she can help around the bar, if she isn't too focused on revenge."

"Wait," Buck said, "You can't leave a ghost here!"

"She's just babbling," Dabney said. "There ain't no ghost, Buck."

Then the glasses in the rack over their heads began to explode, one by one, raining down shards on Buck and Dabney at high speed. They screamed and backed away.

The cash register opened, and all the cash and coins leaped out onto the floor.

I turned and walked away. All around me, an unseen force toppled unoccupied chairs and sent tables sliding across the room. More beer signs exploded and spat out showers of sparks. The bar patrons stood up, shouting in surprise at the wave of unexplained destruction.

I didn't know whether Mercy would kill Dabney and Buck right away, or keep them alive to torment for years to come. I leave such matters in the hands of higher powers than myself.

"Well?" Stacey asked me when I reached the door.

"I think Mercy is going to be very happy with them," I said. "Might be bad for business, though."

"You can't please everyone." Stacey smiled and touched Jacob's arm.

"Thanks for all your help, Jacob," I said.

"It was fun," he told me. "This part right here, anyway. The rest of it was unspeakably horrible."

"Welcome to the job," I said. "Now let's get out of here. I heard this bar is haunted."

We walked out the door while Mercy's ghost tore the place apart behind us.

The End

From the author

Thanks so much for taking the time to read *Ellie Jordan, Ghost Trapper*. If you enjoyed it, I hope you'll consider leaving a review at the retailer of your choice. Good reviews are possibly the most important factor in helping other readers discover a book.

The second book in the Ellie Jordan series is already in the works. I hope to write several of these following her different cases and adventures—I certainly had a lot of fun with this one, and I hope you did, too.

Sign up for my newsletter to hear about my new books as they come out. You'll immediately get a free ebook of short stories just for signing up. The direct link is http://eepurl.com/mizJH, or you can find it on my website.

If you'd like to get in touch with me, here are my links:

Website (www.jlbryanbooks.com)
Facebook (J. L. Bryan's Books)
Twitter (@jlbryanbooks)
Email (info@jlbryanbooks.com)

Made in the USA
San Bernardino, CA
09 September 2016